THE CYBORG'S FORTUNE

BOOK 4

Benoit Lanteigne

80 Mapleton Rd, Unit 11-80
Moncton, New-Brunswick, Canada
E1C 7W8

Benoit Lanteigne

80 Mapleton Rd, Unit 11-80
Moncton, New-Brunswick, Canada
E1C 7W8

https://thecyborgscrusade.com

Publisher's Note: This is a work of fiction. Names, characters, places, and incidents are a product of the author's imagination. Locales and public names are sometimes used for atmospheric purposes. Any resemblance to actual people, living or dead, or to businesses, companies, events, institutions, or locales is completely coincidental.

Book Layout © 2016 BookDesignTemplates.com
Edited by Eliza Dee
Book Cover Design by 100 Covers

The Cyborg's Crusade / Benoit Lanteigne. -- 1st ed.
ISBN 978-1-7387526-0-7

CONTENTS

Do you want a free short story that serves as a prequel to The Cyborg's Crusade? Then, join my newsletter on my website https://thecyborgscrusade.com.

The next book, The Cyborg's Identity, is available for preorder and releases on January 6, 2025

AVAILABLE NOW IN THIS SERIES

The Cyborg's Crusade

The Cyborg's Warning

The Cyborg's Riddle

The Cyborg's Fortune

AVAILABLE FOR PREORDER

The Cyborg's Identity

Certain Death

Chapter 1

Hocmar 14, 2072, on the Nirnivian calendar

Knife in hand, Daniel performed a perfect straight cut. Then he jabbed his fork into the piece of crokk steak resting on his plate and brought it to his mouth. As he chewed through the tender flesh, he enjoyed the rich flavor and kept his lips sealed. After he swallowed, he took a short pause before repeating the process, keeping a deliberate pace—not too fast, nor too slow. Whenever thirst showed itself, he reached for his glass filled with water and indulged in a small sip, careful to produce as little noise as possible.

Around Daniel, chaos ensued, contrasting with his calm demeanor. The other students ignored table manners; instead they shoved food in their mouths and let the world witness their teeth crushing it. And the talking—so many conversations reached Daniel's ears, though the content remained incomprehensible. Most voices approached the threshold between speech and screams, and some exceeded it, resulting in a deafening cacophony. And that wasn't counting the laughter. Why, Kelly Johnson chortled so hard her juice came out of her nose. A few burps even echoed. Didn't these people have standards? Of course, Daniel understood the desire for discussion. On this occasion, he sat alone, but sometimes his friend Madeleine ate with him and they talked, though never at such a ludicrous volume.

The differences in behavior between Daniel and his peers didn't stop at the cafeteria. Whenever he took notes, he forced a steady hand and maintained legible handwriting despite the constant pressure to rush. Not every one of his classmates proved so careful. The most extreme had to be a guy named Benedict who often failed to understand his own writing. His locker Daniel kept spotless and ordered while his neighbors' represented pure chaos. At one point, Clark had forgotten an old sandwich in his for a month and only discovered it because of the resulting stench. Daniel expected such carelessness from a child, but not high school students. Perhaps he demanded too much out of them. The meticulousness he imposed on himself required sustained efforts. There were days he wished he could chill just a bit. His mentor claimed that in time he might be able to. For now, however, the discipline helped avoid past patterns.

Before long, Daniel finished his meal, and he gazed at the remaining piece of cake. Dessert, an allowed pleasure if consumed with moderation. Too bad the boys in front of him insisted on tainting the incoming sweetness with their inane banter. To their great amusement, they ranked the girls frequenting this fine establishment. Daniel shook his head at their immaturity. Ah well, in a few weeks he'd graduate and leave this wretched place forever.

"What about Hella? Got a freaking nice butt."

"She's sexy, but Claudine is where it's at. Those eyes can melt me like butter."

"Yeah, right! I've seen you talk to her: you're not looking at her eyes. I'll tell you, if I could bang any chick here, it'd be Madeleine Gainsborough. That bitch got everything in the right place if you catch my drift. And those lips were made for sucking." Daniel's jaw muscles tightened. Madeleine was a pure soul, and that bastard talked about her as if she was a toy to be used for pleasure. An urge to punch the jerk filled him, but he resisted the temptation. Such violence wasn't necessary. Besides, that wasn't his style—not anymore.

"Dude, watch your mouth! That Ricdeau kid is right there. He's always hanging out with that gal. He gotta like her or something. I heard some messed-up shit about him. You shouldn't piss him off."

"Him? Give me a break! Sure, he used to be a badass, but he saw the light of God. He's a wimp now. Besides, I'm saying his girl is hot; in a way, it's a compliment!" Daniel noticed a hint of mockery in the boy's tone. Not that he cared—the words were somewhat true anyway. He'd sent plenty of annoying kids to the hospital during his youth and nearly killed one. Then he'd found God and in his mercy Ulgorack had guided him along the path to salvation. The irritating gang misunderstood his relationship with Madeleine, however. She wasn't his girlfriend, or even a love interest, but rather part of the duo that had saved his soul. He owed her so much.

"Anyway, that Madeleine chick, she must be a sucking machine. You wouldn't believe the messed-up things I'd do to her. Might as well; that's what they're for, right, guys?"

Upon hearing that sentence, Daniel closed his eyes and exhaled. Some people needed a lesson. Quiet as always, he removed his plates from his tray before grabbing it and walking toward the black-haired jerk. Once near enough, Daniel tapped his shoulder. The youth turned his head and asked, "Yeah?"

With full force, Daniel slammed the plastic slab into his face. The asshole crashed onto the floor with a thud. Blood spilled out of his nose as he whimpered. Startled gasps echoed. Everyone stared at Daniel with their mouths gaping, but he ignored them. Instead, he threw his weapon away and said, "You should respect women," before leaving the scene.

***

For Daniel, confronting the principal demanded little courage. He had done so often back in the day. The old man sat behind his desk, fingers joined in a pyramid, and expressed disappointment. Then he followed the familiar speech: yes, Daniel had a history of bad conduct, but that was years ago, and it seemed he had changed his ways. This sudden regression was troubling. Given the seriousness of his actions, there was no option but to expel Daniel. And what if the Tigh family sued? Daniel didn't care about the elder's opinion; therefore, bearing the reprimand proved easy. Now, however, he faced a far more terrifying prospect, and the resulting anxiety caused a mild bout of acid reflux.

School being over, Daniel headed for his mentor's house to report on the events of the day. Normally, Madeleine walked with him and they shared a chat. Since the principal had thrown him out, he returned home early and headed for his mentor's home two hours later. Soon, Daniel arrived at his destination and rang the doorbell. A mere second after the chime relented, the door sprang open, and a hand reached for his collar, pulling him in. The tug possessed considerable strength, and he almost tumbled forward. Thank God he regained his bearings with his secret mutation.

Now inside, Daniel recognized the person who seized him: Madeleine. The teenage girl stared at him, fists clenched. Remove her anger and the black dress she wore would have been cute. Ah, who was he kidding? She was cute anyway... at least until she lifted her hand for a slap. Daniel winced, but Madeleine stopped the motion before contact. Instead of a blow, she waggled a lecturing finger.

"Oh, so you finally dare show yourself!" As his lips twisted in a grimace, Daniel scratched the back of his head and averted his gaze. Despite the girl's small stature compared to his, Madeleine could be intimidating. "Why did you break that poor boy's nose, Daniel? I believed you had progressed beyond such brutish behavior! You have been expelled! Do you have any idea how disappointed my mother will be?"

"I... I'm sorry." A sigh escaped his mouth. "You should have heard the disgusting things that guy said. The jerk talked as if you were a piece of meat!"

"That is no excuse!" Madeleine poked at Daniel's heart. "They are insecure teenage boys who act macho in a pathetic attempt to pass for grown men. I am above their vulgar banter and you should be too." Then she scoffed and crossed her arms. "Besides, I am more than capable of defending myself. There is no need for you to protect my honor, or whatever nonsense you used to justify your behavior."

Daniel groaned. "Listen, you're right, okay? I screwed up and I'm sorry, but it won't happen again." Madeleine turned around and took a few steps away. Was that a tear he glimpsed on her cheek?

"Lately, Daniel, I do not know what to think! You assaulted that boy. You are planning to join NISDA. Why? Is your thirst for blood so great that you desire war?"

"Come on, Madeleine!" Daniel's voice trembled. "It's not like that, I swear. If I spend my whole service sitting on my butt because of everlasting peace, I'll die a happy man."

Madeleine spun around to face him and frowned. "Then why? Tell me, you owe me that much."

"For her..." After closing his eyes, Daniel scowled. "You know more about Sophia's studies than me. She's—" Madeleine pressed her index fingers against his lips. Then she caressed his face.

"I understand. Please forgive me, for I misjudged you, Daniel. Though your motives are pure, you must be vigilant, for you have a darkness within you. My mother and I silenced the taint, but it exists still, buried deep in your heart. This decision means you will forever tempt your demons. Do not succumb to bloodlust. By joining the army, you will sacrifice many of the small pleasures we take for granted. While your cause is worthy, there is no need to sacrifice your soul as well. The Melkar would not want that."

Daniel nodded. "I promise I'll be careful."

Chapter 2

Kotar 23, 2134, on the Nirnivian calendar

Once again, Daniel and Ron used the special red videophone connecting them to Ostark. On the screen, the one they called Doctor Death appeared. As usual, the cyborg adopted a serious demeanor, though Daniel assumed lacking a mouth contributed to this effect. It must be hard to offer a different impression without the capability of smiling.

A few days earlier, Daniel and his Koporal had contacted the president. BBR had begun raiding Nirnivian transports and stores for supplies, an intolerable affront. NISDA had to counterattack and put back those rascals in their place, but a major obstacle stopped them: their treaty with Ostark limited their ability to operate within the neutral zone. Given BBR hid in that area, that complicated the matter. Since the terrorists proved to be a thorn in Ostark's side too, they hoped the mechanical man would cooperate and accept a short-term modification of their previous agreement. At first, this outcome seemed likely. Doctor Death showed interest in the plan but claimed he needed to consult his cabinet before committing—a mere formality, according to him. Now, however, a tingling sensation in Daniel's neck warned him something had gone wrong, a fact the cyborg soon confirmed.

"As promised, I have brought your proposal to my cabinet," he said while shaking his head before continuing in his monotone voice. "I am afraid it has been rejected. Further excursions into the neutral zone beyond what our original treaty permits remain forbidden. Should Nirnivia violate those terms, Ostark will interpret the gesture as a declaration of war."

Daniel joined his fingers in a pyramid as he often did and leaned forward. The posture conveyed a sense of authority and sometimes helped sway detractors, though he doubted it would produce any effect in his current foe. Still, he performed the action without thinking about it. Force of habit, he supposed. "I understand Ostark's position, but BBR isn't just our concern. If anything, they're a bigger problem for you than us. Getting rid of them is mutually beneficial. Will you please reconsider?"

"If there were any chance to reverse the decision, I would. Alas, it is futile. My colleagues made their opinion clear and I am powerless to change their minds. While they agree BBR is a threat to Ostark, they believe granting Nirnivia further access to the neutral zone poses a greater risk. The stunt you pulled with that Orontian launchpad did not help your case either. To be frank, I disagree, but none of my arguments convinced them."

A groan echoed from Tigh. "Oh, please!" The Koporal crossed his arms. "What you mean is, they're pissed because BBR has been messing with Ostark and we wouldn't let you deal with it like you wanted. Now that the shoe's on the other foot, they're rubbing our faces in it."

"That is likely. An immature display from my cabinet perhaps, but alas"—the Doctor threw his hands upward—"such is Gorumar nature."

Ron rubbed his chin. "Hey, can't you override them? You're the freaking president."

"Indeed, but there would be consequences." He shrugged. "The same is true for NISDA. Military matters fall under the Commander's jurisdiction and not the Council's, but they can still make your life difficult. And so it is in NISDA's best interest to maintain a cordial relationship with the Council, meaning that for important decisions, you will likely consult them and heed their advice. For instance, I cannot imagine the nightmare that would be unleashed should NISDA declare war without the Council's permission." The mechanical man stared at Daniel. "Politics is a game of compromise. Do you agree, Commander Ricdeau?"

"Oh yes. If I did that, my career would be over and that'd be the least of my problems."

"And so you understand my predicament. While this situation is not as extreme, going over the cabinet's head would anger them and might cost me later. BBR is a menace that I wish to eliminate, but not enough to justify infuriating those who can impeach me." The smile in his electronic eye turned upside down. "I am sorry. In any event, I am confident you have other matters to attend to. Thus, I shall not take any more of your time." He offered a small nod. "I bid you farewell."

On that note, the monitor faded to black. Daniel sighed and bent his neck. "Well, I guess that's that."

"Don't you dare tell me you believe him." Ron scoffed. "The bastard can blame his cabinet all he wants, but he's playing us for fools. Doctor Death, the master manipulator, can't convince a bunch of old farts? Come on!"

"That's a fair point, but... I have a feeling..." While exhaling, Daniel waved his own comment away. "It doesn't matter, we can't send soldiers in there either way. We're better off evaluating alternatives, like sending more troops along our border and hoping that slows BBR down."

"Yeah, but it ain't gonna stop them."

"Still better than nothing." With that, Daniel rested his hand on the Koporal's shoulder. "How about we grab a cup of coffee? Whenever I talk with him, I need a pick-me-up."

"Heh, count me in! The bastard is like a mix of sleeping pills and laxatives."

***

When Daniel and Ron exited the room after their disastrous conversation with Doctor Death, they stumbled upon Nicky. The officer paced nearby while rubbing her hands. In appearance, she waited for them. The moment the sound of the opening door echoed, she gasped and spun toward them. In a flash, she straightened and saluted as she exclaimed, "Sir!"

Daniel tilted his head. "At ease. Is there something wrong, Nicky? You look flustered."

"Well, not wrong per se." Nicky twitched. "But there's been a new development." She moistened her lips. "Erik Vandelay contacted us." Recognizing the name demanded a slight effort, but within two seconds Daniel remembered. Back during the techs' strike, Ostark had located and assassinated every spy NISDA had managed to infiltrate into their country. Actually, that wasn't quite true, for a single one had survived: Erik Vandelay. With a nod, Daniel gestured for Nicky to continue. "He discovered confidential information."

Ron scowled. "What the freak did he tell you to spook you so much?"

Nicky took a deep breath. "Erik found out Doctor Death is planning a live press conference in two weeks, something to do with an overhaul of health care. What's more, Erik knows the location."

Only on rare occasions did the cyborg appear outside of secure facilities. Whenever it happened, NISDA learned of the occurrence after the fact. This time they were informed early, and perhaps they could use the situation to their advantage. Filled with anticipation, Daniel leaned forward. "Where?"

"At Rasputin Hospital, and here's the kicker: Erik is in the same city."

A slight smile spread on Daniel's face as he considered the implications, and he mumbled, "My, my..."

His Koporal chuckled. "Oh, that's beautiful." Ron slammed his fist into his palm. "That bastard's been playing with us from the start, always a step ahead! But now, luck's on our side! We got him by the balls!" As if to illustrate his point, Ron mimicked seizing a nonexistent object in thin air and yanked.

"Maybe." Daniel rubbed his chin. "We have to act fast. Nicky!" Again, she saluted. "Gather the senior officers—emergency meeting in half an hour in the war room. Sorry for the short notice"—he smirked—"but we're in a hurry."

Chapter 3

Seconds after Daniel instructed Nicky to assemble the troops, he and Ron headed for the war room. A large rectangular conference table lay in the center of the chamber, a golden NISDA logo displaying the famous shield and winged sword on its black wooden surface. Once they arrived, the men sat at each end, showing their positions of authority, the mother and father of the family in a sense, though neither ever debated which role each of them fulfilled.

For every seat at the table, a special cable existed. Plugging in either a minicomp or a laptop computer allowed one to take control of the four large screens mounted on each wall surrounding them. Those displayed the same image, so everyone could watch from any position.

For a while, they waited in silence. Daniel joined his fingers in a pyramid and contemplated the situation. Nicky had offered little information, but he understood what Erik Vandelay's discovery implied. The prospect caused both a tingle of excitement and a shiver to run down his spine, and he wondered if Tigh endured a similar sensation.

Soon, people began entering the war room. Wilburg, Clara, Milton, Tina and more. Each saluted before taking their place, and Daniel greeted them with a nod. Nicky arrived almost last, because she had to locate her colleagues. For a moment, he thought they could begin, but then he spotted an empty seat. By scanning the faces present, Daniel deduced that the missing person was David, and so they delayed. Three minutes late, he showed up. Thanks to his mutant vision, Daniel noted David fidgeted as he flashed an apologetic smile. In response, Daniel gestured toward the vacant chair and said, "No worries, I didn't give you a lot of time."

"Thank you, sir!"

Now ready to begin, Daniel harrumphed. "All right, we should get things started. First, I'm sorry for rushing you, but there's been a major development. Our last remaining spy in Ostark, Erik Vandelay, has sent unexpected information concerning Doctor Death. Nicky, would you mind giving us the details?"

The Perz woman straightened. "With pleasure, sir! As you're all aware, Doctor Death likes to keep a low profile and usually remains safe in high-security complexes, much like it is for Her Holiness. Unlike her, he makes public appearances on occasion, and according to Erik, he'll do so in two weeks at the Rasputin Hospital for a health-care-related announcement. It seems that hospital has historical significance for Ostark and that's why he chose that location. The important part is we can tell where the president will be and when." She paused and everyone leaned forward as the air in the room grew heavy. "That means it might be our only chance for an assassination attempt."

Every officer present except for Daniel, Ron and Nicky gasped and began talking simultaneously. The resulting cacophony served no purpose as it rendered listening to the spoken words futile. In such circumstances, Moderator Doug Thomson would silence the crowd by banging his gavel. Daniel lacked the tool, and so he tapped the table with his palm instead.

"Order, order! Please, calm down and raise your hand if you wish to speak." The whole room did so. While rubbing his forehead, Daniel sighed. "Yes, I expected that. Clara, you were the fastest by a quarter of a second, so go ahead." Praise Ulgorack for his heightened senses, or he would've missed that detail for certain.

"Sir, with all due respect, this is madness! It would be the end of the uneasy peace. With so little time to prepare, success is far from guaranteed. If Doctor Death survives, we're doomed."

Daniel agreed. "Yes, there's no question there. In fact, it's worse than that. Ostark has superior strength and technology. The Doctor is a formidable asset for them, but even without him, we're unlikely to survive." He grimaced. "I'm not convinced we should kill him, but we have to consider it."

"Really? Why?" Poor Wilburg blushed and covered his mouth as he realized he had spoken without being invited to. "Oh, I'm sorry." With a shrug, Daniel waved for him to continue. "Um, well, I don't see why we have to consider certain death. Assassinating the Doctor is pointless if it means sacrificing Nirnivia."

A scowl formed on Daniel's brow as he was about to answer, but a scoff echoed, interrupting him. Everyone stared at the source, the Koporal. "Pointless? Gimme a break, it's the only way we might survive." Ron crossed his arms and smirked. "You guys think the Doctor will let us live in peace forever? He freaking won't. The bastard wants Rose, and he's waiting for an opportunity to get her. Trust me, one day he'll get sick of waiting and he'll attack, and when that happens we're screwed. Remove him from the equation, and we got maybe a chance in a million we'll win. That's damn low, but if you ask me it's better than the zero we'll have with him alive." He raised a disbelieving eyebrow. "Don't tell me you forgot the Kerbell report?"

As Tigh uttered those words, the officers around the table lowered their gazes. When the uneasy peace had been enacted, Nirnivia had stood at the brink of annihilation. They'd had no option but to accept the Ostarkirans' mercy even if they suspected a poisoned gift. Still, several questions needed answers: For how long would the truce last? When it broke, would Nirnivia have any chance to survive? Should they attack preemptively once they recovered, or hope Ostark wouldn't resume the hostilities? Daniel had appointed a strategist named Pascal Kerbell to study the situation. The resulting report had proven so dire it had shattered his spirit for a month when he'd read it.

Based on Kerbell's research, when the war had started, Ostark had already possessed a slight technological advantage. That explained why they'd dominated Nirnivia from the beginning. Once the Doctor had appeared, the disparity had increased. Fueled by his genius, Ostark had made discovery after discovery, increasing the scientific gap inch by inch. The uneasy peace hadn't stalled their progress. If anything, not having to fight had helped them grow faster. As long as the cyborg lived, that wouldn't change. Every month he led Ostark, Nirnivia's low chance at victory diminished. At this rate, Kerbell estimated, their opponent would be invincible in three to four years. For that reason, he proposed that, should the opportunity to kill the president emerge, they had to attempt it. While doing so implied death, not doing so guaranteed it. Two years had passed since his recommendation.

With a sigh, Daniel joined his hands in a manner suggesting he prayed. "The Kerbell report isn't divine truth. He could be wrong."

The Koporal grunted. "Yeah, well, when the highest authority in the field says something, you should listen."

"Oh yes, I agree. That's why we're here. In theory, it's my decision, but no matter what we decide, we better get the Council's opinion before we pull the trigger. It's like Doctor Death said earlier, we have to deal with politics, and pissing off Moderator Thomson and the councillors won't do us any good." He glanced at Tigh, who twisted his lips and nodded.

"Ah yeah, back in the day we called that covering our asses." The old man chuckled. "We were all in on it, so they can't blame us and we can't blame them."

Daniel pointed at his friend in a manner mimicking the firing of a gun. "Yep! Regardless of what we end up doing, we don't have much time left. That's why we should get the Council's permission ASAP. That way, we're ready to act if we choose to. If we want the Council to accept our proposition, we need a plan—something to show them we can pull it off. Otherwise, they'd never agree." Daniel exhaled. "In other words, we have to figure something out during this meeting." Many winces and shudders he spotted as he pronounced that sentence, but he ignored the reactions. "Nicky, I assume you have the info Erik sent us?"

"Yes, sir!" On that note, she rested her minicomp on the table. "There's not much available, but we have photographs of the hospital and basic notes about the Ostarkirans' security plan."

With that, she jammed the special connector cable into the appropriate port. The surrounding screens flashed before depicting a large brick building. Green letters spelling "Hospital" adorned its facade. Two visible doors permitted entrance, the first labeled general admission and the second emergencies. In rapid succession, Nicky went from one photo to the next. The last image was taken from a greater distance and revealed the parking areas on the sides filled with cars plus a few ambulances. A single emergency vehicle appeared to be departing, its flashers engaged. As for the front of the hospital, it consisted of a grass-covered park. Several trees graced the area, accompanied by multicolored flowers, a couple picnic tables and a fountain. Daniel spotted three birds flying around and a pissack running along a branch. The twin-tailed rodent made him smile as he remembered Janice's so-called pet. Other than the gray clouds above, the scene proved idyllic.

"These images aren't too useful, I admit, but they indicate the layout. We also have this." The monitor switched from the realistic setting to a sketch composed of black lines on a white background. Daniel recognized the same building represented as a simple rectangle. In the park, before the fountain, a new structure presented itself. "As you can see, they're assembling a stage right there, along with benches and chairs for the audience." Further drawings offered different viewing angles and extra information about the stage's proportions. "Details about the security measure are sparse. Erik learned that the Doctor will arrive in an armored vehicle two minutes before his speech starts. Once he's done, he'll leave. No sticking around for the celebration, no talking to journalists, he'll hop in his ride and drive away. Erik believes his security service would prefer he didn't attend, but he's insisting and so they compromised by having him there for the shortest time possible. We can expect plenty of bodyguards surrounding the president and several armed troops patrolling the area. They're also planning on having snipers positioned on the nearby buildings. While those are a little far, the distance won't stop a sharpshooter worth their salt from shooting down any troublemaker. In addition, metal detectors will prevent anyone from sneaking weapons in."

The description of the security plans continued for another five or six minutes, but by that point Daniel had a clear picture. He rubbed his chin while he pondered what he'd learned until a female voice echoed, "I've been thinking..." Tina tapped her cheek with two fingers while she adopted a pensive expression. "Is there any way we can blame the assassination attempt on BBR?"

Daniel chuckled. "Oh, we'll try, but I doubt Ostark will be fooled. BBR pulling something this elaborate is far-fetched."

"Fair enough." Tina swallowed hard. "Doctor Death is a difficult man to kill. His body's gone, replaced by machines. A gun wouldn't work well, since a bullet won't put a dent in him. His only weak point is his head, and hitting his electronic eye or speaker wouldn't hurt him. And trust me, Erik will only have a single try before the guards jump on him."

"Yes, that's true," Daniel agreed. "To make matters worse, Erik isn't a sharpshooter by any stretch of the imagination." He sighed. "No, even if we concealed a pistol on the premises to avoid the metal detectors, he'd fail."

A grunt escaped David as he shifted on his seat. "Normally, I'd suggest poison, but he doesn't eat food."

"That'd be difficult anyway. He won't be staying for the after-party." David averted his gaze and scratched behind his head, perhaps embarrassed by Daniel's remark.

Weldon spoke next. "What about a knife?"

A laugh came from Tigh. "Oh yeah, that's amazing! Rush to the stage and stab the asshole in his living eye! Don't worry about the bodyguards, you'll pass through them by magic. Damn, son, Erik's a freaking spy, not a combat expert. That's dumber than the gun, and the poison!"

A large bang resounded as Daniel slammed the table. "That's enough!" Everyone shut up as instructed and glared at him. "You're right, Koporal Tigh, but the sarcasm isn't welcome. This is a brainstorming session, and I won't have your condescending tone stop people from contributing."

"Fine, I'm sorry."

"Good. Anyone else have an idea?"

"Well, about poison—"

Despite their best efforts, poison led nowhere. Every other suggestion ended up being ludicrous. For a while now, Daniel had realized what needed to be done, yet he waited before revealing his plan, expecting a promising officer would beat him to the punch. But none did, and so he opened his mouth when Nicky leaned forward.

"Listen, guys, I've been thinking and there's only one thing that can work. I hesitated to say it because it sounds impossible, but—" She groaned. "What if we replace an Ostarkiran sniper?"

David stifled a chuckle. "Vandelay isn't trained for that."

With a dead cold tone, Nicky replied, "Who said I meant Vandelay?"

A deafening silence filled the room until a slapping sound echoed because of Ron face-palming. "So now we have to sneak a sniper into the neutral zone and past the Ostarkiran border in less than two weeks? Are you kidding me?"

"I share your concerns, old friend, but I don't see any alternatives." Daniel got to his feet and started pacing as he covered his mouth with his palm. "It's crazy, but we have an opportunity. There's a raid on a BBR cell scheduled in two days. It's already arranged with Ostark—they allowed us to send limited troops. It's not close to the border, but the hospital isn't deep in Ostark. Whoever we send could get there in a day—day and a half at most. That gives us over a week before the speech."

Ron scoffed. "Are you mad? Smuggling someone into Ostark ain't as simple as snapping our fingers."

"We did it before."

"Yeah, and it took months of preparation."

Daniel dismissed the Koporal's concern with a wave. "At least we can fall back on our previous experience. Those details can wait. We don't need perfection to convince the Council—a draft on a napkin will do. Let's search for a suitable sniper, shall we? In the meantime, we'll take what we have, cross some *t*'s and dot some *i*'s to make it presentable, and then we can organize an emergency meeting."

Chapter 4

The men behind the desk wore the same uniform as Travis, yet they stood in a different league. Compared to them, he'd achieved almost nothing. When Travis had received a message requesting his presence in the Commander's office, he'd trembled in his boots in anticipation of meeting one of his idols. Sure, he'd spotted the senior in the distance once or twice, but they'd never spoken. Daniel Ricdeau was a legend in NISDA—perhaps the best Commander in history—and even ignoring that fact, he'd earned his fame during his service. How often as a young man had he taken on an assignment implying certain death, only to beat the odds and emerge alive? Too many to count. No mission proved too dangerous, no risk too terrifying for Daniel's determination. To think he now sat in front of Travis, smiling and explaining what they hoped from him while gesticulating. What an honor.

As for Tigh—well, Travis didn't know him on a personal level, but so far he'd lived up to his reputation of being a grumpy old man. During the whole exchange, he'd remained cross-armed and frowning. No sound he produced, except for an occasional grunt. Many times in the past, Travis had heard people complain about the Koporal. He was a mean asshole and joyless, a contrast to the Commander. Most wondered why Daniel valued his friendship. Still, no question Ron shared his superior's impressive record. Whatever madness Daniel headed into, Tigh followed. Perhaps that explained their bond.

Though Travis realized the importance of this meeting, focusing on Daniel's words demanded an effort. His mind kept wandering, recalling his leader's achievements, and he had to remind himself to focus.

"—so you won't have anything linking you to NISDA and won't be bringing any weapon or special equipment. If you fail, we'll blame BBR."

A scoff escaped Tigh's lips as he rolled his eyes. "Yeah, sure, as if the Doctor will fall for that crap."

"It's a long shot, I admit." Daniel shrugged. "But stranger things have happened." He lifted his index finger to reinforce the following point. "Now, my boy, I want to remind you this isn't an order. You can refuse and there's no shame in that. Nobody will judge you." The elder winked. "In fact, it'll be our little secret." He then sighed. "I don't want to pressure you, but we'll need an answer before the end of the day."

Travis swallowed, gulping down all his doubts and fears. His therapist claimed discarding negative emotions instead of feeling them broke your mind in the long run. In this situation, what did it matter? "I'll do it."

"Oh, that was quicker than expected." As he joined his fingers in a pyramid, the Commander leaned forward. "Are you sure? Don't forget this is a suicide mission. You won't be coming back."

Travis nodded. "Yes, sir, I'm well aware of that."

"In that case, welcome aboard."

With those words, Daniel extended his hand and Travis shook it. He hoped Daniel didn't notice his palm's moistness. Afterward, Tigh presented his hand. "You know, badass young'uns like you give me hope for your generation. A bunch of freaking whiners if you ask me, but glad to see there are exceptions."

"Oh, that reminds me." Daniel opened his drawer and rummaged through its contents. "Before you leave, I have a gift for you, son." He fished out a metallic case with a glass cover. Inside rested a golden medal adorned with a purple ribbon. The intricate shape depicted a winged woman, not the current Melkar but the original, Misha. She kneeled and held NISDA's famous shield high in the air.

Upon the sight, Travis recoiled and gasped. The courage medal, the highest honor a soldier could receive. He reached for the reward, trembling. Tears filled his eyes, and he fought them back, refusing to cry before two war heroes. "Th-thank you, sir!"

"No, I should thank you. No matter what happens from here on, you're a hero."

Chapter 5

The large wooden gate closed behind Daniel and Ron. The Council had heard their pleas and now debated the merits of their proposal among themselves. Whatever the politicians decided lay out of their control. Since they expected the deliberation to last for a while, both Daniel and his Koporal rested on the leather sofa installed in the lobby. With a groan, Tigh crossed his arms as Daniel said, "I think it went well."

"Yeah?" Ron chuckled. "I ain't so sure about that. Guess we'll find out, huh? At least your dearest daughter wasn't there to screw us over. No freaking way she'd agree to an assassination."

A sad smile formed on Daniel's face and he nodded. "You're right, if she knew what we were doing, she'd be furious." As Ron claimed, Rose being a councillor spelled doom for their plan, but they'd sidestepped that problem by claiming the possibility of a conflict of interest. In fact, that had worked so well that the Council had not only organized an emergency session without her, they'd hidden its existence from her. As far as Rose was aware, her peers didn't meet on this day. That suited Daniel fine. Rose believed that in his own way, Doctor Death protected Nirnivia. After all, the cyborg had ushered in the uneasy peace, sparing them. Though he wished to capture Rose for his own sinister reasons, he preferred to keep their country out of their personal feud. To her, removing the freak from power implied war, and Daniel admitted he concurred. Where their opinion differed was that he expected the Doctor would someday lose his patience and attack despite his promise not to while Rose trusted his words. Attempting to change her views proved impossible.

For over an hour, Tigh and Daniel waited in the vestibule. At first they talked about various subjects to pass the time. Perhaps because of the nervousness brought by their precarious situation, they soon ran out of conversation topics and fell silent. Eventually, a roar echoed, puzzling Daniel. He turned toward Tigh and found him snoring with his mouth open and drool dripping on his chin. Daniel resisted the incoming laughter out of fear of waking up his friend.

Since Daniel had lost his companion, he began enumerating everything that could go wrong in the upcoming operation. Several potential disasters awaited them. Travis might die in the neutral zone, or be caught by the Ostarkirans at their border. As far as failure went, those weren't the worst alternatives. The first one ensured their enemy wouldn't discover NISDA's deception, and the second—well, occasionally Nirnivians attempted to cross over to Ostark to start a new life. The odds of success were low, and accomplishing their goal implied losing their identity. Immigration being illegal for everyone, a Nirnivian in Ostark had no rights and would essentially become a slave. Still, people desperate enough existed and a few criminal organizations had developed services catering to their needs. Should Travis be captured, he could pretend to be among these poor fools yearning for another chance.

If Travis managed to cross the border, his task then grew in complexity. With Erik Vandelay's help, he'd infiltrate the ranks of the snipers. To be discovered at that stage would spell doom. Even if he succeeded, what if he pulled the trigger and missed? Maybe more terrifying, what if the bullet hit its mark? Both alternatives sent shivers through Daniel's body.

Before long, the scenarios Daniel imagined began repeating. His worries served no purpose, so to combat them, he studied the painting mounted on the wall: a mishmash of colors. Red, yellow and orange mixed in what he deemed a random pattern. No form, no reason, no shape, just pure chaos. Madeleine loved abstract art. He failed to understand it. What was so amazing about a drawing resembling a toddler's work? Once he'd asked, and a disgusted Madeleine had explained that art wasn't only about technique but also the intention of the artist. Fine, he supposed, but what intention could there be? Deep down, he assumed the painters splashed paints without thinking and proclaimed the result a masterpiece. Then they mocked their fans while enjoying their praise.

Daniel still studied the image when the door opened. The Council's secretary poked his head through the gap. "Mr. Ricdeau, Mr. Tigh, you can come back in."

Ron woke with a gasp. "Huh?" He blinked thrice. "Oh..." With that, the Koporal stretched and grunted before jumping to his feet.

***

Again, Daniel and Ron entered the Council room. Under normal circumstances, they assembled around an oval table, but this was a different chamber for when they received guests. Instead, the councillors gathered on the same side of a large rectangular table, similar to the one in NISDA's war room. The visitors sat on the opposite side, facing them. Daniel deduced this arrangement helped convey unity. That they all averted their gazes in various directions, refusing to look at him or each other, reduced the effect. Something told Daniel the deliberations had caused tension.

Only Doug Thomson stared at Daniel and Tigh, and once they were seated, he said, "Commander Ricdeau, Koporal Tigh, thank you for your patience. We considered your proposal and debated the issue at length." He took a deep breath. "The Council feels you two are the best suited for this decision. You are the most aware of the risks Ostark poses, both in the present and in the future. As such, we trust you with Nirnivia's safety and will support whatever choice you make."

Jade Carlson clutched her fists and Daniel noted her mouth twisted in a slight sneer. "Commander Ricdeau, you requested Rose be excluded from this meeting because of a possible conflict of interest. While I understand your reasoning, it could also apply to you." She glared at Daniel. "I hope your decision will be for Nirnivia's sake and not shadows of the past."

"I've taken an oath to protect Nirnivia, and I intend to keep it. Still, you have a point, and if the Council prefers, I will recuse myself and let my Koporal handle the matter."

"That won't be necessary, Commander Ricdeau." Doug fired a reprimanding glance at Jade. "You have our full support."

***

The dealings with the Council done, Ron and Daniel returned to the parking lot, where a black sedan waited. The moment he spotted them, the driver exited the car and walked toward the back. Once they drew close enough, he opened the door and saluted. Daniel thanked him for the courtesy as he snuck inside. As for Tigh, he went for a simple nod instead.

With his passengers now on board, the chauffeur returned to the wheel and turned the ignition key. As commanded, the motor roared and soon they were in motion. Daniel pushed a button on his armrest, resulting in a thin partition going up with a mechanical hiss. In effect, the divider separated them from the driver, preventing him from observing them or hearing their conversation. The Koporal fired an inquisitive glance and Daniel shrugged. "Just in case we talk about what happened with the Council. He doesn't have clearance."

"Yeah, that makes sense." A short pause Ron indulged in before licking his lips. "Shit, Dan, speaking of those assholes, what's that 'we leave it up to you' crap? So much for your plan of sharing the blame if things turn into a clusterfreak."

Daniel sighed. "Ah well, it was worth a shot."

"You think the bastards stole our idea? Like, give us full control so they can pin it on us if it backfires?"

"Probably. That's how politics works."

Tigh groaned and crossed his arms. "Damn straight, they're always covering their asses. A bunch of cowards if you ask me."

Instead of replying, Daniel stared out the window. What a beautiful day. Outside, they passed several stores and restaurants. Quite a few people enjoyed the sun by strolling along the sidewalk. Of particular note, a mutant girl with scales around her eyes noticed their car and with a gaping mouth brought her hand to her brow, mimicking a military salute. The child must have recognized the golden NISDA logo painted on the sides of their vehicles. Despite her young age—he guessed six, seven at most—she nailed the motion with surprising accuracy.

Daniel smiled and returned the gesture before saying, "Hey, Ron, check that out, we have a future recruit there!"

Tigh chuckled. "Heh, cute!" Then he lightly punched Daniel's shoulder. "If we screw this up, she'll be the last fan we'll have left. Everyone else will want to skin us alive."

"Yes, I suppose so." A frown appeared on Daniel's forehead. "Maybe we shouldn't go through with it."

"You're serious?" the Koporal asked, wide-eyed. Daniel agreed. "Damn, I was kidding, Dan."

"It was still true."

"So what? We let the Doctor run the show? Wait until we have no chance of beating him? What then?"

With a groan, Daniel rubbed his chin. "I don't know."

"Ah crap, tell me you ain't turning soft on him too."

Daniel dismissed the notion with a wave. "No, nothing like that. It's more like... the Kerbell report says we should assassinate the Doctor or else Ostark's technology will progress until they're virtually invincible. That's plausible—freak, it might already be too late—but life isn't predictable. Nobody can read the future. If we kill him, Ostark will attack and that could spell our doom. If we don't, a miracle can always happen. He's not a healthy man. He could die tomorrow from natural causes for all we know."

Ron's lips twisted as he considered Daniel's words. "Sure, but that's wishful thinking."

"So is hoping we defeat Ostark once we get rid of Doctor Death."

"Yeah, but to me that's more of a case of making our own luck, and I prefer that." He grunted. "Anyway, it's your call, but if you're gonna change your mind, do it quick. We're sending Travis tomorrow."

Daniel forced a laugh. "That's fine, I can still sleep on it."

Chapter 6

Kotar 24, 2134, on the Nirnivian calendar

The shot glass produced a clink as Daniel dropped it on his desk. Then he grasped the priceless bottle of uisge and poured himself a serving of the alcoholic beverage within. Tigh instead went with a druikinaka juice. Golden versus blue, to Daniel a contest with an obvious winner. Now both served, Daniel raised his glass. "To Travis, the latest in a long list of Nirnivian heroes."

Ron mimicked his gesture. "Hear, hear!"

The toast said, they clinked, and both downed their drink in a single gulp. Daniel let out a satisfied grunt as the uisge burned his throat. "Trust me, I needed a pick-me-up." He grimaced. "I still can't believe we're doing this." A shudder assailed him. "I hate sending good soldiers to their deaths."

"Yeah, we all do." The Koporal shrugged. "But it's part of the job."

"Yes, I guess so, but it doesn't make it easier." Daniel sighed as he recalled an image of Brucie lying on a stretcher. "I feel like I'm sending the poor guy straight into that beast's mouth knowing he doesn't stand a chance."

"Well, at least he won't be mauled to death by a savage animal."

"Too bad the Ostarkirans might do worse than that." A groan escaped Daniel's lips. "Anyway, I think I messed up. If the plan fails, Rose will kill me. If it works, she might do it anyway."

"Nah, she doesn't have the guts for that kind of violence." A chuckle escaped Tigh. "Maybe she'll bore you to death with a speech." He stopped for a short pause. "So, you haven't told her?"

Daniel wiggled in his seat. "Dear God, no! If I had my way, she'd never find out."

"Good! I don't want her busting our balls. There'll be plenty of that once we're at war."

In silence, Daniel nodded. Even if he assumed Travis would pull off the assassination, the future battle would be grueling. With or without Doctor Death, the Ostarkirans were a formidable foe. They had proven that much during their last conflict as they'd brought NISDA to their knees. Nothing guaranteed they'd avoid the same outcome this time. In fact, though Daniel hated to admit it, deep down he doubted their chances. Still, they had to do something, eventually. At least they had one advantage: they knew of what was coming, and so could prepare. For instance, they'd increased defense along their border. Of course, they had to be careful and remain discreet to ensure Ostark wouldn't notice what they were doing. Otherwise, it would seem suspicious. Regardless, a ton of troops waited in a perfect position to invade and defend the neutral zone.

Despite their preparations, so many details could go wrong. Considering the possibilities of failure made Daniel's stomach churn. Filled with desire, he glanced at the uisge bottle. It steeled the nerves, and how he yearned for the courage it granted. However, abusing the stuff at work lacked professionalism and increased the risk of being busted.

Gritting his teeth, Daniel pulled his eyes away from the liquid temptation and instead opened a drawer. As he rummaged through the contents, he said, "I have to keep my mind busy or I'll drive myself insane." Then he fished out a pack of cards and presented it to Tigh. "Are you up for a game?"

"Sure thing, Dan!"

Chapter 7

The sun's rays roasted Travis as he walked down the street. A massive amount of sweat gathered at his armpits and he imagined the dark stains forming on his shirt. His parched throat begged for water and burned whenever he coughed. Though he wished to grant it that mercy, he'd emptied his reserves around an hour ago. He lacked food too, and his stomach growled. However, thanks to his sore gullet, he couldn't imagine swallowing a bite of anything. That helped overcome hunger, a smidge of good fortune brought upon by a desperate situation.

The superior officers had warned Travis of Ostark's high temperatures. The climate was warmer than what he had grown used to, they said. That matched what they'd taught him in school, and so he'd believed them. Still, "warmer" failed to convey the ridiculous heat he now endured. Any more and he'd assume he'd entered a giant oven by mistake. The hoodie covering his head didn't help. He could have removed it, but having his face exposed in enemy territory caused a tightening in his chest and a sickening sensation in his guts. Of course, he realized the pointlessness of his disguise. Nobody here had ever met him. It'd be impossible for him to be recognized. If anything, the hoodie made him appear more suspicious, not less.

Besides the abundant perspiration, a layer of grime and dirt covered Travis, a gift from the trip through the neutral zone, which had also left his clothes torn and ragged. The combination caused a sensation of grossness that covered his body, similar to when he skipped a shower for too long, except ten times worse. The memory of the neutral zone brought a shiver. No civilization there, but plenty of dense forests filled with predators and hostile vegetation.

Somehow Travis had survived and reached the border, but that had proven a far more terrifying obstacle. If the Ostarkirans had caught him, he'd be dead or a slave. His superiors had told him to head northeast once he separated from the troops accompanying him. That would lead him to what used to be the Ostarkiran frontier's weakest spot. Their intel wasn't as fresh anymore. Fortunately, that turned out correct. Well, maybe—Travis couldn't be certain he'd followed the intended path. Perhaps he'd discovered a different entry point. Despite the area being almost deserted, he had encountered guards along with a domesticated warg. For a moment, it seemed like the warg had smelled Travis and it had growled. Thank Ulgorack, a heroic pissack received the blame for the animal's outburst.

An hour after entering Ostark, Travis had stumbled on a farmer who had offered him a ride in his truck until he arrived at his destination: the city of Motokiva. From there, he needed to reach the rendezvous point where he'd meet Erik Vandelay. NISDA refused to let him carry a note with the directions, so he'd committed them to memory. Travis prayed he remembered correctly. At the moment, he strolled down a posh street filled with people. Many expensive business suits and fancy dresses he spotted. He didn't fit the décor and everyone swerved around him, keeping maximum distance without stepping off the sidewalk.

One man walking with his small daughter fired a disgusted grimace at Travis. While stifling his laughter, he approached the guy and extended his hand. "Got any spare change, sir?"

The stranger's cheeks reddened and he pulled his child toward him as if protecting her from the evils Travis might unleash. "Stay away from me, you filthy bum!"

Travis obliged as he cackled. He had attempted this on multiple occasions since arriving in Motokiva. Given he looked like a beggar, he figured he might as well act like one. While most passersby showed little generosity, he had accumulated a few Ostarkiran dollars. Why, he must've had enough for two snacks at least...

As that thought emerged from his brain, Travis mumbled a curse and smacked his forehead. How stupid of him. Laughing at his stupidity, he located the closest convenience store and entered. The customers and the cashier stared at him, mouths gaping. Travis's kind wasn't welcome. Regardless, he ignored them and rushed for the refrigerated drinks, where he reached for a bottle of water. Then he headed for the cash register and grabbed a candy bar. He plopped the items on the counter along with all his change. He had no idea of the worth of Ostark currency, so he'd let the clerk handle it. The worker complied and seized the relevant coins. Meanwhile, he bobbed his head toward the door. Travis understood the hint, and he left.

Outside, Travis twisted the cap off and swallowed a mouthful of liquid relief. When he forced himself to stop, he realized he'd drunk half the thing. Better keep the rest for later. Thirst conquered, Travis continued progressing. Soon he arrived at a less-than-reputable neighborhood. People sharing his clothing style stood around and sat on the sidewalk. Many waved at him or said hi, and he responded in kind. It always astounded Travis how close the rich quarters could be to the slums. You crossed the wrong street, and bam, the scenery wasn't so idyllic anymore. Doctor Death might've been an amazing president, but even he had failed to vanquish poverty.

Soon, Travis spotted a dilapidated sign spelling the words "Harray Alley." That was his destination, 466 Harray Alley. He found the building sporting that number without trouble. No Erik, however. But that smell. What a stench, even worse than himself. With a retch, Travis covered his lips and scanned the area. He noticed a pile of excrement on the sidewalk and expected it was of Gorumar origin. Charming...

For forty-five minutes Travis waited. By then, he'd finished both his candy bar and water. He wondered how long before the spy showed up and considered leaving, except where would he go? Might as well stay and hope for the best. As he pondered that fact, a blunt pain assailed Travis. Something hit him from behind, and he collapsed while screaming. Now facedown on the ground, Travis gasped and attempted to get up. A pressure on his spine pinned him. He glanced over his shoulder. Two men sporting large grins towered above him. Cops? Ostarkiran soldiers? No, they were dressed in rags. One of them brandished a wooden club.

"Sorry, old guy. Ya wanna live? Give us everything you got, even the clothes."

"Yeah, don't be shy! Better naked than dead, huh?" The muggers erupted in laughter. Why did they want his junk? They must have been desperate. But whatever, their motives weren't important. Travis had to get rid of them. The assailants snickered at their lame joke and didn't pay attention to him. Using this to his advantage, Travis rolled away and returned to his feet. His body ached in complaint, but he managed.

The thief with the bludgeon grunted and swung, but Travis dodged by sidestepping. After he avoided the blow, he snatched the robber's arm and pushed against the joint with such strength that the bone snapped. The thug collapsed and cried. Travis knocked him out with a strike to the head. Sure, they'd overpowered him thanks to the surprise, but they lacked the training of a NISDA soldier. In a fair fight, they stood no chance. Or so he assumed when he heard a click. In a flash, Travis spun. The other attacker pointed a beat-up pistol at him.

"Now you die, son o' a bitch!" Before the mugger finished him, a gunshot resounded. A gush of blood emerged from the thug's head and he collapsed. Travis took a deep breath as a Perz dressed in plain black clothes approached. His rescuer wore sunglasses despite the darkness. As for his hair, Travis couldn't say since a bandana concealed it. The man said, "The night is cold and dark."

"Not as much as the heart of the passersby for this poor beggar," Travis replied as instructed. Unless the Ostarkirans had heard of the code, this was his contact: Erik Vandelay. For sure, he didn't resemble a Nirnivian, but that was probably the desired effect. Not taking any chances, Vandelay shot the unconscious thief.

"You must be Travis. I'm Erik."

"Was that necessary?" Travis asked as he eyed the fresh cadaver.

"I'm thorough. That's why I'm the only one who survived."

"And if the cops track you?"

"Don't worry, a gang from around here uses this type of pistol: the Ol-kodo. They always murder the homeless for sport. The police won't give a damn."

Chapter 8

After a short drive in a car far more compact than any vehicle Travis had observed in Nirnivia, they arrived at Erik's rented house. The building lay in a somewhat isolated area, with decent distance between neighbors. A sigh of relief escaped Travis as he noted that fact. The thought of having the operation compromised by a nosy person from next door proved unbearable, and his temporary home's location helped dispel that fear.

In a nonchalant motion, Erik fished keys out of his pocket and opened the gate. Then he swung it open, and they entered. Out of politeness, Travis removed his shoes and followed Erik into the kitchen. There, he scanned the room, mouth gaping. Everything he saw possessed a slickness and aura of modernity Nirnivia's appliances lacked. The stove used a touch-based surface for controls rather than the familiar dials and buttons. The fridge offered a ridiculous amount of space, far more than necessary for a single man like Erik. Even the toaster turned out to be more advanced. It allowed toasting six slices instead of the two such Nirnivian devices permitted. On the counter, Travis spotted a minicomp, except a quarter of the expected depth. Plus, no sign of a stylus! Could it be one poked the screen with one's fingers? How convenient! And what about the TV he glimpsed in the living room. Why, it must've been an inch thick. A pittance compared to the large boxes required back home. How did Ostark manage those feats?

As Travis observed the wonders present, Erik opened the fridge and grabbed a metallic can. He pulled out a prong, and the hiss of escaping gas echoed. The deed done, he brought the concoction to his lips and gulped. Apparently, Ostark had discovered an alternative to bottles. That explained what the strange cylinders he'd spotted in the convenience store earlier had been. Erik then pointed at Travis. "Hey, mate, you hungry?"

For a response, Travis's stomach grumbled, and he chuckled. He had eaten nothing that day except that candy bar. "Uh, try starving." Expecting a meal, he salivated.

"Sorry, no can do. The doc's coming in an hour for your"—the spy winked—"operation. You can't eat till that's done, his orders."

Travis groaned and bent his neck. "Are you kidding me? Why? Can't it be tomorrow?"

"Nope, you need to recover quickly, so we gotta do it fast."

"But a single day—"

"Hey, I'm just following the doc's advice." Erik shrugged. "He's the pro." Then his eyes scanned Travis from head to toe. "No way he can operate on someone that dirty. Take a shower. Bathroom's over there."

***

An hour later, Travis lay on a stretcher in Erik's basement. As instructed, he had showered. The grime covering his body had proven so resilient that, by the time he'd finished scrubbing it off, the doctor had already arrived. Still, he admitted cleaning up felt good. The warm water pouring on his skin had helped soothe his aching muscles. Now, though, the relaxation period was over.

Erik and the surgeon had brought the required equipment to the house before Travis's arrival, realizing that, despite the relative isolation, moving everything in one go might draw unwanted attention. Travis appreciated their foresight. When he asked where Erik had found someone capable of pulling off the procedure, the spy explained he'd hired a mob doctor who specialized in healing criminals. At first, that worried Travis, who questioned the logic of trusting such a dubious individual with a delicate operation. Then Erik remarked that the surgeon had accomplished this task on multiple occasions. Changing appearances served the mob well for their crimes. They'd be hard-pressed to find a law-abiding physician who had their recruit's experience. That seemed plausible, so Travis tried his best to put his fear to rest, with little success. How he wished he could have received this treatment back in Nirnivia in a proper hospital. Alas, they lacked this technology.

While twiddling his fingers, Travis looked to his right, where Erik stood and the doc sat at a computer. A large wooden board supported pinned pictures of Rousseau the sniper from various angles as well as Travis himself. The surgeon typed on his keyboard as the screen displayed a 3-D model of Rousseau he'd reconstructed based on the data Erik had provided. Soon it would begin, and Travis swallowed hard at the thought.

Perhaps noticing his apprehension, Erik stepped forward and said, "Rousseau's the perfect choice, mate. He's a loner, but competent. A guy that they trust, but enough of a stranger that they don't know his personal life. That makes impersonating him easier, especially once you have his face."

"Sure, but I can still screw up. What if I say something wrong, or make a gesture he'd never make?"

Erik dismissed the notion with a wave. "No problem there, mate. I'll give you acting lessons. Besides, people will be busy and in a hurry. There won't be much chitchat anyway."

"If you say so."

The spy patted Travis's wrist. "I do."

Then the doctor's voice echoed. "All right, I'm about ready to begin."

"Already?" Erik let out an impressed whistle. "That was quick. So, how hard will it be to change our buddy here into Rousseau?"

"Not too bad. They're around the same build. Their arm length is similar, so I won't have to resize them. That's excellent because it should lessen recovery time. The biggest problem is the legs. Rousseau's shorter, but that's fine: it's easier to shorten than lengthen. Though I'm afraid Travis will need physiotherapy to walk again."

"What?" Travis blinked twice before frowning. "That won't do—we're in a hurry."

While he expected the surgeon to answer, Erik replied instead. "It's okay, mate, Ostark has some nifty medical tech. You'll recover before you know it."

"I hope so."

"Trust me, I studied the procedure. I'm thorough, that's why I survived."

Though unconvinced, Travis nodded. He deduced he had no other alternative if he wished the mission to succeed. Not long after, the medic rested a plastic mask on his face. "I'll turn on the gas. Take deep breaths and count to a hundred."

One. Two. A strange smell reached Travis's nostrils. Three. Four. But, not unpleasant. Five. Six. There was a sweetness to it. Seven. Eight. And it was familiar, but despite his efforts, he failed to recall what it reminded him of. Nine. Ten. How silly, he wasn't tired at all. Eleven. Twelve. He'd never fall asleep. Thirteen. Fourteen. Yes, he'd just rest his eyes for a second and then he'd warn them he needed something stronger. Fifte...

***

From Travis's perspective, a whole day passed in a second. He woke the next morning groggy and with a splitting headache. Blurriness served as his lone vision. Distortion rendered spoken words incomprehensible. And his mind refused to work. His thoughts, if you could call them that, proved unfocused and random. For hours he re-emerged into consciousness only to sink again, until at last, during the afternoon, he opened his eyes and discerned concrete shapes. Still felt like shit, though, and the pain in his legs drove him crazy. They weren't paralyzed. He could technically move them, but any attempt at motion hurt to the point that he gave up before budging them a millimeter.

Erik and the doc moved Travis into a wheelchair and handed him a mirror. In this state, he lacked the strength to lift the glass and study his new face. Instead, he watched the surgeon handing an envelope to the spy.

"Here's a list of physio exercises. Make sure he follows the instructions to a T. I gave him a nanomachines injection. Those little buggers will help heal his legs, but they don't last long. They'll be dead by tomorrow. That's why I'm giving you these." With those words, the medic presented a plastic case and Erik grabbed it. "They're extra nanomachine injections. Give him one every twenty-four hours. Do everything right and he'll be back on his feet in five days."

Erik nodded. "That's perfect. Thanks, Doc."

"Yeah, yeah, you're welcome."

"So, we'll see you later for the vocal adjustments?"

"Yup!" The surgeon pointed a menacing index finger. "Don't forget the rest of my money."

A chuckle escaped Erik's lips. "Of course not, mate! Who do you think I am?"

"I don't know, that's the problem. I'll be on my way, I've got business to attend to."

On that note, Erik escorted him upstairs. Their footsteps echoed with less and less volume as the distance between them and Travis increased. Now alone, he gathered his strength and lifted the mirror. The instant he saw his reflection, he almost dropped it. His brown eyes had faded to gray. The black hair on his head had become auburn. A round face replaced the elongated one he expected. And that mustache... to be fair, Rousseau wasn't a bad-looking man, but he preferred his old mug.

"Appreciating the doc's handiwork, huh, mate?"

With a gasp, Travis turned his head toward the source: a smiling Erik. He attempted to respond, but his jaw flared the moment he tried opening it, so much so that his eyes teared up. Thank God for the IV drip the medic had set up, as he expected he wouldn't eat for a while and he had been starving to begin with.

"Oh, right, I forgot about that. No worries, the doc said you'll be talking and eating by tomorrow." Erik winked. "Those nanomachines work wonders."

Chapter 9

Kotar 25, 2134, on the Nirnivian calendar

When Erik assured Travis he'd be eating the next day, Travis remained skeptical. The pain in his jaw he judged too intense for a quick recovery. Fortunately, his doubts proved unwarranted, and he enjoyed a warm breakfast that morning. Well, noon; the operation had sapped the energy out of Travis, so he'd dozed for several hours more than usual. One might expect being knocked out for that long to quench the desire for sleep, but it was quite the opposite.

Erik prepared pancakes for Travis, and now he savored them along with a serving of fresh fruits and druikinaka juice. The spy turned out to be a more than decent cook, though given his hunger, Travis would have gulped them down regardless of their taste. However, the delicious flavor increased his speed. He slashed through the fried dough with a fork and knife at a reckless pace, and his stomach thanked him.

While the meal was great, it lacked company. Erik had vanished. No doubt he had tasks to attend to. And so Travis ate alone. Soon, he finished, and he allowed himself a brief pause to catch his breath before reading through the exercise sheet the doctor had provided. Travis's lips twisted in a grimace as he deciphered the instructions. That would hurt. At least his legs had already improved, and while he doubted he could stand yet, slight movements were possible.

Without further delay, Travis went through the small motions and massages. Some required help, so he hoped Erik would return soon. Mostly, he managed fine, though he winced and swore a lot.

Travis had finished two-thirds of the routine when the spy approached him, waving a syringe. "Hey, mate, time for a fresh batch of nanomachines!" With that, Erik rolled up Travis's left pant leg and rubbed his chin. "The doc said right about there. Okay, let's do this." A slight cold sensation gripped Travis as Erik patted an alcohol swab on the proper area, then plunged the needle into his thigh. Though he felt the prick, Travis didn't react as the pain failed to match what he'd endured since the operation.

"You know, mate, we're lucky to have these babies." Erik smiled. "They passed clinical trials and got approval for treatment recently. Hospitals have been using them for like three months. And they're miracle workers. Yeah, they're new and limited, but it's still impressive. From what I've heard, they can help cure an injury that'd take weeks to heal in two days. In five or six years, it'll heal it like that." To illustrate his point, he snapped his fingers. "Ostark's our enemy, but damn I love their tech."

"Yeah, it's amazing." Then Travis scowled. "Uh, Erik, I've been thinking."

"Always a good idea! What's on your mind?"

"Well, um, I look like Rousseau, but"—he rubbed his chin—"what about fingerprints, or retinal scans?"

Erik shrugged. "Don't worry, mate, I've got that covered. I'll hack the system and replace Rousseau's records with yours. I've done this kind of stuff before. Nobody will notice." The spy indulged in a small pause. "It's funny—Ostarkiran technology is so advanced, we could have had the doc change your prints, and, yes, even your retinas. But that increases recovery time, especially for the eyes, and there's a chance of permanent blindness. Just not worth the risk. But anyway, it'll be fine, trust me."

"What about microscars? NISDA has scanners that detect plastic surgery, so Ostark must have them too."

"Oh yeah, they do." Travis's mouth gaped. After a chuckle, Erik dismissed his fright with a wave. "Do you take me for an amateur? Why do you think I'm the only spy who survived? Because I know my shit. Forget the scanners. Machines can be tricked into doing anything if you understand how they work." He frowned. "Hmm, that might be true for people too." A short silence then ensued.

"I'm not sure that's a comforting thought."

"It is in our case, mate. Makes our job easier. Anyway, how about I help you with these?" Erik gestured toward the instruction sheet detailing the required exercises. "After that, I'll let you relax, but you won't be slacking off for long. Tomorrow, we start your acting lessons, and they're gonna be brutal."

Chapter 10

Kotar 26, 2134, on the Nirnivian calendar

Erik held the bucket in front of his face as Travis retched. Tears in his eyes, he vomited. The puke burned his esophagus as it traveled upward. At last done, Travis coughed a few times, then wiped his mouth. He almost lifted his neck when another round of retching overcame him. Once it was dealt with, he took a few deep breaths before sitting up. "Holy shit, that hurts. What kind of medical treatment is this?"

"It started as a form of torture," the doctor said as he typed on his computer. The screen displayed two vocal tracks, one red and one blue. While similar to each other, they failed to overlap. "It just happened that changing the subject's voice was a side effect. Back then, you couldn't replicate a precise voice, but the process has been refined since. It's not used for torture anymore, though. Pain sticks are more effective."

The statement caused Travis to shudder. "Goddamn, that's hard to believe."

The medic ignored his response and poked at his monitor. "We're close, but we're not there yet. Brace yourself for round four."

"No, no, oh, freak no." Travis lifted his palm as a shield. "Forget it, I'm not going through that again. Screw the mission, I'll pretend I have a cold and it'll go like it'll go."

After a nervous chuckle, Erik patted his shoulder. "Come on, mate, what's the point of suffering through that cosmetic surgery if they bust you 'cause you don't sound like Rousseau?"

"Urgh, I hate you and your logic." A groan escaped Travis's lips. "Okay, fine, but it's your last chance."

"Whatever." With that word, the physician grabbed a long, thin gray tube. Perhaps intending to showcase the tool's flexibility, he twisted it in a curve before straightening it again. "Open wide!"

As commanded, Travis opened his mouth. Without warning, the surgeon stuck the strange cylinder down his throat. Travis's fingers tightened around the armrests of his chair, and he gagged. And that wasn't the worst of it. That would come soon. The premonition came true, and the tube began spinning, scraping his innards. Travis straightened as his muscles stiffened. Tears rolled down his cheeks.

Sensing his distress, Erik seized his hand. "Hang in there, mate, it's almost over."

Not long after, the doctor pulled out the instrument. Right on cue, Travis coughed and covered his lips with his palm. Once the coughing bout was over, he removed his hand and spotted red stains on his skin. Blood. When it had first happened, he'd panicked, but by now he had grown used to it. Besides, the medic assured him it was normal given the procedure he endured.

Once again, he spoke into the microphone and the surgeon returned to the computer. This time, the two vocal tracks merged into one and turned green. Travis closed his eyes and exhaled in relief.

"That's it," the doctor said. "You sound like him now. We're done." He got on his feet, stretched a bit and glanced at Erik. "Give me my last payment and I'll be out of your hair."

"With pleasure, Doc!" With those words, Erik fished a miniature gun out of his pocket and fired. A shocked expression appeared on the surgeon's face as he collapsed in a crimson pool.

"What the freak!" Travis recoiled, and his chair tumbled backward with him still in it. He struggled to get up from the floor. Though his legs had improved a great deal since the operation, they weren't one hundred percent, and that made standing difficult. Thankfully, Erik helped him out.

"Relax, mate, before you hurt yourself."

"You"—he gulped—"you killed him!"

"Yeah, didn't want to, but he's a loose end and I prefer tying those up." Erik sighed. "Told you: I'm thorough."

Chapter 11

Kotar 28, 2134, on the Nirnivian calendar

Inside the living room, Travis straightened and saluted. "With valor and courage!"

From the couch, Erik waggled a lecturing index finger. "No, no, mate, that's garbage!" Then he paused. "Oh, hang on, I have to watch this." The spy returned his focus to the TV and popped what he called a crisp into his mouth. It consisted of thin slices of mishusq fried and packaged into a bag. Nirnivia also cooked mishusq by frying it, but never in a form allowing such convenient snacking. The screen displayed a game show Travis didn't understand. One contestant spun a large wheel, and it turned, turned, turned. Erik literally sat on the edge of his seat, fists clenched. After a while, the wheel stopped with the arrow pointed at a red space. With a groan, Erik slapped the cushion under him. "Ah, crap, she lost her points. She was doing well too. I hate seeing people screwed over by bad luck right at the end." He touched his chin. "Where was I? Oh, yeah, the Ostarkiran salute. Listen, mate, you nailed the intonation, but the words are 'With courage and valor.' Reverse them and you're dead! Plus, your hand isn't at the correct angle. And your posture is weak! Put conviction into it!" A crunch echoed as Erik munched on another crisp. "Try again!"

For days now, Travis had been learning to mimic Rousseau's body language. Erik insisted on perfecting every single detail, from his manner of speech, subtle movements and stance to his way of breathing. The process proved excruciating. After mastering all that crap, Travis assumed he'd have no issue imitating a simple salute, but somehow he kept messing up. "Fine. With courage and valor!"

"Better! You're getting it, mate. Here's a reward." With that, Erik presented a crisp to Travis, who seized it.

"A single one? That's not much of a reward." Still, he ate it and the salty flavor tickled his taste buds. These couldn't be healthy, but Travis supposed it didn't matter at this point.

The spy chuckled. "Yeah, I'm a tough teacher. Mate, when you put a bullet in Doctor Death's brain, you'll thank me for having been so hard on you. Now, go ahead, one more time. Show me it wasn't a fluke and you get another!"

***

When Travis entered the kitchen, a delightful aroma tickled his nostrils, and he salivated. Erik rested a plate containing what seemed to be pan-fried fish on the table. Not that it served as the only food. Among other things, Travis counted a roast, mishusq puree, a variety of vegetables, and what he believed to be a bottle of Calva, an Ostarkiran alcohol considered fancy and reserved for special occasions. As he spotted Travis, Erik smiled and winked as he pointed to the dish he had just carried.

"Estalgio. The Ostarkirans consider it a delicacy. We don't have them in Nirnivia, so I figured I'd give you a chance to try it."

"Thanks, that sounds great." Travis scanned the table. "You put effort into this."

"Yeah, mate. It's our last dinner, might as well live it up while we can."

A frown formed on Travis's brow. "That's true, I kind of forgot about that."

"Hey, don't look so glum. Who knows? Maybe we'll get lucky." He forced a chuckle. "Anyway, how about we dig in while it's hot?"

***

Once they finished supper, Travis and Erik went to the living room and watched a movie before going to sleep. The spy possessed a considerable collection of films, and for a while they debated what they should watch. War or action flicks reminded them both too much of the upcoming mission, while drama felt too sad for their last evening. Before long, they settled on a comedy. If they reached the end, might as well finish on a laugh. About halfway through, Travis noted his hand drew closer to Erik and their skin brushed. Perhaps taking the hint, Erik rested his fingers upon his. Soon after, they began kissing and eventually abandoned the TV in favor of the bedroom.

Chapter 12

Kotar 29, 2134, on the Nirnivian calendar

With a gasp, Daniel opened his eyes, heart racing as he looked around and recognized his bedroom. He took a few deep breaths to calm himself. A nightmare...

In the dream, he found himself confronted again by the black beast he'd vanquished. Except this time, the bullet he fired failed to pierce the creature's weak spot. As punishment, it mauled Travis the sniper, trapping the man in its jaw, resulting in intense blood splatters and a horrendous scream. Then the monster aimed its tail at Daniel. He tried dodging, but the spikes tore through his abdomen and he fell to his knees. The last sight he saw before waking was of the visitor dashing toward Valardir's exit and reaching the outside world, now free to hunt down countless victims.

Daniel moaned. Ever since that incident, the beast visited his dreams on occasion. Now it seemed his brain had decided to mix that catastrophe with his newest predicament. Beside him, Madeleine lay on her side, her back to him. Careful not to wake her, Daniel sat up and glanced at the clock. Four thirty in the morning, or half an hour before his alarm would ring. He indulged in a low groan, well aware he wouldn't fall asleep again. Resigned, he got out of bed and turned off his alarm. This clock offered two of them, and since Madeleine didn't need to rise as early as he did, hers was set for later. No point having the sharp beeping intended for him tearing her out of her slumber. Though Daniel considered kissing her brow before exiting the room, he chose not to given she was a light sleeper. Instead, he slipped through the door while minimizing the resulting sounds.

Without delay, Daniel walked to the bathroom. Inside, he removed his pajamas, entered the shower and turned on the water. The icy streams hitting his body startled him and he yelped, as always. Despite starting this morning ritual in his late teens under his mentor's advice, the shock never lessened. Many disliked a cold shower, but the rush of adrenaline it brought helped him face the day. Besides, back when he had begun the practice, he'd soon discovered it allowed him to manage stress better, and that proved essential to control his condition.

While Daniel scrubbed, his mind recalled the date. Today, Doctor Death might fall. Whether or not the mechanical freak survived, the war would restart, perhaps spelling Nirnivia's end. If so, he'd be to blame. Sure, Tigh supported the assassination attempt, and the Council had decided not to stop it, but he was the Commander. He'd made the final call. The bulk of the responsibility belonged to him and that drove him mad. Was he mistaken? Had he doomed them all? Impossible to tell, except by letting time pass and waiting to see.

Though doubting himself served no purpose, Daniel's brain refused to let the questions go. His mind nagged him, pointing out why he'd acted like a fool. He tried to focus on something else and settled on what he should eat for breakfast. Too bad his stomach churned the instant he considered having a meal. To say he wasn't hungry was an understatement. Still, he supposed he'd force food down his throat before leaving. Maybe eggs. Yes, that sounded fine—light and easy to cook. Problem solved, but that meant his worries returned. While biting his lips, Travis the sniper popped into his head. Even if he had been put in that situation on countless occasions, Daniel hated sending soldiers to certain death. By God's grace, he'd survived until he reached old age. Would the same hold true for Travis? Somehow, he doubted it. His reminiscing made him recall Major Kiras, the officer that had started his journey. A useless digression, but the past helped avoid the present and so he indulged in it.

***

On a bench near Major Kiras's office, Daniel waited. The superior had asked to meet him, and as always he'd arrived at least ten minutes in advance. No matter the task assigned to him, he went a step beyond. That served him well as a cadet, for he earned a superb reputation. Soon, he'd finish training with honors, one of the top of his "class" so to speak. Not that his diligence was meant only to further his career. As his mentor explained, keeping perfect control over every aspect of his life helped calm the darkness within. Now that he was learning combat techniques, that proved more important than ever as he became stronger, faster, and deadlier.

Thirty seconds before the appointed time, a short black-haired man arrived on the scene, walking with his hands in his pockets. After a groan, he dropped into the seat in front of Daniel and linked his fingers behind his head. Daniel resisted a frown. The figure seemed familiar, and he believed he recognized an infamous cadet. Because of his lack of discipline, his notoriety had grown over the years as the most punished recruit in history. Somehow, the chastisement failed to improve his behavior. Tigh was his name, or something similar. Exactly the type of person Daniel attempted to avoid in daily life, so he intended to ignore this new arrival, but soon Tigh leaned toward him and whispered: "Hey, aren't you that Ricdeau guy I keep hearing about?"

"Probably, yes."

Tigh let out a discreet whistle. "Boy, if half of what they're saying is true, you're goddamn amazing. Nice to meet you. What do you think that freak Kiras wants?"

"That's not a proper way to address a superior officer."

"Come on, it ain't no problem, it's just between us—"

Before he finished, the door opened and a Jonilan woman with long brown hair emerged, dressed in a well-decorated uniform. Though she attempted an amicable smile, the eye patch and the hook replacing her left hand countered the effect. Many wondered how she'd ended up disfigured, but anyone who dared ask received an abundance of push-ups as an answer. Because of this, several ludicrous theories circulated. "You two can come in now."

With that, Daniel and Tigh followed her into the office and Kiras returned behind her desk. "Please, take a seat." They obeyed. "You must wonder why I summoned you here. Cadets, I have a special mission for you if you will accept it. We are beset by unusual predicaments, and so we turn to you. Since you didn't finish training, you can refuse. However, if you accept, you will be generously compensated." She paused for a moment and licked her lips. "Cadets, have you heard of the Tiberna Desert?"

"Yes, sir!" Daniel Ricdeau replied with a salute. "Tiberna is the largest known desert in the world. It isn't claimed by either Nirnivia or Ostark and is beyond the safe zone, meaning it's irradiated. However, radiation levels are low. There is virtually no food there. Unprepared visitors would die of radiation poisoning or starve if the thirst didn't kill them first, sir!"

The major nodded. "Impressive, cadet! But I should point out I didn't ask for a geography lesson."

"I'm sorry, sir! I let my enthusiasm get the better of me, sir! It won't happen again, sir!"

"That's okay, Cadet Ricdeau. Everything you've said is correct. Tiberna is a death trap of zero interest. No one goes there, except..." Major Kiras frowned. "Well, we found evidence of Ostark setting up a base there. We can't tell what they're doing, but we're worried. They must have a damn good reason. Now, we're not at war with Ostark, so maybe we're panicking over nothing. Still, we have to investigate. Our plan is to send a nightwings to scout the area and get intel. Trouble is, because of unforeseen circumstances, there's no pilot available. Of course, that's temporary, but we feel we have to act ASAP."

"Please, sir, I have a question, sir!" Tigh said. Daniel suppressed a sigh. Such behavior could land you in hot water. The guy was lucky the major didn't punish him for his insubordination. Wait until invited to ask questions if you have them. That was basic etiquette. "No one can fly the nightwings, sir? But NISDA has thousands of soldiers available!"

Kiras closed her eyes and sighed. "Yes, I realize it sounds impossible, but it's true."

"But, sir, it's ridiculous! Um, I mean, with all due respect, sir!"

At last, the major's patience ran out, and she brandished her hook at Tigh as her cheeks reddened. "Cadet: never, ever, ever question a superior unless you're invited to. The reason is classified. You are to obey orders and enjoy it. Is that clear?"

"Yes, sir!"

"Lucky for you I'm in a good mood, Cadet Tigh. Now, Cadet Ricdeau, while you're not a full-fledged pilot, I believe you received lessons and can fly a nightwings?"

"Yes, sir! While I'm not certified for battle, simple recon shouldn't pose any problem."

"And you, Cadet Tigh, can handle the cameras?"

"Yes, sir!"

"Perfect! We feel given our situation you are our best bet. Risk is low; compensation is high. You have until tomorrow morning to decide. Dismissed!"

Chapter 13

When Travis woke up that morning, a sickening sensation assailed his stomach, and he hoped it wasn't a bad premonition. Strange dreams had invaded his slumber. Not nightmares per se, but weird and filled with uneasiness, the result being a less-than-satisfying rest. Still, he doubted tiredness would be a problem thanks to the excitement awaiting him. Erik didn't seem to share his uneasy sleep. The spy lay beside him after the unplanned night of passion and snored.

For a while, Travis didn't dare get out of bed, as taking his first step of the day would seal his fate. Eventually, he gathered his courage and slipped out, careful not to wake Erik. Based on the loud sound escaping the spy's mouth, he succeeded. The moment he stood, Travis kneeled and linked his fingers. Then he started praying to Ulgorack, begging the god to grant him success. Once done, he stretched and walked to the mirror. As he studied the reflection, he caressed his cheek. Though he'd had a while to grow accustomed to his new appearance, it still troubled him. Not that it mattered. Soon he'd be dead, after all. As he pondered those gloomy thoughts, a voice echoed behind him.

"It's your big day."

With a sigh, Travis turned toward Erik. "Yeah... I'm so nervous. I'm not sure I can make it."

"Don't worry, you'll be fine. Just pull the trigger. If the bullet misses, it's its fault, not yours."

A smile spread on Travis's face. "Ha ha, I doubt the Commander sees it that way... hey, Erik, thanks for last night. It was nice to, you know, one last time."

The spy winked. "Was a pleasure, mate."

***

The nightwings flew above the desert, invisible to the naked eye and they hoped to whatever equipment the Ostarkirans possessed. Daniel piloted the jet in silence, but Tigh kept trying to start a conversation. That proved annoying, in part because of his obnoxious personality, but also because there was a reason Daniel stayed quiet. He needed to concentrate on the controls. While he'd received piloting lessons, he showed greater confidence in his skills than he felt.

Back in Major Kiras's office, the thought of commanding the nightwings had left Daniel in a cold sweat. Every bit of his self-preservation instinct had begged him to refuse, yet he'd accepted. One might assume the reason to be the promised compensation, and, yes, that had tempted him given his lacking finances. However, that wasn't his main motivation. No, he hoped success here would boost his career. To accomplish his goal, he needed to rise through the ranks as fast as possible. Thank God the mission didn't require any fancy flying. Go in a straight line, let Tigh take some pictures, then return home. Simple enough. Besides, the computer system handled most of the work. Still, Daniel's heart had beaten at an accelerated rate ever since he'd stepped aboard. At least Ron at last closed his trap for longer than five minutes. The instant that realization popped into Daniel's head, his unwanted companion's voice echoed from behind.

"Hey, don't you think it's weird? No one to fly the plane? That's bullshit and I won't swallow any of it. Kiras's hiding something."

Daniel almost yelled a profanity-filled warning for Ron to shut up but chomped his tongue. Remain in control. Like his mentor had explained, such outbursts must be acknowledged but restrained. To give in risked letting the darkness take over. "I don't care. They're our superior officers, we're their pets. We follow their orders and they're allowed to lie." Despite himself, he shrugged. "That's how it is."

"Oh, what a good little soldier you are!" A chuckle escaped Tigh's lips. "Are you serious? Damn, man, they freaking brainwashed you!"

"Not really. I knew the rules when I signed up and I accept them. Anyway, please stop talking and let me fly this thing. I'm a novice."

"Fine." Ron stilled his tongue, but only for a moment. After that brief respite, he started yapping again. "I'm just saying, there's something fishy and that worries me 'cause our asses are on the line."

Daniel groaned. "You had a choice. If you don't like it that much, why did you accept?"

"What do you think? Because they gave me a shitload of money! Don't tell me that's not why you're he—" Blazing alarms interrupted the young cadet as a red light flashed on the dashboard. "What's that freaking sound? What's going on?"

"Mechanical trouble. Something broke down." Daniel scowled and his adrenaline spiked, yet he kept a calm tone. "It's serious. I lost control. We're crashing."

"What? Are you shitting me? You said you could pilot this damn bird!"

"I can, when it works. Listen, we have to eject. Brace yourself."

Chapter 14

Travis couldn't believe it had been so easy. Barely any-one had spoken to him. A doctor had asked him to take a special scan that detected microscars in case he was an im-poster who had received plastic surgery. Like Erik had promised, the machine had declared him to be the genuine Rousseau. The spy's act of sabotage had succeeded. Should the results be verified by a Gorumar, then the deception would be discovered, but that manual approach required time. Even if they did it as a precaution, no way they'd re-view everyone's files before the speech.

Travis now lay in position on top of a building, watching the stage built on the hospital's ground through his sniper rifle's scope. People scurried around as preparations were underway, but no sign of the Doctor. Not that he'd be there so early. No problem, Travis had learned patience. With that thought in mind, he swallowed one of the tran-quilizers he'd brought. These helped keep a steady aim. They could ruin your health, but it wasn't like it mattered anymore. Success or failure—in both cases he was dead. If his bullet found its mark, he'd make it into the history books and that was enough for him. Like many soldiers, he'd always dreamed of becoming a hero.

While Travis had worried earlier, he'd now returned to his element, and he felt comfortable. The rifle he held was like an old friend even if he'd never used it before. This was something he knew he could do well, unlike imper-sonating Rousseau. He'd handled the hardest part. About ten minutes after he took his pill, spectators began entering the vicinity. It wouldn't be long before the president arrived, and when that happened, it'd be over in a flash.

***

Ejecting scared the crap out of Daniel, but on the surface, he maintained his composure. That didn't hold true for Tigh. Poor Ron had begun screaming before the seats had been propelled upward and he'd continued during the entire trip down. Though they'd survived the landing without a scratch, both men had ended up entangled in their parachutes. The path to freedom had demanded some wrangling and contorting, but they'd managed, though the effort forced a flow of swearing out of Tigh. In fact, he kept firing off expletives long after he'd loosened himself.

Afterward, they returned to the nightwings' wreckage. Thank God the bird had crashed close by. Without delay, they inspected the plane's remains. Ron searched for the radio, hoping to send a distress call. To be honest, Daniel doubted that would be possible, as it had likely been toasted. Still, it was worth checking out. Tigh located his mark in mere minutes and then attempted to get it working. Meanwhile, Daniel sought whatever supplies he could gather. That turned out to be very little. They had no food, though that was the least of their concerns. The radiation, while weak, would kill them before they'd starve. Sure, they'd received special injections before the mission to protect themselves and Daniel held a few precautionary syringes his superiors had provided, but would it be enough? Far worse, they had almost no water, only two small gourds. In Tiberna, thirst served as their deadliest foe. Why, already the sun's harsh rays pounded his body, drenching him in perspiration and drying his throat. If he listened to his instinct, he'd swallow half of their water in a single gulp. Not a good start. Oh, but he discovered a map and compass. While not his priority by any means, at this point he'd enjoy any victory he could get.

Too bad it ended that way. Daniel had had such grandiose plans. He'd intended to serve his country and Ulgorack himself. Alas, God had decided otherwise, it seemed. So be it, he couldn't fight the will of a divine deity. However, he still aimed to use what precious time remained...

As Daniel considered his options, Ron approached him. "The radio's hopeless. We're not contacting anyone."

"Can't say I'm surprised." Daniel wiped the sweat off his brow. "We won't get out of here."

"Come on! Maybe they'll send a search party, and we can always walk."

"You're so naïve." Daniel scoffed. "We don't have enough water. We'll never make it. And they're not coming for us. They'll declare us dead: why waste time and money on two cadets who most likely didn't survive? No, we face certain death."

"Well, that's a freaking downer."

With that, Ron fell silent and Daniel appreciated the change. After a grunt, he grabbed his map and compass. They were roughly there, and... yes, that was his destination. It'd be tight, but possible. "That way," he announced as he pointed east.

"Huh? I thought we were dead anyway. You figured something out?"

Daniel shook his head. "No. That way to the Ostarkirans' base. We might be able to reach it."

"Oh, and then what?" Ron chuckled and rolled his eyes. "Let them shoot us? Why not just stay here until the sun roasts us alive? Same outcome, less work."

"Ostark's not necessarily our enemy. Officially, we're at peace. What if they're here for innocent reasons? If that's the case, they might help us out."

"Oh, right! They set up a base in this godforsaken place in secret for innocent reasons. Keep dreaming, pal."

Daniel sighed. "Look, what else can we do? Anyway, my real plan is to complete the mission."

"The mission?" A derisive laugh came from Ron. "The mission's freaking over. We screwed up! What are you going to do? Infiltrate the base like a super spy and send back your findings by magic?"

"Something like that."

"You're insane! You're not an action hero, you'll get yourself killed."

Daniel nodded. "Yep, but I'm dead no matter what. I signed up to serve my country, and that's what I'll do. Or at least I'll die trying." Then he started walking east.

"I'm stuck with a goddamn over patriotic asshole. Wait up, I'm coming with you." And so Ron followed him, though Daniel almost wished he didn't.

Chapter 15

Erik Vandelay walked along a corridor in the military complex he'd infiltrated long ago. Though the setting had grown familiar, on that day anxiety gripped him. How he wished to be far away from the place, but he feared his absence would raise suspicion. Better play it safe until Doctor Death had been disposed of. With any luck, nobody noticed the large sweat stains marking his shirt's armpits. Given the air conditioning ran at full power, those might appear dubious.

As Erik headed toward his office, he sensed someone watching him. Curious, he turned his head and spotted a trio of soldiers approaching him. He almost jumped out of surprise and reached for his weapon but forced himself to stay calm. No reason for concern; soldiers crawled all over the place. To their knowledge, he was an ally. Then one of the men yelled, "Officer Marcod, wait." That was Erik's fake name. No doubt about it, they followed him on purpose. "Could you please come with us? We have a few questions."

Just by the tone of his voice, Erik deduced they'd discovered his true identity. They'd learned everything. No, they'd determined his status as a spy, but the assassination attempt remained hidden. He had a sixth sense for those things. He could smell it.

If captured, Erik would be tortured. While he'd received training to resist such crude techniques, he'd witnessed the Ostarkirans' methods and realized even he wouldn't endure for long. He had to delay the inevitable until Travis completed the mission. With a hard swallow, he grabbed his pistol and swallowed the barrel, tasting cold metal. Before he pulled the trigger, a loud bang echoed, and a bullet struck his left shoulder. The force of the impact propelled Erik face-first to the floor. He dropped the gun, which now lay several inches away from him. Tears filling his eyes, Erik whimpered as his fingers grazed the weapon. Right when he was about to snatch it, a foot crushed his hands and he yelped. The soldier smiled. "Thanks for confirming our suspicions."

***

Daniel and Ron advanced one step at a time, feet sinking in the sand. That cursed desert made progress difficult. During the day, the sun scorched their skin. Meanwhile, the nights froze them to the bone. And walking in sand demanded so much effort. Daniel's calves and thighs ached and burned. Yet the worst of their torments remained the thirst. Water supplies being low, they rationed it to the extreme. While enough to go on, the amount they drank failed to satisfy. A constant dryness assailed their throats, turning their voices so hoarse that speaking resembled torture. At least that kept Ron's big mouth shut.

On top of the lack of moisture was the radiation poisoning. They'd injected themselves with special drugs, but they'd since run out, so the symptoms started showing themselves in the form of nausea and headaches. Had they been eating, Daniel suspected they'd also suffer from diarrhea. Perhaps the absence of food had turned into a blessing, given frequent bowel movements implied more dehydration. Without treatment, dizziness and confusion should follow. Not ideal when navigating a wasteland. At least their queasiness somewhat distracted them from their other ailments.

Around noon, Ron eyed Daniel while shaking the gourd he held. That was an attempt at asking for permission while avoiding uttering a single word. Daniel nodded his agreement. Overjoyed, Ron brought the gourd to his lips enthusiastically, only to groan and throw the container on the ground with a swear.

"Empty!"

"Mine's low too... we'll have to fill them up."

Tigh frowned. "How? There's no water here." Then his mouth gaped. "Oh, goddammit, tell me you're joking."

"No. It's not so crazy. I've heard of miners trapped underground who survived that way. It might work for us too."

"Freaking disgusting!"

Daniel shrugged. "It's that or death. If you'd rather die here, that's fine with me. I won't stop you. So, would you?"

"Nah, I guess not." Ron grimaced before clenching his fists. "But I'm telling you, if by some insane miracle we get back home, I'm breaking Kiras's neck, and don't you try to change my mind."

"Oh, I won't. In fact, how about some extra motivation? It's standard procedure for any mission in the wild to give soldiers decontaminating tablets in case they need to drink from unsanitary sources. Now, with urine it wouldn't be a perfect solution, but it'd make it better." On that note, Daniel forced a chuckle. "Guess what? Somehow, our survival kit didn't have any."

"What?" Tigh's cheeks reddened with rage as he gritted his teeth. "That's it—screw murder, I'll tie up that asshole major and piss in her mouth."

Daniel patted Ron's shoulder. "Sounds like poetic justice to me."

Chapter 16

Travis feared something had gone wrong. The ceremony didn't begin on time. Delays happened, but the worrying part was that when the service finally started, Doctor Death remained absent. A lone fat guy stood on the stage and blabbered.

At least Travis had an excellent view of the scene. Once the president stepped behind the podium, scoring a headshot would be a simple matter—an important fact given that his mechanical body proved invulnerable to bullets. Travis would only get one try, but he grew confident he'd succeed. Unless the cyborg decided not to show up. Travis stared at the giant screen. Maybe the freak planned to use that instead. Erik assured him he'd arranged for a live appearance, but the Doctor might've suspected foul play and changed his mind. Then the mission would fail and he'd die for nothing.

***

Daniel and Ron walked and walked. Keeping track of time posed a challenge, but Daniel estimated six days had passed. By then, the radiation poisoning was in full effect. Another week and it'd be over, assuming they survived that long. As Daniel contemplated that prospect, he frowned at the reddening sky. The sunset implied the cold would return. Between that and the exhaustion they suffered, they needed to settle for the night.

In the distance, Daniel spotted a structure. That puzzled him; nobody lived here. Whoever had built it had done so before the war. He glanced at Ron and pointed at his discovery. "I have no idea what it is, but how about we set up camp there? That thing might provide decent shelter." Ron nodded in agreement and they kept going. Once they arrived, Daniel realized he had discovered a large statue depicting a deformed man surrounded by ruins. Elongated arms, short legs, mismatched eyes. The sight brought shivers, but ugly or not, it would protect them from the wind. Beyond exhausted, Daniel limped toward the effigy and sat back against the stone forming it. A second later, Tigh joined him.

"How long?" Ron asked with a destroyed voice.

"A day or two and we'll be there."

Tigh considered those words in silence while rubbing his chin. Then he stared at Daniel and opened his mouth. Whatever sentence he planned to utter turned into a gasp. "Son of a bitch! It's you! I knew I'd seen you before! Now I remember: you're the dickless shit who hit me with his freaking tray back in high school!"

Astounded, Daniel recoiled. Could Ron really be the jerk who'd said those horrible things about Madeleine? Rage surged through his veins and he formed a fist, ready to strike. No, keep control; focus on your lessons. He didn't have the energy for a fight. Besides, he had grown beyond futile violence. He had to remain calm and contain the darkness in his heart. "I... I'm sorry about that. I shouldn't have broken your nose."

"Nah, it's fine. Don't worry about it, I dissed your gal."

"No, Madeleine is only a friend. And it's not right, I lost control—"

Ron dismissed his objection with a wave. "Whatever, it was a long time ago. Anyway, I deserved it. I acted like a misogynistic jackass, but I didn't mean it, you know? I was trying to impress the boys. Make 'em laugh. You remember how it was back in high school?"

"Yeah..."

"Besides, we can't fight. Guys who chug down piss together are friends for life."

Daniel frowned. "I wasn't aware of that rule."

"Well, you can't risk having the other guy spread the story." To Daniel's surprise, he laughed out loud and Ron joined him. Pain ravaged his throat, and no doubt the same held true for Tigh, but they couldn't stop. "Dan, we're a mess. We can't take down Ostarkirans. It's pointless."

"Feel free to give up, but me, I'll keep going on my own."

"You got a plan?"

A sad smile formed on Daniel's lips. "Get shot and die."

"Damn, man, you're like the perfect soldier. You target your objective and don't deviate no matter what. It's not natural. You're beyond motivated; you're driven. What's your story? Why is this so important?"

***

As it had often happened during those days, Sophia Gainsborough, Madeleine's mother, invited Daniel for dinner. The meal comprised a delicious roast along with mishusq puree. For dessert, Sophia had baked a trotleberry pie. Once the three of them finished eating, they retired to the living room. A pang assailed Daniel as he sat on the couch. This was the moment he dreaded. Ever since he'd arrived at Sophia's house, his nerves had played tricks on him. He wondered if his two hostesses noticed his anxiety.

If so, they remained tactful and didn't mention it. Either way, Daniel had a big announcement, and their potential displeasure frightened him. That was why he delayed until after they ate, as he feared making his announcement beforehand might have ruined supper. A large part of him wished to keep his actions secret, but that wouldn't be right.

Now seated, Daniel gathered his courage and prepared to speak. Madeleine joined him on the couch while Sophia went for a chair facing them. After a hard swallow, Daniel began talking, though Madeleine didn't give him a chance to finish as she jumped to her feet, threw her hands in the air and yelled, "Have you gone mad, Daniel? What are you trying to accomplish?" Then Madeleine crossed her arms and sneered.

In truth, Daniel had expected such a reaction. That was why he hadn't consulted with either of his "mentors" before enlisting. No question they'd disapprove, but he refused to abandon his newfound goal. It pained him to disappoint these two women as he owed them so much. Thanks to them, he'd learned to control his violent impulses.

While Madeleine made her discontent clear, her mother, Priestess Sophia, remained unreadable. Ever since Daniel had arrived, she'd presented the same enigmatic smile she always adopted. The smile that suggested she understood the intentions of God himself. Sophia took the news with no outward reaction. Not a twitch, no sign of a grimace, not even a slight tremble. Perhaps she'd expected it, but Daniel couldn't imagine how that could be possible.

Though Sophia served as a minor priestess ridiculed by her peers, Daniel assumed that soon they'd regret their skepticism. For years, she'd studied religious texts and predicted the Melkar's imminent rebirth, ushering in an era of prosperity for Nirnivia. Head Priest Christopher had disagreed, and so had everyone except rare allies like Madeleine and Daniel.

Madeleine groaned. "Perhaps it is not too late to annul this. You in the army, Daniel? Are you serious? Is your bloodlust so intense?"

Daniel shook his head. "No, it's not like that!"

"Madeleine, you should not be so harsh." Sophia waggled a lecturing finger. "Those who join the military guard our country. While on occasion they extinguish sacred lives, it is to protect our own sacred existence. They must tread carefully, for they stand at the brink of nothingness. They take a great risk for everyone's sake. Do not judge them so quickly."

"I did not mean to! I am grateful for their sacrifice, but Daniel is too unstable for that. Oh, and what is the point? Neither of you ever listen." With those words, Madeleine rushed out of the room. Hurting her broke Daniel's heart. She worried about him and he understood her feelings; still, her lack of trust proved painful. He started to follow her, but Sophia stopped him.

"Do not worry, Madeleine will come around. For now, it is best if she sorts out her emotions by herself."

"Priestess Sophia, she's wrong. This isn't about bloodlust, I swear."

"No need to explain. You joined the army because of the second coming."

For a moment, Daniel's mouth gaped as he stared at Sophia. When he recuperated, he nodded. "The Voice of God will return. This world is sick and twisted. Last time, infidels slaughtered her like an animal. She'll be a defenseless child, so I must make the world a safer place. I want to protect her so she fulfills her destiny. The Melkar died thousands of years ago, but she played as big a part in saving my soul as you or Madeleine. I owe her that much."

"No, you do not, Daniel. The holy prophet does not expect compensation for her actions."

"Even so, I have to do this..."

As Daniel finished his sentence, Sophia stood up and approached. Once near, she rested her palm on his shoulder. "In that case, Daniel, you have my blessing. However, Madeleine is not wrong. If you take this path, you must remain vigilant."

"I will, Priestess Sophia. Don't worry, you taught me well."

***

Through Daniel's whole story, Ron had kept rolling his eyes, and he still did by the end. "The second coming, huh?" A snort escaped his nose. "That's a fairy tale."

"No, it's not. You can't understand, you have no faith!"

Tigh scowled. "Hey, that's not true! I'm not a religious nut like you, but I believe in the Melkar. Don't ask me if all those texts are accurate. Maybe the facts got screwed with. Anyway, Misha came thousands of years ago for God's sake! She hasn't returned so far and she ain't gonna. Ulgorack gave us one shot, and we blew it. We have to accept that."

"You're wrong, Ron. Ulgorack is merciful. He'll give us another chance. The Melkar's coming soon, Sophia said so."

As he heard Daniel's words, Ron burst out laughing and slapped his knee. "Sophia Gainsborough's a dumbass who was demoted from high priesshood and almost excommunicated. And why? Because Sophia's too freaking stubborn to admit she made a mistake." Perhaps Tigh then noticed Daniel's stare, for he gulped and averted his gaze. "Um, sorry. Listen, Sophia helped you and that's awesome. I'm just saying, that doesn't mean everything she says is an absolute truth."

"Of course not, but her logic is sound. If by a miracle we survive this, in a few years a winged baby girl will be born and you'll feel like an idiot."

"Doubt it, but, hey, I wish. That'd be sweet! A new Melkar? Amazing! Tell you what: if it happens, I'll organize a press conference and declare I'm the stupidest goddamn son of a bitch ever." Ron smiled. "Sounds good?" Back then, Daniel hadn't believed that claim. He had no way of knowing that upon Rose's birth, the Koporal-to-be would fulfill his promise. "So, Dan, you enlisted to make the world safer for her?"

He nodded. "Yep, but I'm just a powerless grunt. That's why I'm 'driven.' The Melkar's coming soon. I have to rise in rank quickly so I can change how things are. Too bad I messed up. Now we'll die here. All I can do is complete this mission. Maybe somehow, she'll be safer if we succeed."

"That's a long shot, pal. You're an honorable man, Dan; much more than me." Daniel didn't reply. Both stopped talking. Sleepiness finally grasped Daniel, and he drifted toward slumber when Ron opened his mouth again. That guy needed to learn to shut up. "Hey, Dan, you got the hots for Madeleine, huh?"

Daniel shook his head. "No, she's a friend who helped me and I'm grateful."

"Yeah, sure, but I've seen you look at her." Ron winked. "Come on, I won't spill your secret. Yeah, I'm a complete shithead, but I ain't no snitch. Besides, we're both dead anyway."

There was no argument against that. "Fine. Yes, I love her, so what? You want Madeleine for yourself?"

"Nah. The gal's freaking gorgeous, but those priestesses, they're too righteous. It gets on my nerves. With them it's always do good, be nice, don't hurt others. It's like they don't understand this world is made of shades of gray. Pisses me off." Ron paused for a moment. "Madeleine doesn't know, right?" Again, Daniel shook his head. "Why not?"

Daniel shrugged. "Because I don't enjoy being shot down. What's the point? Madeleine's special—a gentle soul who abhors violence. Me, I'm a messed-up bastard. I have these dark impulses. A desire to hurt people. When I was young I"—he winced—"almost killed a kid once for crying out loud. Yes, I'm under control now, thanks to Sophia, but... Madeleine deserves better than that."

"Yeah, you got that right, you're a douchebag, but she should decide for herself. I'm no prophet, but I'd bet if you ask her on a date, she'll say yes. She likes you too, buddy."

"Oh yeah, why are you so sure?"

A large smile formed on Ron's face. "Because, when you joined the army, she bitched about it! Forget that crap about bloodlust Madeleine fed you, she didn't want to admit she worried you'd get hurt. Freak, she probably daydreams about marrying you and having kids."

Daniel chuckled. "Nice fantasy."

"Hey, I made you a promise, you should do the same. If we get out of here alive, you'll declare your love to Madeleine, all right?"

"Yeah, sure, whatever. Now shut up and let me sleep." Daniel closed his eyes and turned his back on Tigh.

"By the way, it's only fair that I tell you my story too. You must wonder why a guy like me joined the military."

"Nope."

"Well, my family has a history of joining only to wuss out during training. So I decided—"

Daniel sighed. "I don't care, shut up."

"—I'd reclaim our honor by... ah, never mind, no one gives a crap about my story."

Chapter 17

Chains attached around Erik's wrists suspended his dangling naked body from the ceiling. Uncomfortable by nature, the position proved even more excruciating as it pulled on his shoulder injury. Four Ostarkirans surrounded him. One after the other, they poked him with pain sticks in various sensitive areas. Though the impacts were gentle, each time the torture instrument touched his skin, Erik let out an agonizing scream. He had no idea how they worked, but they spread an intense burning through his muscles, resulting in a purer pain than he'd ever endured before.

Keeping a few meters of distance between his men and himself, the officer in charge of the interrogation stared at Erik through his glasses. His face remained blank as he stood there with his hands linked behind his back. Eventually, he presented his palm as a signal for his underlings to stop and they obeyed. "Listen, you are making this harder on yourself than necessary. We already know you hacked our computer system and sabotaged the microscars scanner. Tell us who you are and what you're planning."

Erik forced a chuckled. "And miss out on the fun? No way."

"Very well." With those words, the officer gestured for his men to carry on. The poking resumed. Each contact caused a flinch that sent Erik dangling in a different direction. Beyond the resulting churning stomach, the movement stressed his damaged shoulder, and he winced. After about ten minutes of intense agony, the man stopped them again. Tears ran down Erik's cheeks. Somehow, he'd kept them at bay until then, but no more. "So, did that finally change your mind?"

"Screw you!"

"It appears it did not." The officer sighed and shook his head. After that, he headed for a nearby table and grabbed a syringe, which he presented to Erik. "There's a shortage of the stuff, so I would have preferred not relying on it, but you're getting on my nerves. Let's see how long you resist after I inject this in you."

Erik swallowed hard. Ostark's infamous truth serum. Despite their efforts, no Nirnivian lab produced a substance that came close to achieving the same effectiveness. The concoction stimulated pain receptors, lessened inhibition and messed with your capacity to lie. Everyone who had been subjected to it had broken sooner rather than later. No question he'd suffer the same fate, but if he focused, he might buy Travis another ten, or even fifteen, minutes.

***

As they lay on a dune, Daniel and Ron gazed upon the so-called Ostarkiran base. The whole thing comprised a few tents, though they spotted some vehicles. One might have guessed they had chosen their current position to survey the area without being detected, and that was the case. However, even if they had wished to stand in full view, that would have been difficult to accomplish. By this point, exhaustion overwhelmed them. Every muscle hurt. Beyond that, the radiation poisoning grew ever more serious. Their skin tone turned pale. Minor lesions covered them. The itching the abrasions caused served as the worst part thanks to the fact that they realized scratching would only aggravate their condition. Constant nausea also assailed their stomachs. Had they possessed any food, Daniel doubted he could have kept a meal down.

"Dan, I gotta hand it to you," Tigh said in an unrecognizable voice. The thirst, along with their sickness, ravaged their throats. "I never imagined we'd make it this far, but here we are. Problem is, we're screwed. I can barely move. How are we supposed to infiltrate that place?"

"No idea, Ron. I'll try to figure something out."

"You boys need assistance?" a voice resounded from the side. Daniel's heart skipped a beat. While his brain commanded him to turn his head this second, his body refused to obey the order, and a ridiculous amount of time passed before he spotted the three men approaching. Slowly, he reached for his gun, wrapped his fingers around the grip, pulled it out and dropped it. Though he wished to pick it up, he lacked the strength to do so. What did it matter? He couldn't aim in his condition.

"You're right, Ron, we're screwed."

"Heh, we were from the start."

With a sad laugh, Daniel stared at the approaching Ostarkiran soldiers. To his surprise, they wore the same blue shade as he did. What were the chances? He'd expected different colors. In fact, the similarities went further. The fabric appeared similar; the pockets were in the same places. And wait... Daniel squinted. Was that the famous NISDA shield embroidered on their uniforms? As if to confirm he didn't hallucinate, one soldier yelled, "Relax, cadets, we're on the same side!"

"What the freak?" Ron mumbled. No doubt if his vocal cords had permitted it, that whisper would have been a shout.

"Yes, we're sure you have plenty of questions. Major Kiras will explain everything soon, but first, we need to patch you up. You're a mess, cadets."

Chapter 18

Finally, the moment Travis awaited arrived. The fat man presented the president and gestured him forward. While he waved, the Doctor approached the podium. Travis almost pulled the trigger but resisted the temptation. Though his anticipation flared, he had to wait until the mechanical freak stood in the optimal position to maximize his chances. Soon.

Then footsteps echoed. They'd found him out. No more time—he squeezed the trigger, and a bang resounded. The bullet hit the cyborg in the head and he collapsed onto his back. Despite the large distance, the crowd's screams of terror reached his ears, and he smiled. He'd succeeded. Mission accomplished! But if he didn't act, he'd be captured, and that'd be tragic. The Ostarkirans had mastered torture. If interrogated, chances were he'd reveal his identity as a NISDA soldier. Sure, they'd probably figure that out regardless, but if there was any possibility he could conceal Nirnivia's role in the assassination, he had to try. And so, Travis grabbed his pistol, swallowed it and, confident he'd earned his place as a hero, he fired.

*****

The Nirnivian soldiers showed mercy on Daniel and Ron and carried them to the camp. First order of business when they arrived, they visited the doctor. While they were hungry and thirsty, the medic explained, their stomachs couldn't handle food and drink at the moment. They'd vomit everything up, so he made them lie on stretchers and set up IVs for hydration. The solution also contained nutrients and medication for the radiation poisoning. According to the physician, they were in better shape than they looked and would be fine. Somehow, Daniel doubted his diagnosis, and Ron downright mocked it. Thanks to their exhaustion, both men soon fell asleep.

Daniel woke up sometime later with a cough. He couldn't tell how long he'd slept. Though he was groggy, his nausea had vanished. He sat up, opened his eyes to a blurry mess. Then he rubbed his brow. By the touch, he deduced the lesions had already improved. Perhaps the doctor had been right. As Daniel's vision cleared, he spotted someone standing in front of their stretchers. After blinking, he recognized Major Kiras. She stood there smiling, with both her hand and her hook behind her back. Daniel was about to salute her when groans echoed from the side and he heard Ron mumble, "Oh goddamn it, my head is killing me."

"That will pass," Kiras said. "Excellent job, cadets! You were magnificent!"

"We were, sir?" Daniel frowned. "But we did nothing. The plane crashed, sir."

"Yes, you deserve an explanation. The mission was all a setup. As you can see, this isn't an Ostarkiran base. The truth is, I am in charge of a secret military organization so hidden that officially, it doesn't exist. We handle special cases no one else can take care of, and we need the best of the best. Because of that, finding recruits is a challenge. You two showed potential, so we arranged this charade. The nightwings was rigged to crash, and you were given insufficient supplies on purpose. If you could survive and make it here under those conditions, that'd mean you're the kind of soldiers I'm looking for. Cadet Ricdeau, you performed admirably. Cadet Tigh, you complained every step of the way, but you never gave up and that's enough for me."

"Whoa, whoa, wait, sir!" Ron scowled as his jaw tightened. "Are you saying this whole goddamn ordeal was a test?"

"Yes, that's exactly it."

"What? How did you know we'd survive?"

The major shrugged. "We didn't."

"This is ridiculous! Is it even freaking legal? You're a lunatic! What's wrong with you?"

"I told you before, Cadet Tigh, never, ever, ever question a superior officer," a red-faced Kiras replied. "Now, calm down. I realize this is shocking, so I'll ignore your breach of protocol, but don't push your luck. Listen up, you both did so great, I'll give you the opportunity of a lifetime. You can join my crack team. I won't lie, it's dangerous. We do the craziest missions, and if you accept, you'll either die young or rise through the ranks faster than you can imagine."

Tigh rolled his eyes. "Oh, yeah, I'm so interested, sir. Can you at least tell us what your secret club's name is?"

"No, the name is classified."

"Ah, come on. Are you serious? This is complete bullshit! You want me to join your crack team and I can't even hear its name?"

As she glared at Tigh, Kiras brandished her hook in a motion implying a desire to slash his guts open. "How many times do I have to repeat myself? Never, ever question a superior officer!"

Daniel had bitten his tongue during the whole exchange. The revelation infuriated him so much he didn't dare utter a word. In an effort not to break the major's neck, he recited prayers and mantras in his head. He used every relaxation technique Sophia had taught him. Eventually, he cooled himself down.

At first, Daniel refused the offer. The major was an insane woman and he preferred to stay far from her. After a few days, he figured she'd delivered his goal on a platter. Ulgorack had approved his plan and offered the means to fulfill it. Kiras promised if he survived, he'd rise through the ranks. Then he could make the world a safer place. Confident God stood on his side, Daniel returned to Kiras and joined the secret organization. Even then, she declined to reveal the name. When the news reached Ron's ears, he assumed Daniel had lost it and tried to change his mind. When that proved impossible, the Koporal-to-be enlisted too. Daniel asked why, and his friend explained that piss drinkers needed to stick together. On this so-called crack team, they faced certain death constantly, but somehow they cheated the odds.

Though the major had deceived them once, her promise was genuine. Both had distinguished careers. Plus, thanks to Ron's pushing, Daniel married Madeleine, and in an improbable twist of fate he became the Melkar's adoptive father. Ulgorack removed every obstacle in his way. However, despite all this, Daniel wasn't convinced he'd succeeded. Had his effort helped to protect Rose? Maybe someday he'd learn the answer.

Chapter 19

It happened so fast. A bullet flew straight into the Good Doctor's brain, and Evelyn witnessed the tragedy from the front row. Despite the medical breakthroughs he'd granted Ostark, that served as a death sentence. People started running, most trying to escape the scene before the shooter struck again. A few proved so distraught, they dashed in random directions. As for Evelyn, she fell on her knees and wept.

What a nightmare. The president was our hero, how could he be gone in a blink? Ostark would never recover.

—Thoughts of Evelyn Losier, Hocmar 28, 2134, on the Nirnivian calendar

While clenching her fists, Evelyn promised herself she'd make the Nirnivian scum pay. It had to be them. Everyone else loved the Good Doctor. Then the large screen mounted on the stage turned on and displayed an image of the beloved cyborg. Evelyn gasped as she wondered what it meant.

She didn't have to wait long. As soon as he appeared, the mechanical man said, "Attention, please remain calm. Though it might seem like you have witnessed my assassination, I assure you I am alive and well. The secret service informed me they suspected an unknown entity prepared to infiltrate this event to murder me. At first, we considered canceling, but we decided that holding the event would offer us the chance to capture the culprits and interrogate them for much-needed information. As such, I have been replaced by an elaborate robotic double."

I whimpered as I heard his words. Could this be true? Without delay, I dashed toward my car, ignoring the rest of the president's message.

—Thoughts of Evelyn Losier, Hocmar 28, 2134, on the Nirnivian calendar

***

Once Evelyn arrived at her destination, she rushed inside the building. She ran through the corridors at such speed she almost stumbled into several people, avoiding them with a last-second dodge. One of the poor passersby even dropped his coffee because of her mad dash. Evelyn mumbled an apology without stopping, and the innocent victim replied with what she assumed were curses. She hurried too much to hear his words.

After what seemed like an eternity, Evelyn arrived at the laboratory. She opened the sliding door with her key card, and there he stood, his back turned to her, the Good Doctor. Twice she blinked to confirm the robotic figure wasn't a hallucination conjured by her desperate mind. Against all hope, his metallic body remained visible, and a strained giggle escaped her lips, followed by a smile. As usual, he didn't greet her or even glance at her. Tears in her eyes, she sprang toward the president and wrapped her arms around him. Her cheek brushed against the metal, spreading coldness through her skin. Though the sensation brought a shiver, Evelyn kept her embrace tight.

"Dearest Evelyn, while I appreciate the intention behind your gesture, you should be more careful. I sometimes work with dangerous chemicals."

Upon hearing those words, Evelyn stepped away and realized he had been stirring a mixture when she'd seized him. She brought her fingers to her mouth. "Oh, I'm sorry, I didn't notice."

"No need for concern, this liquid is harmless."

"Good Doctor, you're okay! I can't believe it. I was so scared! Ostark would be lost without you."

"With time, you would have adapted. It is not as if I am a holy prophet." Was that a joke at the Nirnivians' expense? With his monotone delivery, Evelyn couldn't be certain, but she assumed so. "Rest assured I will not die, not until I have accomplished my goal. To be honest, I am surprised nobody found the lack of blood suspect."

"Everyone was shocked."

"Yes, now that you mention it, that is understandable."

The president started stirring his mysterious solution again. The burst of joy I'd experienced slowly transformed into embarrassment, and I blushed. I'd just hugged my direct superior, a strange gesture given our professional relationship. Not that my awkwardness lasted for long. Two seconds later, an incriminating detail popped into my brain and I scowled. Prey to a sudden rage, I clenched my fist and punched him. A loud metallic bang echoed as a sharp pain spread through my arm. With a wince, I recoiled.

—Thoughts of Evelyn Losier, Hocmar 28, 2134, on the Nirnivian calendar

The Good Doctor shook his head. "That was not a smart move. You could have broken a bone or two. Be grateful you did not strike me with your full strength."

Evelyn ignored him and instead rubbed her hand. "Why didn't you tell me about the assassination attempt? I'm the vice president and should have been informed! You worried me so much. Don't you trust me?"

He didn't answer. At first, that made me madder, but then I spotted a glimmer of shame in his remaining eye. A year ago, I might have assumed it was because he regretted deceiving me. By then, I understood him better and figured out the real reason immediately. The Doctor's surgical skills weren't his only gift. He had many others. In particular, he was a master of psychology even without formal training in that domain. He prided himself on being able to predict people's actions. Often, he guessed the Nirnivians' plans as if by magic.

—Thoughts of Evelyn Losier, Hocmar 28, 2134, on the Nirnivian calendar

"So, you didn't know?"

"No. My spiel about the secret service discovering an infiltration attempt was a complete fabrication. The people feel safer when they believe their leaders are a step ahead of their enemies. The truth is, the assassination was a total surprise. Some officers noticed strange occurrences, but too late to warn me."

Evelyn tilted her neck. "Then why send that double?"

"Ah, you mean my drone. I am working on several projects including that one. It is intended as a tool for remote surgery. The robot copies my movement exactly with negligible delay, allowing me to operate without being physically present. Countless lives I can save with such a system. While that is the primary function, there are other potential uses. I promised a live appearance, but I was making great progress on my Alcharia cure and wished to continue. I figured this would be a perfect occasion to test the drone and none would be the wiser. My deception saved my life." He paused. "Evelyn, I apologize for not telling you and promise that I would have had it not been a last-minute decision. I swear that if I had foreseen the assassination attempt, you would have been among the first to know."

"Oh, I see..." Evelyn gasped, then frowned. "Wait a second!" She presented an objecting index finger. "Did you use that drone in cabinet meetings and other official business by any chance? Everyone knows how much you 'love' those."

"Alas, it has not been available for long, so no." The cyborg rubbed his chin. "That is an amazing idea, however. Perhaps I shall."

"Don't you dare."

"Oh well, it was a brilliant idea. Too bad you insist on leaving it unused, but I forgive you."

"Good Doctor, there's something else." Evelyn's lips twitched. "NISDA tried to kill you. This is the equivalent of a declaration of war. The cabinet and the military will demand we attack. I understand you don't want to, but Nirnivia isn't giving us any choice."

The president shrugged. "Ah, but you are being hasty. At this instant, nothing proves NISDA is responsible."

"But who else would be?"

"BBR for instance. Another possibility is a political rival who decided they would benefit from my death. Or a businessman I angered with my stricter legislation and higher taxes. Though I am popular, I have my share of detractors."

"None of those sounds as probable as NISDA."

"I agree, but I would rather make sure that is the case before risking another genocide."

Chapter 20

Before long, the vice president left, and the Doctor continued his experiment. An assassination attempt—what an unexpected turn of events. Evelyn had assumed NISDA to be responsible, and they were the most likely suspect. It seemed he'd have to chat with Daniel Ricdeau soon. As he pondered that fact, a familiar though unwanted presence filled the room. The Doctor straightened as his brain wished for him to grit his teeth. Alas, the broken body he'd received couldn't obey the desire.

"Gwa ha ha. Ain't you a lucky bastard? Almost croaked today. Hey, how 'bout thanking me? Without my gift, you'd be dead meat! Gwa ha ha ah!"

That said, the presence vanished, leaving him in peace. The Doctor allowed himself a second to recuperate and then returned to science.

***

As he gazed at the picture of Rose that sat upon his desk, Daniel downed a shot glass of his precious uisge. Then he caressed the photo and mumbled, "I'm sorry," while he wept. He hadn't cried since... to be honest, he wasn't sure. Probably since Rose had almost died from Alcharia. Oh well, if any situation deserved tears, the end of their country must've been one of them.

Ten minutes ago, he'd received a message from the special beeper connecting him to Doctor Death. The text explained they needed to schedule an urgent talk concerning a botched assassination attempt—so urgent it requested a phone conversation in a quarter of an hour. That implied Travis had failed his mission, and the cyborg had survived. No question—that spelled Nirnivia's doom. Attempting to murder Ostark's president had been a clear declaration of war. They would attack, no way around it. In fact, Daniel wondered why his nemesis had asked to speak to him given the circumstances. Why not let the troops do the talking at this point? He supposed he'd find out soon.

Again, Daniel focused on Rose's image. He'd have to explain the situation to her. That prospect left him sick to his stomach. She'd be furious, though she'd forgive him. Such was her nature. Still, disappointing her would be like stabbing his own heart. As he shuddered at the idea, he poured himself another glass, his third so far, and gulped it down. After he did so, his eyes fell on the picture of Janice hanging on the wall.

Through her adult life, Janice had leveled plenty of accusations against him, both as a father and as a man. Perhaps he'd apologize, accept the responsibility for everything she deemed his fault. In truth, he deserved a fair share of her blame, yet a lot of it she exaggerated, or pulled out of pure fantasy. But, whatever, why not admit to every sin he hadn't committed if it led to peace with his daughter before Nirnivia burned?

The moment Daniel asked himself that question, his interphone beeped, interrupting his reverie. "Commander, the Koporal is here."

"Please let him in."

With that, Daniel served himself a shot once more. Tigh entered his office as he swallowed the alcohol. Without delay, Daniel poured another drink.

"Whoa, Dan, pace yourself. Getting stupid drunk ain't gonna help with that call."

Daniel shrugged. "Some situations require more courage than others."

"Yeah, well, trust me, relying on that stuff leads to dangerous places. I should freaking know."

"What does it matter?" Daniel shook his head. "Rose will die; I killed the Voice of God, the one I swore to protect."

"Heh, the whole country's going to shit and you worry about Rose? What about your other daughter, remember her?"

"Of course, but we're all nothing compared to the Melkar." Daniel shuddered. "Ulgorack will never forgive me." A sad smile formed on his face. "And you're in the same boat, old friend. We're in this together."

With a scoff, Ron dismissed the notion with a wave. "Ah, I'm not here to make God happy, I'm here to protect Nirnivia and that's what I'll freaking do. Listen, we crapped the bed, and that's depressing, but it's not the time to fall to pieces, ya hear me? Nirnivia needs us more than ever. Whatever happens in that goddamn war we just started, I'm sure it'll be a lot worse without you. You're the genius tactician. I'm nowhere near your level. You want Rose to survive, well, you better get out of this funk and quick."

After a sigh, Daniel nodded. "Yes, I suppose you're right. Doctor Death might destroy Nirnivia, but it won't be without a fight." The second he finished uttering those words, the red videophone rang. Daniel straightened in his chair and cleared his throat before accepting the call. He used the speakerphone option so Tigh could take part.

Soon after, the mechanical man appeared on the screen. As always, the electronic eye that replaced the one he'd lost displayed a smiling face. "Commander Ricdeau, Koporal Tigh, thank you for accommodating me so quickly. I realize how busy you are, so I shall dive directly into the matter at hands." Daniel's muscles tightened, and he resisted gritting his teeth. "Earlier today, a sniper attempted to take my life. By pure luck, he failed."

Daniel faked a shocked expression by staring at the cyborg with his mouth wide open. No doubt his nemesis had determined they were responsible by now, but he refused to confirm that fact as long as the Doctor pretended otherwise. What if his ignorance ended up being real? "What? Hard to believe there'd be anyone foolish enough. Let me assure you I'm appalled by what happened, and my Koporal and I are overjoyed you survived."

"As you should be, for I am maintaining this so-called uneasy peace. If I disappeared, it is likely that Ostark would destroy Nirnivia." The president then shrugged. "But I digress. In the beginning, most assumed NISDA to be the perpetrator."

"That's absurd."

"Perhaps, but who else possesses both the resources and a potential motive? Because of this, my cabinet pressed me for retaliation, but I held strong and insisted on further investigation before we act. It is fortunate that I did, since it revealed the true culprit to be BBR."

Daniel had to bite his tongue to keep a straight face. Given he expected Ron to burst into laughter, he stepped on the Koporal's foot, and instead the imminent chuckle morphed into a grimace. "BBR?" He scowled and rubbed his chin. "If they're capable of this kind of scheme, they're a bigger threat than I thought."

"Indeed. There is good news, however: this attack opened my cabinet's eyes. Though earlier, they declined your request for greater access to the neutral zone to hunt down those terrorists, they have changed their minds. We will grant your request and cut back on the related red tape, provided you reciprocate. Am I correct in assuming you will agree to those terms?"

Daniel nodded. "Yes, quite so."

"Perfect!" The Doctor bowed his head. "And with that, I—" He paused and raised his index finger. "Oh, actually, I just remembered. There is one last thing." The emoji within his robotic eyes went from a smile to a furious glower. Shivers assailed Daniel as he glanced at Tigh, who swallowed hard. "Do not think for a second that your pathetic attempt at framing BBR fooled me. Why, I had to plant evidence or my cabinet would have discovered your deception and war would have been inevitable. I have been beyond generous with you and stopped Ostark's massacre even when you refused to grant me my principal demand. For years, I maintained this uneasy peace in the hope you would see the light and deliver Rose to me. Believe it or not, it has not been an easy task, yet I toiled and toiled to achieve it. Though I am still committed to peace, my patience has limits. You have crossed a line. Do you have any idea how close to annihilation you have come today? Get rid of me, and Nirnivia will be destroyed. Nobody else in Ostark cares about your people's fate. Now, you do not deserve it, but I decided to give you a final chance. Be aware: if you ever try pulling something like this again, I will crush Nirnivia and slaughter your precious Melkar like an animal." He paused and his emoticon returned to a neutral expression. "Do I make myself clear, Dad?"

A whimper escaped Daniel's lips as he closed his eyes and massaged his temples. So he'd only pretended to be fooled. Part of him had realized that from the start. Still, how he wished that part had been wrong. "Yes, very much so."

"Excellent."

At last, the screen turned dark and Daniel clenched his fists and took several deep breaths. Once calmer, he stared at Ron, who stared back. Though they exchanged no words, they both understood how close to annihilation they had come.

Timanites Crisis

Chapter 1

Kotar 33, 2134, on the Nirnivian calendar

The computer took a long time as it performed a multitude of calculations to determine its next move. The Ostarkiran president interpreted this as a sign his strategy was working since his opponent couldn't keep up. He glanced at the clock as he waited. Three in the morning; still early. At last, the program decided. A piece budged on the screen, accompanied by a beeping sound effect. What an interesting twist; the Doctor considered the new board with amazement. This required thought.

Kuhard... how he loved Kuhard. The word *game* seemed inadequate—too frivolous to describe the sublime activity. Nothing else like it existed. The complexity proved so daunting that most lacked the patience to learn even the basic rules. Whoever had invented it was a pure genius and perhaps insane. Luck served no purpose in Kuhard. Only skill mattered. If you lost, you only had yourself to blame. That wasn't special—many games incorporated chance in some way, but a good number didn't. The source of Kuhard's uniqueness was the amount of skill it expected.

The Doctor had played Kuhard for several years now. He'd started when he had a normal body and had shown considerable prowess, for he never lost. The best he'd challenged, and he'd defeated them. Despite this, he hadn't fully understood the game. Flaws riddled his strategies, though less so than his opponents'. Ever since his first match, he'd tried to perfect his technique, without success. Of course, he improved, but there was still so much missing. It was an impossible task, but he enjoyed the undertaking.

Yes, the computer provided an interesting test. The Doctor studied the screen as his doubts lingered. He considered various potential alternatives: none seemed adequate. Then he noticed a possibility... could it work? For the short term, this would give him the upper hand, but it might come back to haunt him later. Everything depended on the opponent's reaction. Nonetheless, he didn't see any better alternative. With a click of the mouse, he moved his piece.

Decent Kuhard players were rare. Few enjoyed the game, and its popularity had waned in modern days. People preferred not thinking anymore, it would seem—such a pity. Since the president only had time for entertainment during the night, competing with a living, breathing being was impractical anyway, so he battled against software instead.

This arrangement was far from ideal. Defeating a machine offered rare thrills, in part because the computer didn't care if it won or lost. Beyond that, though programs had defeated Kuhard masters, they lacked skill. On a technical level, the AI performed with infallible logic. Yet, something was missing... maybe intuition?

The Doctor had tested every off-the-shelf Kuhard program available. They'd all turned out unsatisfactory until by pure luck he'd discovered a homebrew programmer who'd developed the most impressive AI he had ever witnessed. Even this one he vanquished with ease; however, a wonderful occurrence had happened. The developer had released his code as an open-source project. The president had changed it several times, improving it in incremental steps. Now he fought his latest creation, and the outcome eluded him. In a strange way, no matter who won, he'd earned a victory.

The computer ran slower than usual. With a touch of annoyance, the mechanical man studied the board more. Then he spotted it: a critical mistake. How had he missed it? If his opponent noticed the error, the Doctor would lose his first match. Torn between the fear of losing his perfect record and the delight of having created an AI capable of defeating him, he waited. The most desirable outcome felt... uncertain. For sure, if he had been capable of sweating, perspiration would have covered his brow.

And so he stood at the brink of death. The Doctor had been there before, except it hadn't been a mere game. No matter how he sliced it, he shouldn't have survived. He'd suffered severe injuries and hadn't received immediate medical attention, but he'd lived, a miracle. Nobody understood how. He himself wasn't surprised. He wouldn't die. Not yet. He had one last mission to accomplish, and he refused to rest until it was done. Luckily, the laughing fool's actions guaranteed his survival until he succeeded—not that the sick bastard had intended it that way.

Occasionally the Doctor wished he had died. He had lost so much, like his sense of touch. Of his original self, only the head remained, and not even in a complete form. The incident had ravaged his eye and his mouth. They'd had to be replaced. Metal couldn't feel, and the strange chemical allowing the fusion between flesh and machine had rendered his skin just as numb. He couldn't feel the soft wind blowing around him, nor the gentle water splashing on him, nor the delicate caresses of a loving woman. The concept might frighten a normal person, but they couldn't imagine its true horror unless it became reality.

The Doctor also couldn't eat anymore. How he missed that one: food used to be his guilty pleasure. Tender meats, salty treats, sweet fruits, even sweeter pastries: he loved them all and wouldn't savor any of them again. Of course, he still had biological parts, so he needed nutrients, but replacing a special capsule in his body every two weeks lacked the delight brought by a proper meal.

Besides that, the president used to appreciate a variety of physical activities—particularly rock climbing. Technically, those weren't lost, yet they didn't provide satisfaction anymore. His robotic form removed the challenge, making them boring.

Perhaps the cruelest aspect of his physique was that he endured constant pain. He'd lost his sense of touch, so there shouldn't have been any aches; however, the Doctor suffered the full-body equivalent of phantom limb syndrome. The torture was in his mind, yet all too real. Countless medics had attempted to correct this problem. None had succeeded, and so he lived with everlasting torment. In truth, it was maddening. If his will hadn't been so strong, he would have gone insane long ago.

Nothing is black or white: his mechanical form provided significant advantages. For one, he had grown stronger, and faster. For a second, compared to organic beings, he was almost indestructible. A bullet hitting his torso would ricochet. On a lighter note, he never needed to use the bathroom. A silly but convenient perk.

Another benefit people attributed to his new body was that he didn't require sleep. This was misleading. Indeed, his metallic parts endured intense work without fatigue, yet his mind wasn't immune. His brain demanded rest. Even before the incident, he'd slept less than normal. Four hours a night and he woke refreshed in the morning. With his robotic form, this decreased further to forty-two minutes per day. Not quite the zero the urban legend claimed, but impressive.

Of everything he'd lost, the Doctor missed his identity the most. Oh, he remembered his past, but the incident had changed him. He didn't behave like his old self, and he wasn't sure what that made him. He was nameless. The moniker given by his parents became inappropriate, and he found himself unable to choose a replacement. The Nirnivians called him Doctor Death, but he judged that unfair. He didn't seek their death, nor was he fighting them—they fought him. If only they understood that. In contrast to the Nirnivians' beliefs, he had little interest in conquering them or the world. Fools relished such violent endeavors. He only wanted to accomplish his final mission, then he'd rest. The Ostarkirans, on the other hand, called him the Good Doctor: a pleasant title he didn't deserve. Good Doctor possessed a virtuous quality, yet sin tainted him.

As the president considered those thoughts, the computer at last moved a piece, resulting in an arrangement so flawed, it was equivalent to the software having forfeited. The program had failed to recognize its opponent's error. A strange mix of joy and disappointment filled the Doctor. Crucial flaws still crippled his AI. Really, it was fortunate: he grew tired. Forty-two minutes of slumber awaited him. Afterward, he would handle annoying paperwork, and then he'd read before the working day began.

Chapter 2

Kotar 35, 2134, on the Nirnivian calendar

A new painting had been hung in the chapel and Rose asked James if he'd go with her. Now, he stared at it while wrinkling his brow. The painter showed considerable technical prowess, but the scene proved surreal despite the realistic style. The portrait depicted a shining white creature. Crystal-like cyan balls served as its eyes, and multicolored wings spread out of its back. Their shape reminded James of a butterfly. The entity soared while a crowd gathered below, gazing and pointing at it.

"It's beautiful," Rose said in a whisper. "The artist deserves praise."

James nodded. "Yes, he does."

The work was flawless. I might not have understood what the image represented, but I appreciated its beauty.

—Thoughts of James Hunter, Hocmar 28, 2134, on the Nirnivian calendar

"I just don't get what that white thing is supposed to be."

In a rapid motion, Rose spun toward James. Her hands rested on her hips, a posture she often adopted when angered, though the laugh she stifled revealed she did so in jest. "Thing? Please, show respect for what might be my previous incarnation."

"Sorry." A scowl formed on James's brow. "Uh, wait? You mean this is Misha, the original Melkar?" He scratched his head. "But wasn't she that black-haired woman in the other paintings?"

Rose smiled. "Yes, glad to know you've been paying attention! I'm impressed you remembered her name." A light blush appeared on James's cheeks. In truth, he would've forgotten, but he had been reading a novelization of her life. "Misha possessed a special power reserved for the direst circumstances. You see, Hunter, she could transform into the Papillon, an entity invulnerable to any weapon or force. Ulgorack realized that the Melkar would have enemies and gave her the means to defend herself. But she had to be careful, as using this gift without necessity could doom her soul to nothingness."

As Rose told me of the Papillon, I recalled that book contained a scene where Misha transformed and subdued criminals. The image standing before me matched the description of the creature, yet I didn't recognize her until Rose spelled it out. Then an unsettling thought popped into my mind, and I scowled.

—Thoughts of James Hunter, Hocmar 28, 2134, on the Nirnivian calendar

"Can you... uh, do that?"

"Sure, wanna see?" The seriousness of her tone caught James off guard, and he recoiled so fast he almost stumbled and fell. Rose giggled at his nervous demeanor. "Hunter, I'm kidding! I can't transform into anything." She forced a sad face. "Not even a cute pissack."

James exhaled. "Good. There's enough weirdness around here."

"Actually, my inability to transform is a major reason I don't believe I'm the new Melkar."

"That's a fair point." James rubbed his chin. "So, why do people still follow you?"

She shrugged. "When people want to believe, they'll invent excuses to ignore incongruity. Some say I can't transform because I'm not ready yet. Others claim I lost my ability because of a mutation." Rose grinned. "There are even those who assume I can transform into the Papillon and pretend otherwise for whatever reason; it's so crazy."

"I don't know, it sounds fishy. What if you really are pretending?!"

"Oh, please, Hunter, you don't have to compensate for Brucie's absence. He's coming back tomorrow. We'll get our fill of questionable humor then."

James gasped. "Oh, right, I forgot. It'll be nice to see him, I missed him."

"Yes, he's a jerk sometimes, but Brucie's part of the family, like it or not."

Chapter 3

Bacdor 1, 2134, on the Nirnivian calendar

As promised, Brucie returned the next day. To celebrate, a bunch of soldiers organized an arm wrestling tournament in the rec room. Many showed up, including Janice, Charlie, Patricia, and Dylan. Both Rose and I declined to participate and instead watched from the couch. It was a small miracle that she was there, but she explained she'd cleared her schedule to encourage the bodyguard and friend who had been absent for so long.

—Thoughts of James Hunter, Hocmar 28, 2134, on the Nirnivian calendar

The soldiers were a festive bunch, and the competition drew out that side. People cheered and yelled as the contestants brawled it out. Whenever their preferred participant secured a victory, they pumped their fists or even performed mocking dances. Conversely, defeat resulted in disappointed headshakes and curses.

At the moment, Brucie battled Charlie. A considerable amount of perspiration covered both men's brows. James noted dark stains near their armpits. Between the sweating and the grunts they indulged in, he judged the match posed a challenge for both opponents. For a while, they appeared evenly matched as each gained the advantage for seconds before losing it. Then Brucie gritted his teeth. In a savage motion, he slammed Charlie's hand against the table with such force James flinched at the resulting bang.

His victory assured, Brucie pumped his biceps, showcasing their size. "Freak yeah, those guns ain't lost any strength even with that beast messing me up. Ya can beat me down, but I'll be back stronger than ever!"

"Great match, Brucie!" Charlie rubbed his forearm and winced as he spoke. "But don't gloat too much, or it'll sting a lot more when I win my rematch."

"Ah, no way, ya gonna try again, dude? That's freaking dumb, but brave as shit. Whatever, it's your funeral, bro. So, who's next?"

Shaking her head, Rose sighed. "Arm wrestling and trash talking. Brucie's back in his element and crushing it."

"Yeah, and Janice's doing well too." The gigantic woman had annihilated everyone in her bracket, starting with Patricia and finishing with Dylan, securing a position in the finale. Now she stepped forward and fired a defiant stare at Brucie. "That would be me, buddy. If you have the balls."

"Gimme a break, gal, I ain't gonna bail." He grinned. "You're going down!"

Janice giggled and winked. "Yeah, I'm planning to later, but not with you, bud."

They took their respective positions and James sat at the edge of his seat. Right before the referee began the match, Rose's voice echoed. "I'm sorry to interrupt, but could you stop for a minute? I need to watch this."

Thanks to the reverence Rose commanded, everyone hushed and looked at the TV. James followed suit. On the screen appeared what he guessed to be a church. The statue of Rose, familiar paintings and benches suggested that much, except multicolored scribbles covered everything, from the walls and floor to the furniture. Some depicted crude images; others spelled words no scripture would use. A reporter said, "—perpetrator is unknown, but the extensive damage suggests a grudge against the priest or the parish itself. Many unique works of art worth a fortune have been ruined, and it's doubtful the church will ever be restored to its former glory. So far, the cops have no leads; however, those living in the neighborhood are quick to point the finger at a Timanite family."

The picture switched and showed an interviewer speaking to a heavyset balding man. He glared at the camera, cross-armed. "Yeah, of course it's them. Who else would do that? They're the only ones who don't care about our church. And come on, they hate our god Ulgorack and his prophet the holy Melkar. That's enough of a motive."

The point of view then changed to a frail senior woman using a cane to support her petite physique. "Well, I don't mean to accuse them without proof, but the Timanites have very different beliefs from us, so it might've been a hate crime."

Rose groaned. "That's ridiculous! There's no evidence it's them. This is religious intolerance, pure and simple." The redheaded Melkar rubbed her chin as she considered the issue. "Perhaps I'll remind them what they're doing is wrong during my next sermon."

"Will ya now?" Brucie scoffed and crossed his arms. "Don't get why ya worry 'bout the Timanites. They ain't gonna appreciate your help, ya know."

"Maybe not, but we shouldn't accuse them just because they have a different faith."

"Didn't say we should; I agree with ya. Just saying ain't no need getting your panties in a bunch for a guy who'll thank ya by spitting in your face."

Now the camera filmed a closed door. The journalist pounded on it, but the homeowner refused to open. A frightened feminine voice came from inside: "Please, leave us alone. We did nothing wrong. We never even set foot in your church!"

James scowled. "Um, what's going on? What's a Timanite?"

"That's right, you wouldn't know, Hunter." A sigh escaped Rose. "In short, they're kind of the fourth branch of our main religion, though they're not recognized as such and there's a major difference. The progressives, orthodox and centrists all worship Ulgorack. Timanites, however, are Timagoron's disciples."

"Wait, isn't that the god who hates people and wants everyone banished into nothingness?"

Rose nodded. "Yes, that's close enough for government work." A smile formed on her face. "I'm impressed that you remember."

"But"—James scratched his head—"why would anyone worship that guy?"

"It's simple if twisted. Timanites feel Timagoron is correct and that Gorumars are evil, selfish creatures unworthy of existence. They believe attempting to achieve a virtuous life and attain the afterlife is doomed to fail, regardless of Ulgorack's efforts. To them, the only chance to avoid nothingness is accepting their nature and begging Timagoron for forgiveness, but they admit the chances of that happening are low."

James swallowed hard. "That's rather gloomy."

What a depressing religion. If they hated people, did that mean they hated themselves? Their children, even? How were you supposed to love anyone with such radical beliefs? The thought made me shiver.

—Thoughts of James Hunter, Hocmar 28, 2134, on the Nirnivian calendar

"Despite their views, they aren't dangerous. In fact, their crime rate is lower than average. They rarely cause trouble. However, they are hated. Long ago, Timanites didn't have legal rights. They were persecuted and enslaved. Nowadays, the laws have changed and technically they've obtained the same privileges as everyone else. In reality, they are often victims of discrimination. At least their situation has improved. I disagree with their doctrine, but they are still people. Besides, when we mistreat the Timanites, in a way we prove their point." Rose turned toward the group of soldiers. "Again, I'm sorry for the interruption. Please continue."

"All right!" Brucie pumped his fist. "Janice, I'm gonna kiss your ass!"

"Huh, don't you mean kick, big fellow?"

A wink came from the bodyguard. "Both are fine with me, ya know?"

"Oh God!" Janice slapped her forehead. "You're as disgusting as ever. Never mind, I forfeit. I want nothing to do with you today."

Guttural laughter escaped Brucie's throat. "Ain't that sweet, baby? Who's the arm wrestling champ, you losers?" He pointed both his thumbs at himself. "This guy!"

"Correct, and here's your prize!" With those words, Janice dashed toward him, formed a fist and punched him straight in the crotch. After a pain-filled whimper, Brucie fell to his knees as his eyes watered. For a moment, several gasped echoed through the room, but then the soldiers started clapping and cheering. With a smile, Janice bowed for the crowd. "Ah, Brucie, I missed you, you big pervert." She kissed her knuckles. "Without you, the girls get no exercise."

Chapter 4

Bacdor 5, 2134, on the Nirnivian calendar

When Anya entered the office, Tania sat at her desk and typed. Her fingers moved at a slow pace, far from their maximum potential. The lack of speed betrayed Tania's low interest. Other signs showed themselves too. These days, the incredible energy she normally displayed vanished. She barely spoke or smiled, and she walked in a hunched posture that contrasted with her usual enthusiasm. Under normal circumstances, Tania possessed great vigor and adopted a jovial demeanor. However, whenever work didn't thrill her, she grew somber and depressed. That thought in mind, Anya caressed the yellow folder she carried. Perhaps this would help.

"Hey, sis, you're almost done with your current assignment, right?"

A nod came from Tania. "Yeah, I'm just reviewing the final data." She sighed. "It's so boring. Ever since the president pulled me off the strange plant project, all he has for me is junk science."

"Well, I might have something more interesting for you." With that, Anya dropped the folder on her sister's desk.

"Huh?" Tania blinked twice. "What is it?"

"Reports about the clinical trial."

"Come on!" After a groan, Tania crossed her arms. "You call that stuff interesting?"

Anya nodded. "In this case, yes. The trials had been a resounding success, but then a patient suffered from strange rashes after the operation. We haven't been able to figure out the cause, though it looks like an allergic reaction."

"What?" A frown formed on Tania's brow. "That shouldn't be possible. The skins are generated from the patient's own cells. The body can't see the difference. Are you suggesting he's allergic to himself?"

"And that's why it's interesting! Frankly, I can't make heads or tails of it. The Good Doctor figured you could help me out."

At that point, Tania didn't listen anymore. She hopped to her feet and paced around while rubbing her chin. Various observations she mumbled to herself until she snapped her fingers and a large smile graced her lips. "That's it!" But the grin disappeared. "No, no, never mind." Tania sat down again and opened the folder. "Better read through this." Anya stifled a giggle. The funk had been dealt with.

***

"This is getting ridiculous," Plague said, staring at his computer monitor. While his broken eyes interpreted the image as a hazy blur, he understood both Diabo's and Stalker's pictures appeared on the screen. "Six attacks this week. NISDA is out for blood. The bastards are more ruthless than Ostark. BBR can't take this crap for long. Something's gotta give."

Stalker groaned. "Told you attacking Nirnivia would backfire."

"Ain't like we had a choice." Though he couldn't see him, Plague imagined Diabo crossing his arms and glaring at Stalker. "Needed the resources, boys. Simple as that. Pissing off NISDA's worth it if it means we ain't gonna starve. 'Sides, Plague, didn't ya tell me we got a lot of our supporters back?"

Plague nodded. "Yes, I contacted them after we raided Nirnivian transports and explained that their pulling their support had reduced us to this. It took some convincing, but many decided it was best for everyone to let bygones be bygones and return to our old arrangement." He paused for a second. "Frankly, I couldn't have done it without Stalker. He got BBR in contact with those guys. Thank you for the help, I know you don't enjoy stepping into the spot-light."

"No biggie, gotta do what we gotta do." Those words came with a shrug from Stalker, or so Plague assumed. Hard to be certain given his condition.

"There ya go, problem solved." Diabo chuckled. "Ain't no need to steal from Nirnivia no more. When NISDA sees we're backing off, they'll chill."

Plague resisted a sigh. "I doubt it, boss, things ain't so simple. That's like trying to stop a fire by removing the match. It's too late. BBR crossed a line and NISDA won't forgive it easily."

"Nah, those wusses ain't gonna keep on risking their lives for a useless fight. They'll calm down. Just looka how they groveled to Ostark."

"That's true, but we don't pose the same threat as Ostark and they know that."

"Psst." A dismissive wave must've accompanied that sound; Plague could've bet it did. "Yer overestimating 'em. Bunch o' freaking cowards if ya ask me. 'Sides, even if you're right, what do you wanna do 'bout it?"

After an exhale, Plague bent his neck. "I can't think of anything that'd get us back to how it was with NISDA."

"Then no point arguing 'bout it."

Deep down, Plague hated admitting it, but the crimson beast was correct. "Guess not. Still, we gotta figure something out. Either we calm down NISDA, or we find a better way to defend ourselves, or BBR will be dead meat in six months, top."

"Well, I ain't gonna pretend I got a bigger brain than ya, Plague, so I'll leave that up to ya. Keep me posted, won't ya?"

"Of course, boss."

***

After a hard day of work, Rose decided she'd relax with her trusty old violin and she invited me to listen. I accepted. Mostly, she played her usual repertoire, and the songs felt familiar. Not that I complained. They were so beautiful, it didn't matter if I heard the same pieces a million times.

—Thoughts of James Hunter, Hocmar 28, 2134, on the Nirnivian calendar

The hair on Rose's bow tickled the instrument's strings to perfection, resulting in a wonderful melody. James appreciated her performance. It brought back various memories from his past—some pleasant, some sad. Music did that to him. It possessed a magical quality that allowed him to relive previous moments of his existence. Whether or not he wished to, it took him for a nostalgic trip. After the fourth song, Rose stopped and glanced at her clock. "Sorry, I want to check the news. They might talk about that church."

"Sure, no problem."

Having received his blessing, the prophet grabbed the remote and switched the TV on. A journalist materialized on the screen and babbled about unrelated topics. For a quarter of an hour, James and Rose watched a story about the continuing epidemic of child kidnappings until at last the reporter said, "There's a new development in the case of the vandalized church. The police have identified the paint used and discovered that a teenage boy named Frederic Sysco bought the same kind at a nearby store days before the incident. It turns out, Frederic is part of the Timanite family suspected of the crime. As expected, the neighborhood is in an uproar. Most residents criticize the police's decision not to arrest Frederic. They believe the paint confirms his guilt and that he might strike again if he remains free. Officer Frank Murphy offered this comment."

With that, the image changed to a heavyset mustached policeman standing behind a podium. After clearing his throat, he leaned toward the mike. "There's not enough evidence to arrest Frederic. Yes, he bought red paint, but it's a popular brand. Thousands of people use it. I have some in my garage myself. Frederic and his family have been beyond cooperative." He adjusted his glasses. "They let us search their house even though we couldn't secure a warrant, and Frederic answered all our questions of his own free will. He says the paint was for his motorcycle. We tested the bike: it was painted recently."

As the cop pronounced the word *motorcycle*, James shuddered. Perplexed by his reaction, Rose frowned. "Something wrong?"

He shook his head. "Um, no, no—just a bad memory." James paused for a second. "This doesn't look good for the Timanites, does it?"

"No, it doesn't. It's meaningless circumstantial evidence, but people will blame them even more now." Rose sighed. "Well, I can't do anything about it tonight."

And so Rose returned to her violin. As I observed her, I realized she chose a strange instrument for someone who looked like an angel. On earth, angels played the harp. Um, one of them played the violin, but he fell from grace and became something different. Or at least that's what some TV show I watched a while back said. With a smile, I noted maybe Rose should offer Diabo her violin as it might suit him better.

—Thoughts of James Hunter, Hocmar 28, 2134, on the Nirnivian calendar

Chapter 5

Bacdor 7, 2134, on the Nirnivian calendar

Late in the evening, Rose sat at her desk and read letters people had sent her. She received plenty of mail daily. Some asked questions she used as material for her sermons. Others expressed their appreciation for her guidance, or requested prayers. As she toiled, a muted TV played in the background. She paid no attention to it.

Done with the current document, Rose reached for the next envelope and opened it. She grasped the page inside, unfolded it. She studied the words and realized another one of her followers pleaded for her to condemn the Timanite family. The memo claimed that, thanks to her influence, she could convince the cops to do their job. She sighed. That was the sixth or seventh similar message so far. She'd have to do something about it before the situation degenerated into total chaos.

As Rose put the paper away, she peeked at the nearby screen. A picketing crowd assembled, brandishing signs displaying messages such as "Justice for our church" and "Lock up the Timanite bastards." The way the protesters' lips moved as well as their glares suggested they also screamed less-than-flattering slogans. Behind them, a house stood, and it seemed familiar to Rose. Then it clicked, and she recognized the Timanite family's home from a previous news report. With a groan and a grimace, she grabbed her remote and turned up the volume. As expected, a multitude of voices echoed from the speakers, most furious. The general chaos made it difficult to distinguish any words, but she discerned a few, including "Timanites" and several insults and curses. Often, the passing cars honked in support, adding to the cacophony.

A reporter attempted to speak over the noise. Thanks to his microphone, he managed, but barely. "As you can see, the situation spiraled out of control over here." He gestured toward the crowd. "This group of protesters accuses Frederic Sysco of vandalism and calls for his arrest. They feel the fact he is a Timanite and the red paint he admitted buying confirm his guilt. However, the police insist there's not enough evidence against him. The protesters warned they wouldn't stop until justice was served."

Prey to a sudden headache, Rose rubbed her brow. They behaved like intolerant fools—not that it surprised her at this point. Though she'd intended to denounce Timanite discrimination from the start, she had been so busy. She couldn't delay anymore and had to act before it became even worse.

Chapter 6

Bacdor 8, 2134, on the Nirnivian calendar

Rose paged Kristina, asking her to come to the office ASAP. As usual, the assistant arrived less than five minutes later. She always proved so punctual and dedicated. Rose admired her sense of professionalism. No matter what was asked of Kristina, she performed the task and excelled. Rose admitted she occasionally requested services touching issues outside of Kristina's job description, not that she ever complained. Often, she deduced what needed to be done and accomplished it before receiving instructions to. Without her, Rose would be so lost. Even now, summoned at the last second, Kristina stood in front of Rose holding a minicomp, ready to jot down notes before they exchanged a greeting.

"Kristina, thank you for coming." Rose welcomed her with a beaming smile. "I'd like you to do some research for a speech I'm planning to write."

The assistant nodded. "Not a problem."

"I'm sure you've heard about the vandalized church by now and how people blame a Timanite boy." A slight frown appeared on Rose's face. "There's no reason to think he's guilty. He's a scapegoat because of his beliefs, and I can't let that happen, so I'll remind everyone what they're doing is wrong during the next sermon. I'd like you to find relevant passages in our sacred texts so I can back my words up with scripture. There should be plenty of ex—"

"No! I refuse!" As Kristina said that, she performed a rapid motion suggesting she waved the request away. In addition, her lips contorted in a disgusted expression, and a flash of rage glimmered in her eyes.

Stunned by the act of disobedience, Rose recoiled. "What did you say? My ears must deceive me."

"I said no!" Kristina repeated at a volume dangerously close to a shout. "I won't help write pro-Timanite propaganda!" Then she scowled and proceeded in a calmer tone. "Rose, I'm sorry, but I can't do this. The Timanite beliefs are heresy. They despise life. They worship Timagoron. I won't take part in this, it'd be immoral."

Rose's surprise vanished, replaced by an intense frustration. Her beloved assistant spewed hate speech and accused her of sins she did not commit. "It's not pro-Timanite propaganda," she countered while resting her hands on her hips. "I'm only trying to protect an innocent. The Timanites' doctrine is disturbing and I don't condone it, but they are still people and have the same rights as everyone else!"

"Don't get me wrong, I feel bad for the boy, but if you deliver that sermon, some will assume you support the Timanites' faith. I won't be part of it." Kristina paused for a fraction of a second as she gathered her thoughts. "The Timanites don't deserve your compassion. They hate what you represent and they hate you! Trust me: if they had the chance, they'd kill you!"

"Kristina, that's ridiculous!" an outraged Rose shouted. "Most Timanites aren't violent, let alone murderers."

A shudder assailed the blond woman. "Oh, Rose, you have no idea how much they despise you. To them, you're foolishly leading people toward nothingness by pursuing Ulgorack's senseless dream of proving that Gorumars deserve a chance. Make no mistake, they see you as the enemy."

"Come on, Kristina, you're exaggerating. Since when are you so intolerant?" Rose rubbed her temples. "I've had enough. Kristina, I'm just asking you do to your job. If you won't do simple research, why should I employ you?"

The assistant scowled at the implied threat, opening her mouth only to close it. Then she whimpered and nodded. "Fine, I understand." Without further ado, she turned around and left. Once she was gone, Rose sighed and sat on her bed. She regretted yelling at Kristina, but she didn't have much of a choice. As she wondered what had gotten into the blond woman, she hoped it wouldn't happen again. This wasn't like her at all.

***

Janice sampled a sip of her blue paradise. Delicious, and that ended up reassuring. This kind of establishment received few patrons requesting fancy cocktails, and so ordering it had been a risk. In front of her, Gareth Stevenson held his beer. Unlike her, he'd opted for the safe option. Tons of voices filled the area, from drunken clients seeking a one-night stand to Rubarg players accusing each others of cheating. Janice had picked a somewhat isolated table, however, and so the cacophony failed to interrupt their conversation. In fact, she hoped it might prevent curious people from overhearing, as she meant to discuss personal matters.

Earlier today, Janice had learned that Gareth had passed his psych evaluation. In other words, he'd be allowed to resume active duty and be sent on missions. Under the pretense of celebrating, she'd invited him here, though her true intentions proved less joyful. Janice's lips twisted in a grimace as she considered bringing up the question. Gareth wouldn't be pleased. Then he said, "All right, Ricdeau, you can stop pretending now. I know what's on your mind." He chuckled. "So, you think I'm crazy, huh?"

Janice exhaled in relief. She wouldn't need to broach the subject. "No, buddy, but not long ago we had a talk that freaked me out." A shudder assailed her as she recalled the event. Gareth had spoken of how returning to a "normal" life felt off and how they'd let their deceased comrades down by abandoning the war effort for the uneasy peace. "No way Nigel would've okayed you then, and it's hard to believe you're cured so soon after."

"Heh, I've been going through intense therapy. It's done me a world of good. Don't worry, I'm much better, I promise. Besides, they wouldn't have cleared me if I wasn't ready for duty."

Janice frowned. "BBR has been causing trouble, and tensions with Doctor Death are higher since the assassination attempt. What if NISDA is pressuring Nigel so he passes borderline cases? Wouldn't be the first time that kind of shady stuff happened."

"So you're saying NISDA will risk sending a guy into the field who might get a PTSD attack and jeopardize the mission?" With a laugh, Gareth waved her concerns away. "Not bloody likely."

"That's not quite it." Janice closed her eyes and sighed. "I'm afraid you're looking for a place to die."

"Well, I'm not. Yeah, when I said those things I was depressed and maybe..." He groaned. "But whatever, that's the past. I'm fine now, I swear."

***

As Gareth headed for the bar's door, he pondered the discussion he'd shared with Janice. Despite his efforts, he'd failed to quell her concerns. She'd pretended he'd reassured her, but he realized she doubted his words. Yet he had been one hundred percent honest. He felt ready. Ah well, you can't stop other people from worrying.

Gareth had almost exited the building when he spotted a familiar face sitting at the bar hunched over. Ken Marcella, a fellow soldier who sucked on his beer with little enthusiasm. The poor guy had lost his wife recently. Catherine had been contracted by NISDA for the Orontian launchpad project. The very one the Ostarkirans had discovered during the strike incident. The ensuing raid had killed her. Gareth walked over to Ken, patted his shoulder and said, "You shouldn't drink your sorrow away. It leads to dark places. Just ask Koporal Tigh."

A smile formed on Ken's lips. Though he attempted to adopt a joyful demeanor, the sadness glimmering in his eyes shattered the illusion. "Nah, I was getting bored at home, and I figured I'd come here and relax." He gestured at the TV. "And check out the game." Ken winked. "Hey, they didn't pull me off active duty, so maybe I should be the one worried about seeing you here."

"Actually, as of today Dr. Nigel Crane cleared me."

Ken recoiled a bit. "Really?"

With a grunt, Gareth crossed his arms. "What? It's that hard to believe?" Then he burst into laughter and Ken joined him.

"Nah, I didn't expect it is all. But it's great news!" Ken pointed at the stool next to his. "How about celebrating by joining me?"

Gareth nodded and sat down. Sure, he'd celebrated with Janice already, but that had ended early and he could use a second, and even a third or fourth, beer. Besides, he sensed Ken needed the company.

Chapter 7

Bacdor 9, 2134, on the Nirnivian calendar

The next day, Rose sat at her desk and filled out some obligatory paperwork. As she toiled, the door slid open and a swooshing sound echoed. Rose lifted her eyes from the page she consulted and confirmed Kristina had arrived at the office. Few people entered this place thanks to the limited security access, and so guessing the visitor's identity posed little challenge.

Instead of looking at Rose, the blond woman hung her head in shame as she approached. Rose expected she'd completed the requested task and would now present the results as a peace offering. The prophet smiled as she prepared herself to accept the apology, but Kristina handed her an envelope. Then she turned around, sobbed and started to leave. Beyond Kristina's behavior, the material seemed light compared to the detailed work she usually delivered.

"Kristina, please wait. What is this?" she asked as she brandished the document. Kristina stopped and gazed at her employer. A sorrowful glimmer haunted her eyes. A gulp escaped Rose's lips as she realized what it meant before her assistant confirmed it.

"It's my letter of resignation." Kristina forced a smile. "Rose, it's been a pleasure and an honor working for you. I'm sorry it has to end this way."

"Kristina, don't do this. It's only research—"

"I don't have a choice," the blond woman countered in a whisper. "Rose, you're a wonderful person. You preach tolerance and open-mindedness and accept different beliefs—even when they're wrong. I respect you for it, and in most cases I agree." A touch of anger invaded Kristina's voice. "But the Timanites... are monsters. I won't help them. I can't help them." The bit of rage morphed into a furious yell. "Some beliefs shouldn't be tolerated!"

A chill ran down Rose's spine. She gritted her teeth. Incredible loathing she witnessed. Kristina didn't easily succumb to intense emotions. In normal circumstances, she maintained a calm, even cold demeanor. Many ridiculed her for it—called her an iceberg. For her to react like this, something horrible must have happened. "Kristina, what in the world did the Timanites do to you?"

"To me?" A nervous giggle came from the assistant as her fingers covered her mouth and her eyes darted left. "Oh, they did nothing to me. It's what they did to another." She sobbed. Tears rolled down her cheeks. Having never seen her cry before, Rose gasped. "There was this girl at school, Emma. She was very smart and so nice. We worked on assignments together and we got close. Emma was my only friend." Kristina paused, sniffled. "One day, she told me she and her family were Timanites. It was a secret; she made me promise not to tell anyone. Timanites despise life. Her parents had filled her head with nonsense and showed her the worst side of people. She resisted, and they punished her. I tried to help, but I didn't know how. In the end, they broke her. They killed Emma's cheerful personality bit by bit until hatred consumed her. I couldn't bear to see her like that, so we drifted apart."

The tale finished, Kristina hushed. While she rubbed her chin, Rose reflected upon what she'd heard. The silence continued for several minutes. "The Timanites are misguided, not evil. By hating them, you validate their beliefs. If you offer them compassion instead, they might realize how wrong they are and change for the better. That being said, I understand your anger." Rose then seized the envelope Kristina had given her and tore it in half. "I'll handle the research. Now, that means I won't have time to write the rest of my sermon, so you will. Don't worry: it's not about the Timanites, and I have notes that should guide you."

After an exhale, Kristina nodded. "Of course, it will be my pleasure, Rose." She began drying her tears. "I haven't been professional and handled this all wrong." The assistant chuckled. "I deserve to be fired."

"After years of brilliant service, I figured I should be lenient." Rose then adopted a severe expression and brandished a menacing index finger. "Don't let it happen again. Even my patience has limits." Done with the warning, Rose smiled. "Kristina, I'm a reasonable woman: you don't need to scream for me to listen. Remember that. Next time you have a problem with your tasks, please let's have a civil discussion." Rose winked. "You were so angry yesterday I feared you'd go Flanders on me."

No doubt Kristina understood the reference, and Rose hoped the exaggerated claim would lighten the dire atmosphere. The Tom Flanders incident was infamous. Years ago, not long before Ostark had attacked, the overworked aide of a councillor had murdered his employer during a fight. Back then, many had joked that the treatment of assistants then improved out of fear the tragedy might repeat itself. Going Flanders had become a common threat for when a boss made ridiculous demands. While not in an official capacity, the date of the disastrous event had sort of turned into a day celebrating aides and their support.

Though Rose feared her attempt at humor might've been too dark, Kristina burst into genuine laughter. "Oh, don't worry, I'm not quite there yet."

Chapter 8

I still had difficulty believing I sat in a bar with Brucie. For so long, I'd remained inside Valardir. In fact, I believe I only had exited the complex by choice three times since my arrival. The first time had been to visit a child who'd caught a disease called Alcharia. The second, a trip to a library where I'd researched Project Ekelon, an endeavor that had achieved no results. Finally, I had gone to a restaurant with Janice. I missed the fresh air and enjoyed being outside, but between the brutal greeting I received from the general population and BBR's kidnapping attempt, doing so felt unsafe.

—Thoughts of James Hunter, Hocmar 28, 2134, on the Nirnivian calendar

For certain, James didn't expect to go out that evening. He planned to stay in his room and finish reading the book about Misha he'd checked out. The due date approached, and he preferred not to bother the soldier who'd borrowed it with the renewal. Bad enough he'd have to return the volume. Then Brucie rang his doorbell and asked if James wanted to hang out. At first, he declined, but the bodyguard proved insistent, and always the pushover, James eventually agreed.

To be honest, James wasn't thrilled by the idea. Brucie could be a jerk. While James had warmed up to his antics, he wondered if Rose's absence would encourage Brucie's less pleasing qualities. Beyond that, he feared Diabo might still be searching for him. When he shared that concern, Brucie guaranteed he'd protect him. Besides, they wouldn't stay long, an hour or two. What were the chances Diabo would find out? Even if he did, no way he'd manage to send someone considering the short notice. That quelled James's worries.

Moments after they ordered, a waiter brought their drinks. James took a risk and chose an unknown alcoholic beverage. Lucky for him, it tasted more than satisfactory. As for Brucie, he picked a simple druikinaka juice. Based on the server's face, those weren't popular with the regular clientele. Five minutes passed, and a waitress dropped a plate containing pieces resembling wings on the table. Brucie had requested those. Though James had no idea what animal they came from, they smelled similar to chicken, and so he tried one. The meat turned out to be tender and cooked to perfection. Plus, the sauce made him lick his lips in delight. A perfect mix of savory and spicy, enough to offer a kick without being obnoxiously hot. Despite the food's quality, few patrons filled the area. An old guy sitting at the bar and sucking on his beer, two women chatting and themselves. Then again, they might be early. Perhaps more people would arrive later.

"So, man," Brucie said, "not a bad li'l place, ain't it?"

"Yeah, it's nice. Um, don't ask me what I'm eating, but it tastes good! I—" Before James finished his sentence, Brucie brandished his index finger.

"Sorry, bro, just a sec."

The bodyguard stared at the TV screen mounted on the wall. Some kind of sport played. Men armed with sticks chased a ball. By the cheers of the crowd, a crucial event had occurred. One player struck the projectile, and it flew toward the goal but hit the post and rebounded, missing its mark. Brucie clenched his fist while shaking his head. "Damn, 'twas freaking close. Can't believe he missed that shot, it was wide open, ya know."

"It looks interesting, but I don't understand the rules at all."

Brucie shrugged. "Ah, it's easy, dude. Ya know, gotta put the ball in the goals using those sticks. There's a bunch o' other crap, but that's the main thing." The description sounded like a mix of hockey and soccer, and James figured he'd catch the finer subtleties with time.

"Anyway, James, thank ya for coming. I wasn't sure you'd come, with my stupid jokes—well, people think I'm an asshole and don't like me much. They ain't getting that I tease 'cause I love."

A nervous laugh escaped James's lips. "Then you must adore me."

"Ah, freak yeah! You're kinda cool for a lame-ass human." Brucie winked. "But seriously, man, what happened to ya is messed up. I mean, I'd go crazy as shit. You hold up damn well now, ya know. You're freaking tough, bro; no muscles but you're tough as nails."

"It was hard at first. Still is, actually. This place is so weird. No offense." The more he progressed, the more James's voice became charged with emotion. "And I've lost so many people. I miss them a lot, especially when I'm alone. Hell, they must be worried sick about me. But, after a rough start, you guys welcomed me here with open arms. It makes it all easier."

Brucie brought his glass to his lips and sipped the blue liquid. He savored the flavor for a moment. "'Twas what I thought. Like, I needed a break from Rose, 'cause o' the shit going on about the Timanites. Anyway, man, since she gave me the evening off, figured why not ask that James dude if he wanna hang out, he ain't got much to do."

"Thanks for thinking of me." James paused and hesitated for a second. "Um, you don't like the Timanites?"

"Ain't hating 'em or anything. It's just, they creep me out. Like, they worship Timagoron, that's weird as balls. I don't get it." He scowled. "And I've heard some scary stuff. People say their religion encourages child abuse and crap like that. Dunno if that's true, but it gimme the shivers just thinking 'bout it. Still, I ain't nothing next to Kristina. She blew her gasket 'cause Rose wanted her to do research to help that family. Now that's hatred if ya ask me. Didn't think she had it in her. But whatever, they patched things up, no worries."

"Where is Rose anyway? You're usually right by her side."

"Oh yeah, man, I'm her perso bodyguard. Shit, if something happened to her I'd be screwed." Brucie gnawed a wing, then continued. "But it's fine, a bud o' mine's covering for me; Rose signed off on it. The guy's a soldier, so he can handle her." He chuckled. "'Sides, he's in charge, so if it goes wrong it's his fault." A frown formed on his brow. "Ya know, I got some crazy-ass hours, but the job's all right. I mean, Rose's kinda cool."

"She's very nice, I enjoy spending time with her." Or at least he did when the Doctor's tricks didn't mess with his brain.

"And she's damn hot too, ain't she? Hey, pal, I saw ya two together. Ya got a thing fo' her, don't ya?" Brucie winked. "Come on, ya can tell me, I ain't gonna squeal."

"No, um, she's my friend. I don't think of her like that."

I wouldn't have gotten a more incredulous glare out of Brucie if I'd pretended my dog had three heads. Some people can't comprehend the concept of a platonic relationship be tween a man and a woman, and it appeared that was Brucie's case.

—Thoughts of James Hunter, Hocmar 28, 2134, on the Nirnivian calendar

"Ah, come on, you gotta be shitting me." The bodyguard snapped his finger. "Oh, ya play for the other team, huh? No problem!" He pointed both his thumbs toward his own torso. "This guy can get you laid either way!"

"Uh, no, and didn't you make that joke before?"

"So what? Repetition's part of comedy."

"Yeah, but it's not funny. And it might be homophobic? I can't even tell."

The bodyguard shrugged. "Everybody bombs once in a while. But, nah, I was kidding, ya know. It's because of that chick, what was it, Nadine?"

James nodded and then sampled his drink. "Close, it's Nadia. And I guess so." As he realized what his words implied, James blushed. "I wouldn't be interested in Rose that way even if I didn't have a girlfriend, but yes, I'm not planning on dating anyone because I have Nadia back home."

"Damn, dude, that's dedication right there." A giggle escaped Brucie. "Is she that scary, bro? 'Fraid she'll cut your balls if ya stray?"

"Maybe the concept's foreign to you, Brucie, but for some, fidelity is important."

"That's cool, man; respect ya for it. That kind o' stuff's so freaking hard for me, ya know. Still, dude, you're trapped here; probably won't see the gal again. Shit, she might not wait for ya herself. The chick couldn't blame ya too much, right? I wouldn't anyway. Sure, sometimes sleeping 'round is cheating, but hey, sometimes it's more like moving on with your life."

James sighed and rubbed his eyes. He hoped the bodyguard didn't notice he wiped a tear. "Uh, I guess so. Maybe

I'm holding on to Nadia because, well, I'll never see her again, but I'm not ready to accept that yet?"

With a grimace, Brucie scratched his neck. "Ah crap, man, I'm sorry. So tactless o' me. I got plenty o' class, but no tact." That brought a smile back to James's face. Brucie's definition of "class" must have been special. Determined to rid himself of his sorrow as fast as possible, James grabbed his glass and downed the contents in a single shot. "Whoa, dude, calm down! That's strong stuff. Ya don't wanna puke later."

"Ah, I won't, I had my share of parties on earth."

"Cool." Brucie hesitated for an instant. "Good thing ya ain't hot for Rose, bro. Never got over that Miguel guy and that ain't 'bout to change for anyone. Not even you." He sighed. "Rose's been down for a while. She's depressed 'cause... I dunno, I guess she's tired o' all the crap going on around here. Ya can't blame the gal. Ain't gonna happen, but if ya got in her pants, it might help take her mind off things."

"Right, nothing solves a woman's problems like a dick, huh, Brucie?"

The bodyguard raised an eyebrow and gave him a cocky smirk. "If it's mine, sure! Heh, whatever, I wanna see her happy again. Don't care if it's 'cause o' dicks or not."

As usual, Brucie's words were crude and perhaps even offensive, but he felt genuine concern for Rose. For all the talk about her being depressed, she mostly acted happy around me. Still, I had to admit that sometimes I wondered if she faked joy so others wouldn't worry about her. There was this sadness in her eyes that never went away.

—Thoughts of James Hunter, Hocmar 28, 2134, on the Nirnivian calendar

"You care about her a lot, don't you, Brucie?"

"Course I do! She's a damn nice lady and I spend a crap ton o' time with her, ya know. We're kinda like friends, I guess. Work friends, but heh... and, hey, she's the freaking holy Melkar. The whole bloody country cares 'bout her."

"This religion, it's important to you, isn't it?" James then asked.

"Sure is, man. Ya think I'd bust my ass like I do if it wasn't? What's so damn wrong with being religious, anyway?"

James swallowed hard and raised his hands as a shield. "Uh, nothing at all; it's, um, great. It's just that you didn't strike me as the religious type at first."

Brucie snorted and took a sip of his juice. "Yeah, I'm used to that. People think, 'That Brucie dude, he ain't got no smarts. He's a clown.'" The bodyguard adopted a serious expression. "But that ain't true." He lifted a lecturing index finger. "I'm a deep guy, ya know. I've got some freaking layers. Ya see, first there's the asshole layer everyone talks about, then there's a dickery layer, similar, not quite the same. After that, man, there's a religious layer and a trotleberry pie layer—"

"That's a good one."

"Ah yeah, the best, dude. And after that there's a meat layer. Kinda clash with the pie, but what can ya do? And then the last one: another asshole layer. All this crap gives us, well..." Brucie winced as if he'd forgotten how he planned to finish his pointless monologue.

"Complex psychological shit?" James proposed after a little while.

Brucie mimicked firing a gun with his hand. "Yeah! Ya nailed it!" Both men started laughing at their immature humor.

Afterward, Brucie glanced toward the TV. One of the teams must have scored, because he cheered. Then the bodyguard pointed at James's empty glass and said, "Wanna get another? It's on me..."

"I might take you up on that." James eyed Brucie's juice. "You don't drink alcohol, do you?"

"Nah, not anymore. Used to get shitfaced like crazy. Always hanging out in bars, drinking myself stupid, having sex with a bunch o' chicks, man; was the bomb. I even tried some drugs. I was wild, my mom didn't know what to do. My brother was the respectable one back then. Things change. It's all over now. I'm busy protecting Rose, no more fun. I haven't been laid in months, man. It's so rare these days, special occasions only, ya know."

"You can try to get lucky if you want."

"Ah man, I ain't gonna leave ya alone. Guess we could both get some, but ya got Nadia and look at this crowd. There's only those two gals and I'm pretty sure they're a couple."

They stopped talking for a moment after that since Brucie focused on the game. It was in its final moments. The team Brucie rooted for led by one point. In the nick of time, the opponents scored, and the bout ended in a draw. This outcome drew a groan out of Brucie, but he didn't dwell on it. With the match over, James restarted the conversation.

"Say, how did a party guy like you become Rose's bodyguard, anyway?"

"Compromising photos." The deadpan delivery proved so convincing that James gasped. "Ha, nah, I'm shitting you. Ya see, once I had grown up, I realized I had to do something with my life. That sucks, but it's how it is. My grades were crap, dude, and most jobs don't consider beer chugging a skill; freaking stupid of 'em. Didn't have much prospects, what I'm trying to get to. Lucky for me, my big bro took me to this charity event hosted by Rose, something 'bout orphans. Some jerk pulled a gun on her. Saw him before Rose's bodyguard, tackled him and got shot. Nothing too bad, the hospital patched me up."

"Wait, what? Why would he want to kill Rose? She's beloved."

"'Twas a kidnapping attempt. Some crap about using her as a hostage for some bullshit. Anyway, Rose visited me at the hospital. We talked and, ya know, she found out I was searching fo' a job. She freaking offered to hire me as a bodyguard. My stunt impressed her. Paid for training and everything." Brucie giggled. "The other guy bitched 'bout that. 'That asshole ain't qualified' and stuff. Her dad also wasn't too thrilled at first. Rose didn't give a damn, though." He emptied his drink, then proceeded. "'Twas a nice gig. Rose didn't have enemies. People loved her like crazy. Shit, they still do. Then the war started, but she wasn't a target, so it didn't change much for me. But then that Doctor Death douche showed up, and Rose moved into Valardir. Didn't need many bodyguards there, so she only kept one and she chose me." Brucie scoffed. "Don't ask me why. Things got busy, but I ain't got any regrets. Nirnivia needs Rose, ya know. And it made my mother proud too. On her death bed, she told me I was her favorite son. Since my bro became a terrorist, that ain't too surprising, but whatever. Anyway, it's 'bout time we go back or ya won't be able to enter Valardir."

"Oh, yeah, good point."

Chapter 9

Bacdor 11, 2134, on the Nirnivian calendar

Rose gazed at the camera and smiled. The lecture proceeded well. Not that she'd expected otherwise; so far, she'd performed the routine she'd perfected through years of performance. She'd read some texts, answered questions and led a group prayer. Now, however, she'd reached what she deemed the crucial part of the sermon. No more tiptoeing around the issue. She paused and gathered her thoughts before resuming.

"I would like to address a terrible incident concerning a vandalized church. It is an atrocious crime, and anger is warranted. The police are searching for the culprit but have made little progress. In their desire for swift justice, many accuse a Timanite family living nearby, without serious evidence. I understand why the Timanites' doctrine is unpopular, but that does not mean they deserve persecution. For years I have preached tolerance and argued that religious differences are no reason for hatred. Today, I wonder if my efforts were in vain. Though the Timanites are easy suspects, you should not condemn them before they are proven guilty. Don't the Yldrad scrolls say: 'You will not be judged by your faith, but by how you treat each other'?" She sighed. "However you feel about the Timanites' teachings, they are people, like us. What's more, they are Nirnivians. Ulgorack and Timagoron will consider how you treated them in their final judgment. Besides, condemning them only validates their beliefs. You are acting like the monsters they assume Gorumars to be. Instead, show them respect and accept them as they are. Perhaps this way, they'll realize life isn't inherently wicked. Perhaps they'll see how wrong they are and embrace their existence. This would be a greater victory for our cause than jailing a few innocents. Saint Augustus said it best: 'You can save far more souls leading by example than by reciting prayers and performing sacred rituals.'"

And so Rose continued her speech, citing divine sources in support of her arguments. She could only hope her message got through.

***

While rubbing his chin, Fabio studied his cards. An annoying bug flew around the room and the resulting buzz sapped his concentration. Part of him wished to squish it, but that'd be a waste of time. Those things moved so fast and saw you coming regardless of which direction you approached from. So instead of interrupting the game and running around with a swatter, he remained sitting and redoubled his focus.

This latest turn offered him a favorable assortment of shapes and colors. In particular, that red lozenge and the green square had arrived at the perfect moment. They'd serve him well in helping secure a win. Despite this, Fabio lacked interest in the game. The same held true for Lucas and Abacus. They all sat at the table mostly in silence, sipping from their beer bottles. Under normal circumstances, these weekly card games caused quite a ruckus. Constant trash talk filled the air, and a victory led to a fair amount of bragging, and even the occasional accusation of cheating. This evening, though, enthusiasm remained low. When

Abacus won a round ten minutes earlier, he celebrated with an incomprehensible mumble while Fabio and Lucas responded by shrugging.

"Hey, Lucas, what's taking so long?" Abacus asked.

With a frown, Lucas scratched his shaved head. Then he grunted and dropped his cards. "Nah, screw this, I'm done. Guys, how about we stop pretending we're having fun and talk about what's going on? That sermon was bullshit. What's wrong with Her Holiness?"

"Don't ask me." Fabio adjusted his glasses. "The Timanites are guilty, it's obvious."

Abacus nodded. "Damn straight. The paint alone is proof. First, the cops refuse to arrest them, so people like us pick up the slack. Shit, I missed work to protest, and I need the money. And now the Melkar comes and condemns us for doing what's right? The world is going insane."

"Yeah, and did you hear from Justin? They're calling off the protests." A bang echoed as Lucas slapped the table. "How are we supposed to stop those bastards from vandalizing our churches when the cops and Her Holiness protect them?"

Fabio sighed. "I know, and it's strange. The Timanites are followers of Timagoron. The Melkar is Ulgorack's prophet. They're enemies by definition. She can't be on their side: it's impossible, so why is she defending them?"

His comrades remained silent. They pondered the question, in search of a reasonable answer, but they found none until Lucas snapped his fingers. "What if it's a test... like, to see if we have enough faith to continue?"

Impressed by the idea, a smile spread on Fabio's face. As for Abacus, he leaned forward and said, "Oh, that's some crazy shit there, but it kinda makes sense."

"Yes, the Voice of God works in mysterious ways." Fabio tapped his chin. "Her Holiness is always talking about the importance of different points of views and interpretations. And she's always saying we shouldn't take sacred texts at face value but think about their meaning. Maybe we shouldn't take her words literally either."

Abacus shook his head. "Goddammit, you guys are geniuses. And we all gave up like a bunch of cowards. She must be so disappointed in us."

A chuckle escaped Lucas's lips. "Well, boys, why don't we show her some people are paying attention?"

***

Bacdor 13, 2134, on the Nirnivian calendar

The Good Doctor was stuck in an obligatory meeting with his cabinet. As the vice president, I was also present. Sometimes, I hated being a politician. We weren't doing anything useful. Instead, we argued about various subjects to defend our own interests. We were allies in theory, yet we were at each other's throats. Politics as usual.

—Thoughts of Evelyn Losier, Hocmar 28, 2134, on the Nirnivian calendar

The cabinet met in a large conference room decorated with statues and paintings. In the middle, the politicians gathered around an oval table. Small signs displaying their names rested before each of them. Most wrote notes with minicomps, including Evelyn. Those less familiar with technology preferred old-fashioned notepads.

The Good Doctor sat at one end of the table, his seat raised a touch above the others as a symbol of his authority. Everybody wore expensive outfits; even the mechanical president sported a black suit and tie. He usually remained "naked"—garments were pointless for him since his robotic body had little to hide and couldn't feel cold. Regardless, people often seemed more comfortable when he was clothed, and so when in public he indulged them.

A middle-aged blond woman named Eliza Springtown was speaking. A few nodded along in agreement.

"Our education system is in shambles. The simple truth is we are underfunded. Children are our future. It is imperative we increase funding, and I believe I hold the answer. The medical field has made a lot of progress thanks to the Good Doctor's hard work. Medicines and medical procedures are cheaper than ever. We offer public health insurance to help the most unfortunate in this time of war. However, now fewer and fewer people require assistance. We should cut public health insurance and invest this money in education—"

"Hold on," a man named Anthon Landry objected with conviction. "Public health insurance is necessary. Yes, we've made progress in this area, but many still need help. Are you really suggesting we take away their support?"

Both gave a great performance. To the untrained eye, they appeared concerned with the well-being of the people, but I knew better: both had special interests influencing their opinions. Eliza was sponsored by insurance firms who despised the public health system as it cut down on their business. And dear old Harold had contacts with pharmaceutical companies who would hate seeing it disappear since that might decrease their sales.

—Thoughts of Evelyn Losier, Hocmar 28, 2134, on the Nirnivian calendar

The Good Doctor's monotone voice then echoed. "Education is indeed a priority, but it is not in such a dire state. Dropout rates are down, national averages are up. Still, I agree we must do better, and a greater budget is necessary. Nevertheless, we worked hard to create a health system that provides care for everyone while remaining affordable. I understand most Ostarkirans believe people are responsible for themselves and see public insurance as a temporary measure. As president, I strive to lead this country in accordance with the population's expectations. Unfortunately, cutting the healthcare program would cause more harm than good. Too many could not afford the medical treatments they require. Children are our future; we must prepare them adequately. However, we must also ensure their survival or they shall only be our past."

General Torn snickered. "In that case maybe we should cut the military budget to fund education. We're hardly fighting a war now anyway."

Evelyn understood his position and even agreed with him on rare occasions, but that despicable man gave her shivers. In an uncharacteristic display of frustration, the defense secretary slapped the table with his hand, causing a large thud. "That's asinine. I'm well aware you're being sarcastic, but that kind of potshot is counterproductive."

The cybernetic man nodded. "Mr. Cursak is correct. General Torn, I—" A high-pitched screech echoed through the air. Pain assailed Evelyn's ears and so she covered them while gritting her teeth. The rest of the cabinet followed her lead. Despite covering her lobes, the sound still pierced her eardrums. Evelyn's eyes watered and she lowered her neck. When at last the squeal relented, she gasped in relief. "I apologize, I got careless and attempted using a contraction."

"Speech synthesizers have made great progress these last couple of years. You should have yours updated so you don't have to worry about that quirk."

"If a software patch sufficed, I would. However, my model is so outdated it would require an operation to replace the old module. Alas, my time is precious and I refuse to sacrifice any for such a cosmetic endeavor. Regardless, as I was saying, General Torn, you should kindly keep your sarcasm to yourself: it contributes nothing to the debate. Your objections about our current strategies are noted. Let us proceed, please."

The whole thing was a total pissing match. It used to be even worse. Before, an opposition party worked against the president and his cabinet. This system kept the leaders in check. Then President Laforge disbanded the opposition party as a special measure reserved for wartime. The move had its critics—some feared it gave the current administration too much control. They also claimed the opposition party would never be reinstated. I can understand the concerns, but it was necessary: everything progressed slowly to begin with, we didn't need more bickering. Besides, President Laforge was of questionable character, but the Good Doctor wasn't the kind of man who'd abuse his power.

—Thoughts of Evelyn Losier, Hocmar 28, 2134, on the Nirnivian calendar

***

Why had he chosen that path? As a bloodied Frederic lay on the ground, he couldn't help but wonder. His mother had sent him on an errand. By the time he had finished, night had fallen. Eager to return home, he had shortened his walk by cutting through a small alley. He had done so often in the past and nothing bad had ever happened. His parents had warned him that since their family had fallen out of favor, he should avoid secluded spots: they were perfect for ambushes. Like a fool, Frederic had dismissed their concerns as misguided. Now he wished he'd listened.

Two shadows had attacked him along his way. The darkness had concealed their features: he had no idea who they were. They'd cornered Frederic and pummeled him with punches and kicks. Though outnumbered, the young man had held his own and landed quite a few blows. He doubted he could've won, but he'd offered a brave resistance. The real trouble had started when a third assailant armed with a club had approached from behind. After the weapon had struck his head, pain had crippled Frederic, and he'd collapsed. Unable to get up, he'd lain in the street, defenseless. The thugs had shown no mercy: they'd stomped him and had no intention of stopping. Just when Frederic reckoned they'd kill him, a strong voice echoed through the air and ordered the bullies to surrender. Police officers stepped on the scene, brandishing their guns. The goons obeyed and Frederic realized he might yet live. In his mind, he kept repeating the same question: was the five minutes he would've saved worth the risk of broken bones?

Chapter 10

What complete clusterfreak.

> —Thoughts of Wrathchild, Hocmar 28, 2134, on the Nirnivian calendar

Emerging from behind the rock she used for cover, Wrathchild fired a spray of bullets with her automatic weapon. Normally, she favored a simple pistol, but given the circumstances, she'd traded up. Most of the projectiles missed any living target, instead hitting the walls, resulting in sparks. A few, however, struck flesh. In particular, a young man grimaced, clutching his chest as red stained his fatigues. Before he collapsed, she spotted the winged sword and shield sewn to his clothes and winced. A reminder that Melissa fought not Ostark, her sworn enemy, but NISDA. The armed force defending Nirnivia. The country she had grown up in. The one she and everyone in BBR had sworn to protect despite their unwillingness to resist. A sickness filled Wrathchild's stomach. What a cruel joke.

How had it come to this? To be honest, she knew the answer. NISDA had fought BBR from the start to keep the uneasy peace going. Fair enough, she supposed, except these days they had stepped up their efforts. Not long ago, NISDA's assaults against those they labeled terrorists had proven lacking, a mere farce. That had since changed. The previous week had brought six attacks from NISDA, and this week they'd assailed two other cells, with devastating results. Wrathchild's and Diabo's cell marked the third. So many comrades had died. BBR lacked the resources to sustain such losses. Soon, they'd have to find a solution, or face extinction.

The whole nightmare had started because of that damn apartment complex. Plague had found evidence an Ostarkiran spy lived there, but they couldn't be identified. Enraged, Diabo had insisted BBR blow up the building. Everyone, including Wrathchild, had protested, but the boss had stood his ground. The result ended up being a fiasco. Several rich Nirnivians had funded BBR in secret, but this sudden act left them cold. Many had pulled support and their limited supplies became downright scarce. Soon enough, they had little choice but to find alternative sources. In other words, they had begun stealing from Nirnivia in addition to Ostark. That failed to please NISDA, and these recent raids served as the consequence. Stubborn as always, Diabo accused the Nirnivians of foolishness as BBR was their only hope of getting rid of the Doctor. Maybe so, but in Melissa's opinion, how had he expected them to react? As much as she hated to admit it, NISDA's move made sense to her.

As the crimson beast entered her mind, Wrathchild glanced at Diabo. He hid behind a table mounted on its side as a barricade. Once in a while, he popped out and fired a volley, like every BBR warrior present. Unlike most, normal ammo posed little danger to him as it bounced off his hard skin. Still, their enemies had learned this and often came armed with special armor-piercing bullets. Though those caused less damage to Diabo than might be assumed, they did injure him.

Diabo must've felt Melissa's glance, since he stared at her after peeping at his watch and said, "Not long." She didn't hear him, however, because of the deafening noise. Instead, she read his lips. An optimistic message, and she hoped he was correct. They couldn't hold on forever. Allison remained their only chance. Too bad she had taken part in a raid on an Ostarkiran convoy and so succumbed to her limitations. As soon as she was able to use her power, Diabo would force her to flood the Nirnivian soldiers with her visions and it'd be over. Even then, they'd lost so many friends.

Gritting her teeth, Wrathchild engaged overdrive and fired at the NISDA troops. Thanks to incredible speed, she aimed with great precision. Plenty of her foes fell. A bullet approached her, but no worries. She waited and kept shooting. When it almost struck her right between the eyes, she ducked, evading it. Then a grenade landed next to Diabo. He didn't notice. With the cacophony going on, Wrathchild doubted he'd understand if she shouted a warning. Instead, using her velocity, she rushed toward him. Midway, she rolled, avoiding a stray bullet. Once near enough, she grabbed the explosive and threw it back at its sender. As a reward, Diabo offered an impressed nod.

Now reallocated, Wrathchild crouched behind Diabo and disengaged overdrive. She took a few deep breaths while her heart still beat at a sped-up rate. Though a neat trick, overdrive sapped her energy. Unfortunately, she didn't rest for long. Her instinct warned her of incoming danger and she triggered it again. Melissa turned her head and saw what had prompted her intuition. A bullet headed for a BBR goon. After a groan, she dashed, slashing projectiles with her sword along the way. That impossible maneuver was one she'd perfected over the years. When in range, she jumped and tackled the guy to the floor, saving his life. Satisfaction filled Melissa for a moment, but it vanished when she spotted three BBR cadavers in the background. Even with her skills, she couldn't save everyone. The only consolation: a greater number of NISDA's soldiers littered the ground. Then again, given that they should be allies against Ostark, that provided no comfort, and what satisfaction remained disappeared when a burning pain spread across her muscles. She'd overdone it.

As she massaged her thigh, Wrathchild gazed at Diabo again. The red mutant reached for the special remote hanging at his belt. With a smirk, he pushed a button. As he did so, Melissa winced. Allison waited hidden in a safe place out of sight, but she imagined the poor girl contorting and screaming. Not that the Nirnivians fared any better than the telepath. The instant she unleashed her visions, their order had fallen in disarray as they'd yelled, run in every direction and rolled on the ground.

Frowning, Diabo howled, "Come on, we gotta evacuate." A wise decision. They only fought as a diversion so others could escape. Despite Diabo's command, his scowl implied he'd rather stay and murder the remaining troops.

Praise Ulgorack listened to reason. Obvious choice, but Diabo reckless. Never knew what expect from him.

—Thoughts of Wrathchild, Hocmar 28, 2134, on the Nirnivian calendar

Chapter 11

Bacdor 16, 2134, on the Nirnivian calendar

This had to be the strangest video conference Rose had ever attended. The screen displayed three shackled men staring at the camera. Several armed guards surrounded them, ever vigilant. Resisting a sigh, Rose matched the prisoners to the pictures included in the report she'd received: Fabio, the potbellied man, fidgeted as much as his restraints allowed; Lucas, lacking a single hair on his head, pressed his lips together; finally, Abacus rubbed his hands.

The police had arrested them for assault. There'd be no point denying the charges; the cops had caught them stomping on an already bloodied Frederic Sysco without mercy. The youth had been rushed into the hospital, and Rose had heard no news since. She hoped the poor soul would be okay and the doctor would provide the best treatments available despite him being a Timanite. The law forced them to in theory, but Rose had grown familiar with the ways people skirted around legal obligations when convenient.

To Rose's surprise, the villainous trio had requested an audience with her. This happened occasionally with criminals. Pushed by a guilty conscience, they'd admit culpability, but only to the Melkar. Rose felt a confessor would be a more appropriate choice, but she always accepted regardless. Extracting a confession helped keep stress off the already clogged legal system. Here, however, the guilt was proven, so talking to them served no purpose.

Rose had almost refused, but a morbid curiosity had made her reconsider. Every fiber of her being screamed she'd regret it, but here she was.

"So yeah, we realized that it was a test," Fabio said, speaking too fast. "The Melkar protecting Timanite vandals? Impossible. So we acted and got in trouble. Since we're the only ones who understood your real message, we figured maybe you'd speak on our behalf? It might help reduce the sentence."

Fabio paused and gazed upon Rose, expectations filling his eyes. The other two followed suit. Rose rested her right palm on her heart and smiled. "Of course I'll speak on your behalf." Then she formed a fist and gritted her teeth. "I'll tell the judge you are ruthless psychopaths and that they should double whatever sentence they planned."

The three men gasped and exchanged worried glances. "But, Your Holiness," Lucas mumbled after a whimper.

Rose's glare held a rage so strong the bald man didn't dare finish, so Fabio continued instead. "We thought you'd be pleased, that it was a test."

Rose hadn't believed her anger could increase; she was wrong. Furious, she stood up and rested her hands on her hips. "That's a lie!" she yelled, and Fabio cringed. "Anyone who's listened to my sermons for all these years knows I don't speak in riddles. Religious texts are complex enough as is. I try to clarify their meanings by being as straightforward as I can. Here's the truth: you attacked a kid. Why? Because you wanted to. And you wanted justification, so you twisted my words and intent until it fit with your scheme. You deluded yourselves until you assumed I'd play along." Rose fell silent for a second and then added, "But I won't." The tirade extinguished the fire in Rose's belly, but the sadness remained and she sobbed. "I have a question. No matter how often I deny it, people say I'm a prophet. They claim they want me to show them the correct path and steer their souls toward the afterlife. They put a lot of stock in my opinion. So tell me: for all your faith, why doesn't anybody listen when it's really important?"

They offered no answer. Instead, Fabio whispered, "Your Holiness, please forgive us."

Rose shook her head. "No, I cannot, for I'm not the one you wronged." A sigh escaped her lips. "Oh, I suppose that as much as I hate doing so, I must forgive the grief you caused me since that's what my beliefs dictate, but I can't forgive your crime. If you seek forgiveness, then I suggest you beg your victim for it."

A scowl formed on Abacus's brow. "Apologize to a shit-face Timanite? What freaking heresy is this?"

Rose didn't bother replying and glanced at the tech that waited in the background along with Kristina and Brucie. "I'm done here. Please cut off the transmission." With that, she spun away from the monitor.

"Your Holiness, please wait! Forgive us! Please don't turn your back on us!"

As instructed, Rose stopped and lifted her index finger, indicating the technician should belay her order. "But I'm not turning my back on you: you turned your back on me. There might still be hope. If you ever truly repent, I shall return and help as best I can. If not, then I see only certain nothingness in your future. I can't save your soul, but you can. Right now, you're not ready to do so, and until that changes, I cannot help."

***

With a sigh, James closed the book sitting on his desk before rubbing his eyes. Then he grabbed the picture of Nadia resting next to the volume and forced a smile. "Well, looks like it's another bust. Um, not that I expected otherwise, but it still sucks."

Since the due date on the books I borrowed was getting close, it was about time to return them. On a whim, I asked if I could go back to the library and pick something else. I figured maybe some of the checked-out books would be back or something. Heh, I even convinced the guard escorting me to go to another library after I struck out. Not much there either. Like at the first place, the oldest newspaper or magazine they had was two years old, and of course nothing about Ekelon other than that conspiracy theory. I did find a copy of one of Rose's biographies, but it was outdated. The whole thing stopped in her early twenties, before she even got married. Still, I took it and skimmed through. Based on that, there wasn't much in terms of controversies, other than her father and Gail, but I already knew about those. Even then, the way they recounted the Gail incident put far less blame on Rose than she did.

—Thoughts of James Hunter, Hocmar 28, 2134, on the Nirnivian calendar

James bit his lip, followed by a groan and a shake of the head. "I won't find anything at the library—it's pointless. Maybe a bookstore? But I don't have money. I guess Rose might agree to pay for a book or two, but I doubt I'd find anything there either." A moan escaped his lips. "Yes, I know, baby, I know... only place I might find something is the GlobalNet, but I can't access that here. The libraries won't let me either, not without a card, and I can't apply for one. I guess I could ask Rose if there's any way I can try the GlobalNet out, just for fun, but... I'd rather not if I can avoid it. Whatever, I'll figure something out."

Chapter 12

Bacdor 19, 2134, on the Nirnivian calendar

Despite Diabo's assurance that NISDA would back down, the assaults continued. In fact, the red monster's own cell had endured an attack. Thanks to him, Wrathchild and Allison, the fight went better than most, but they'd still suffered considerable losses. Again, the three founders organized a video conference to discuss the issue.

"At any rate, it looks like NISDA ain't gonna stop." Plague said while stroking his chin.

"Ya sure love rubbing that kind o' stuff in my face, don't cha?" The words dripped with scorn and Plague expected a bitter scowl accompanied them.

"Nah, it's not like that, boss. I'm just assessing the situation."

"Whatever." Diabo groaned. "Still got the same opinion, boys. 'Twas stealing from Nirnivia or starving. We didn't have a choice, right? Too late to cry 'bout the past anyway. We gotta deal with NISDA."

Plague nodded. "Yes, I agree." Deep inside, he recalled that Diabo had brought this misfortune on BBR by ordering that they bomb that apartment building. So, sure, they had done what they had to, but it remained his fault. Plague understood that bringing that up would only start a fight, so he kept it to himself. He sighed. "Ain't much we can do to stop NISDA, but I've been looking at some options to slow them down. Things like better ways to hide our cells. Improved defense and escape routes so when they find us, they can't hit as hard. If we're lucky, it might give us two more months."

"So eight instead of six?" Plague imagined Stalker frowning. "Not much, but I guess we gotta take what we can."

"Yeah, sounds 'bout right." Diabo grunted. "Go ahead, Plague, we're all ears."

***

That day during lunch, Rose seemed less stressed than she had been lately. As she ate her soup, she explained why.
—Thoughts of James Hunter, Hocmar 28, 2134, on the Nirnivian calendar

"Yes, I'm relieved because Frederic will be okay. The doctors feared the worst, but now they say he'll recover. And the cops proved his innocence. They arrested the real culprit."

"Really?" James scowled and leaned forward. "Uh, who is it?"

Before the prophet could open her mouth, Brucie answered with a shrug. "The freaking priest, dude." Enraged, the bodyguard clenched his fist. "That old bastard got pissed over some shit and destroyed his own church."

Rose nodded. "Yes, that's basically it. He expected to ascend to high priesthood, and when he learned it wouldn't happen, he vandalized the church as revenge. The police suspected him from the start, but he covered his tracks well." She sighed. "Once again, people blamed a minority for a crime they didn't commit. At least the cops kept a cool head and didn't harass the family. There have been cases where—" Rose dismissed her own sentence with a wave. "Ah, whatever, it's over. We caught the bad guy, Frederic will be back on his feet soon: by our standards, it's a happy ending."

"Hey, maybe ya could make it happier fo' me if ya know what I mean."

"Shut up, Brucie."

Negotiations

Chapter 1

Kotar 34, 2134, on the Nirnivian calendar

Plague ran along with his colleagues, their footsteps echoing on the cave's stone floor. His left hand held the hand of one of his companions, the right his trusty white cane. Not that the staff helped. His ally pulled him in a mad dash, and at this pace, probing the environment would be foolish. Every limb cried out in agony, in part because of Plague's lack of exercising, but mostly because his body suffered from years of deterioration. In this state, that he remained standing under constant strain proved to be a small miracle. Each breath burned his lungs, and he grimaced in pain. While this wasn't a new phenomenon, the physical effort he exerted sped up his breathing, worsening his condition.

To think they had hidden from Ostark all this time only to be discovered by the inferior military that was NISDA. How ridiculous. Especially since the country they had sworn to protect when they'd formed BBR now served as their enemy. Damn Diabo and his insistence on stealing supplies from NISDA. To make matters worse, unlike their so-called leader, Plague couldn't rely on Allison to solve his problems, and so he and his comrades sprinted, hoping to flee their pursuers.

At least, other than Plague himself, none of BBR's key members were in danger. Diabo, Stalker, and Wrathchild remained safe in different locations. Maybe their presence would have tipped the odds in their favor, but Plague preferred not to find out, as losing any of them would bring tragedy for the group. That was why they mostly kept top BBR personnel in separate cells.

The more Plague ran, the weaker his legs grew. In several spots, he almost stumbled. At this rate, they better reach their destination soon. A special trap lay ahead. Pull a concealed lever and a section of the roof would collapse, blocking the tunnel. That should stop the Nirnivians and guarantee their escape. However, Plague doubted he'd reach it. He pushed his ravaged body beyond its limits. Any minute now, it would collapse. And what was that strange sensation in his left hand? Like fabric rubbing against his skin. Too late, he understood the meaning. The glove he wore had slipped off. His companion continued running, holding the glove and leaving Plague behind without realizing. With a gasp, Plague attempted to hop forward and seize his pal. As a result, he tripped and fell on the ground. Rocky edges pierced his flesh and hot blood dripped from the wounds. Plague winced and groaned. Thanks to the noise, the others realized what had happened and turned around toward him.

"No, keep going!"

They ignored him and retraced their steps. Plague whispered a curse. Those poor fools doomed themselves. One of the men attempted to grab him, but he lifted his palm in a signal to stop.

"Don't, I'm bleeding! Don't touch me! We don't have any antidote with us." The goon paused just before touching him. "Go, run! Never mind me: I'm screwed!"

As if to confirm his words, footsteps echoed as several NISDA soldiers entered the scene. "Freeze! Drop your weapons and get those hands up or we'll shoot."

After a shake of the head, Plague sighed. "Better listen to 'em, boys. We've lost this round."

Tipped off by the harsh voice, an enemy blur faced Plague. "Be careful! That's Plague: he's poison. Don't touch his skin and especially not his blood."

"Oh, so you heard of me, huh?" Plague chuckled. "Scared? Well, you should be." He pointed his thumb at himself. "You don't want to get dirty with this guy. Plenty of people died that way. Trust me, I know." In truth, he doubted that warning would work, but it was worth a shot, he supposed.

"No need to worry about us: we have the antidote. But I've seen what the sickness is capable of. I'd rather avoid it if possible. Don't think that means I won't bring you in, though."

Plague shrugged. "Sucks to be me. My cursed body might have been useful for once, but no such luck."

Chapter 2

That evening, in a rare turn of luck, Rose was free. Though she suggested a Kuhard match, I felt tired and preferred to postpone since that required mental prowess. If my decision disappointed Rose, she chose not to show it and nodded in acceptance. Brucie then proposed we play Rubarg instead. While I knew Rose didn't enjoy that game, she agreed to watch us, so we went to the recreation room.

Soon, Brucie won the first match, and he suggested a best-of-seven tournament. I figured why not? Then I realized why: because I'd be crushed four times instead of once. And, yes, my prediction seemed to come true: in less than an hour, Brucie defeated me three times. One more victory and it'd be over.

—Thoughts of James Hunter, Hocmar 28, 2134, on the Nirnivian calendar

For the final confrontation, it was James's turn to break. He grabbed his cue, studied the board. Then, with a hard swallow, he bent over and aimed. Though he understood he'd never win the whole thing, he hoped perhaps he'd at least bring the score to 3–1. Still, he doubted that'd happen. So far he'd always lost at Rubarg. Kuhard too, in fact.

With a deep breath, James prepared himself to strike. Right before contact, a loud beep echoed. The sound skewed his aim and the white ball rolled around the table without hitting his target. A laugh escaped Brucie's lips. As he groaned, James straightened and searched for the source, which ended up being Rose's wireless phone. She carried it on her in case someone attempted to reach her.

When she realized what had happened, she covered her mouth with her fingers.

"I'm sorry, Hunter. I better take this." She picked up the phone, brought it to her ear and pushed a button. "Yes? Kristina, is something wrong? Oh, good. Okay, I will." With those words, she hung up and reached for the remote control.

Brucie leaned forward. "What did the iceberg want?"

"Stop mocking her! Kristina told me to check out MegaNews this instant." As instructed, Rose switched on the TV and changed the channel to forty-two. An anchor sitting at a desk before a large MN logo appeared, reading from a sheet.

"—the infamous Maltafas scrolls have always been elusive. Not only are the contents cryptic and debated, the texts are incomplete. For years, archeologists have dreamed of finding the missing parts, to no avail. That changed yesterday when the Etriel church discovered documents assumed to be the sought-after scrolls, though their authenticity remains unverified. While damaged, they are in decent condition."

Rose's eyes widened, and she gasped. "Oh my God! I can't believe it, the Maltafas scrolls completed at last! I must read them!"

James frowned. "Um, what are they?"

"Sacred texts written by Saint Augustin Maltafas thousands of years ago. Such literature is often open to interpretation, but in their case that's an understatement. Nobody agrees on their meaning. Beyond that, an incomplete passage might allude to the multiverse, though that's a wild guess at the moment. If these new documents are genuine, we'll at last understand what Saint Maltafas tried to tell us. Not only that, it could prove our religion knew about the multiverse from the start, but we forgot about it. If so, it fills several holes in our doctrine. Oh dear Ulgorack, I must read them!"

"That's great and all, but"—Brucie scoffed—"ain't gonna be easy."

"True, but I have to try."

Perplexed, James scratched his head. "Why would it be hard? I mean, you're their holy prophet, aren't you? I'd think they'd be thrilled to have your opinion."

"In theory, yes, but it isn't so simple. Our religion isn't a united front. In the beginning there was only one branch, but because of disagreements, various groups split off and there still is some bad blood between them. The Etriel church is part of the orthodox branch. They believe I'm the Melkar and respect me, so there should be no problem, but"—she sighed—"well, even though I'm not allowed to discuss it by law, people assume I'm a progressive. That rumor caused the orthodox to lose many followers, and their influence has been reduced. Because of this, they are reluctant about collaborating with me."

"Ya going easy on 'em!" The bodyguard crossed his arms. "They're freaking assholes 'bout it!"

Rose shook her head. "I wouldn't go that far, but they can be fussy. In a way, I'm glad because the orthodox respect scripture beyond anything. To them, those words are literal, absolute truth. They'll spare no expense to ensure the documents aren't forgeries. The problem is, they'll be reluctant to give me access to them because they'll fear I'll use them to push my alleged progressive agenda." She groaned. "That's not the case at all, but... whatever. They'll try to find excuses for why they won't show me the originals. Like, I'm in Valardir and they can't let the scrolls out of their supervision for security reasons. Copy machines and old texts don't mix well, so as a solution, they'll propose using transcriptions. That's better than nothing, but I'd rather have the originals because copying them manually can introduce mistakes." She paused as she hesitated for a moment. "Besides, there's also the possibility they'll alter them for their own purposes. I doubt they'd sink that low, but it's possible."

"Ain't that bad." Brucie winked. "Can ya imagine if the Timanites found 'em? Those scrolls are getting burned, baby!"

"Don't scare me like that. I pity those poor misguided souls."

Chapter 3

Valar 3, 2134, on the Nirnivian calendar

"Damn, I really bungled that one," Janice said after shaking her head. Then she gestured toward James. "Your turn, buddy."

"Um, yeah, sure." On that note, he grabbed his stick and studied the table. Number eight lined up almost perfectly and should be an easy target. He aimed, striking the cue ball, and as hoped, the chosen orb fell right in the hole. A rare perfect play for him. The next move, however, proved far more difficult, and he failed.

"Not bad, got one." Janice winked.

"Yeah, uh..." James winced as he pondered asking the question that weighed on his mind. It might be a mistake, but at this point he lacked options, and he preferred leaning on Janice rather than Rose for this one. "Say, uh, do you have GlobalNet access at your house?"

The soldier shook her head. "No, I don't like spending my free time staring at a screen, so I don't bother paying for it. Why? You'd like to check something?"

While resisting a hard swallow, James scratched his neck. "Well, um, I'm just curious. I don't have much to do, and I figured browsing around would be a decent way to spend an afternoon. I tried the library, but they won't let me because I don't have any ID."

"Oh, right. There are a few places you might be able to access the GlobalNet, but you'll run into the same problem. Maybe we should look into getting you an ID. Not sure how it'd work since you're a visitor. I'm a little busy right now, but give me a week or two and I'll set something up for you."

That never actually happened, but considering how things went down afterward, I don't blame her.
—Thoughts of James Hunter, Hocmar 28, 2134, on the Nirnivian calendar

"Thanks."

"Don't mention it, buddy. Like I said, you did a good job on your last turn. But not good enough. Check this out!" With those words, she bent over, and James averted his gaze, as usual. She pulled back her cue, ready to strike, when a swoosh echoed as the door swung open. Distracted, Janice forsook her shot and straightened. James sighed. Of course, for her the disruptive sound happened before the critical moment. "Hey, big guy!" She waved at Brucie as he entered. "Fancy a game?"

He dismissed the notion with a headshake. "Nah, got, uh, a favor to ask ya."

"Oh?"

"See, it's..." The bodyguard scratched the back of his neck while staring at the floor. "Well, kinda heavy."

Janice chuckled. "So? Come on, stop imitating James and spit it out."

And that made me blush. While it was a cheap shot, I had to admit I saw the resemblance. That was beyond out of character for Brucie.
—Thoughts of James Hunter, Hocmar 28, 2134, on the Nirnivian calendar

"The shy look is cute for him, but it doesn't work for you, bud."

"Fine, it's like... my dad croaked last night."

After a gasp, Janice covered her mouth with her hand. "Oh no, I'm so sorry."

James recoiled. "Um, I'm sorry too. That's horrible."

"Nah, it's okay." Brucie shrugged. "Ain't like we were close. The guy bailed on us when I was six or something. Barely remember 'im, so ain't gonna miss him or anything."

"Still, it must be a shock."

He nodded as a grimace appeared on his face. Perhaps James imagined it, but he heard a slight sob. "Yeah, ya could say that. Funeral's in a couple days. I'm not sure I wanna go." Then he scowled. "It feels like I should, it's my last chance to see the bastard." Brucie gritted his teeth and closed his fist. "The coward freaking ran away, left us fo' dead. Didn't come back, not even once. Found 'im when I got older. Still thought maybe he had a good reason, ya know. Wanted to hear his side o' the story, but he wouldn't talk to me. Freak, he deserves I just forget 'bout him, but"—he shook his head—"I dunno. Not sure if I'm gonna say goodbye or spit in his coffin, but it's like I gotta go even if I'd rather not. Ya get me, babe?"

"Yes, I do."

"Good. Problem is, I'm gonna be alone. Yeah, there'll be people, but not those I care 'bout. Ain't got many friends left, Mom's dead, Pierre's gone, Rose can't leave Valardir. Not many options, ya know, and I can't handle it on my own, so I was wonderin' if ya'd come with me."

Janice closed her eyes and then exhaled. "Oh, Brucie..." While rubbing her brow, she swallowed hard. "I wish I could, I swear." She frowned. "But, with our past relationship, I'm not comfortable doing that. Especially after what happened when the beast attacked."

A gasp almost escaped James's lips. Did he just learn they used to date? If so, that might explain the bodyguard's behavior around her. For instance, when James had danced with her at the new year celebration and Brucie had displayed hostility.

"I don't want to give you the wrong idea," Janice went on. "It's better if we're casual friends for now and don't meddle in each other's personal lives. I'm so sorry."

For a second, Brucie's mouth gaped and tears glimmered in his eyes. Without delay, he closed his jaw again and nodded. "No worries, babe, I dig it."

As Brucie turned around and began to leave, I winced. Witnessing the big oaf so down brought a pang to my heart. Yes, Brucie could be annoying—an asshole, even—but deep down there was a tenderness to him. My decision made, I stepped forward.

—Thoughts of James Hunter, Hocmar 28, 2134, on the Nirnivian calendar

"Um, Brucie, I'll go with you." He scratched the back of his head. "If you want me there, that is."

Upon hearing that, Brucie stopped in his tracks. "Ya will?" He spun and faced James with a large smile. "Bro, that's awesome!"

Filled with gratitude, Brucie seized him in an embrace. While James appreciated the sentiment, as usual the bodyguard displayed too much enthusiasm and squeezed so hard it pushed the air out of his lungs. With a gulp, James said, "No need to thank me by choking me."

A laugh echoed as Brucie set him free. "Sorry 'bout that, dude. I'm just so glad, ya know." He patted James's shoulder and for once restrained his strength. "You're a true pal." While extending his tongue, he pointed his thumb in Janice's direction. "Not like that traitor."

"Ooh la la, the old Brucie's back already! Impressive progress through grieving!"

"Heh, no point living in the past. And ya know I'm kidding. Anyway, better go check on Rose. Thanks again, James."

Chapter 4

Valar 5, 2134, on the Nirnivian calendar

I'd left Valardir on rare occasions, and even then I had seen nothing comparable to the church of Onel. Right from the entrance, the décor impressed. In the distance, past several rows of pews, a large altar rested. Behind it, gigantic statues of Rose and Misha stood. Not only did their size dwarf those in Valardir's small chapel, the material proved different. Instead of gray stone, they were sculpted from the Nirnivian equivalent of gold and glimmered as the light struck them. On top of the altar lay many objects made of the same metal. As for the walls, detailed paintings and smaller figurines decorated them. Stained glass formed the various windows, coloring the rays that beamed through them. Even the benches, graced with complex carvings depicting religious scenes, served as works of art. In the background, a solemn organ played and complemented the luxurious setting to perfection.

—Thoughts of James Hunter, Hocmar 28, 2134, on the Nirnivian calendar

Ever since James and Brucie had entered the premises, they'd lingered near the door. Brucie stood in place, staring at the floor and fidgeting. He showed no desire to proceed. People circled around them, their footsteps echoing in the vast empty space of the church. Though a few exchanged words, they did so in whispers and kept conversation short. Nobody could be fooled into thinking they assembled here for a joyous occasion.

"Um, are you okay?" James asked after a moment of silence. While he intended to give Brucie a chance to reconcile his feelings, the bodyguard had delayed for a while and so he figured it might be a good idea to check on him.

"Oh, yeah, just, uh"—Brucie forced a nervous laugh—"it's kinda intimidating, ya know? Not sure what I'll do when I see the old man in his coffin."

"Do you want to go outside to get some fresh air? We got time."

The bodyguard dismissed the suggestion with a wave. "Nah, it's fine, bro. Gotta face 'im eventually."

"Brucie, is that you?"

James turned toward the one who had spoken. It ended up being a large senior with gray hair. Several misshapen lumps covered his cheeks and, upon further observation, his lower arms too. Was it a mutation, or some other condition? Regardless, James wouldn't dare pose the question and so he'd remain ignorant of the answer.

Brucie scowled. "Yeah, that's me."

A tender yet hesitant smile spread on the elder's face. "I'm your uncle Robert, Hank's brother. Boy, no way ya 'member me. Last time I saw ya, ya were like this tall." He positioned his hand a meter above the floor. "Looka you now, ain't so small no more. Freak, you gotta be as heavy as me"—the old man winked—"but not for the same reason. So, how's life treating ya?"

"Ain't too shabby."

"Heard you're the Melkar's bodyguard. That's awesome, Brucie, your dad would be so proud o' ya." Perhaps realizing his faux pas, Robert grimaced and lowered his gaze. An awkward silence lasted for a few seconds. "Listen, Brucie, Hank screwed up. I ain't gonna pretend he was a good father." He sighed, closed his eyes. "Your dad, he loved ya in his own way, but... he had issues, if ya get what I mean." Robert mimicked a person drinking from a bottle. "And other stuff too. Guy was messed up. I tried to tell him not to bail on ya, but Hank thought you'd be better off without him."

A humorless chuckle escaped Brucie's lips. "Yeah, well, maybe we were."

"Yeah, maybe. Sorry I didn't get in touch. Your mom didn't like our side o' the family. I don't blame her, mind ya. Hank treated her bad, a real shame. But, it's good that ya came. If ya didn't, you'd regret it later. Poor Pierre ain't gonna have the chance to say goodbye."

While Brucie nodded, he turned his head slightly, concealing his visage. James suspected the mention of his brother brought a tear or two. Again, they all fell quiet for a moment, until Robert stared at James. "Oh, didn't notice ya there. Don't remember seeing you before."

"He ain't part o' the family. That's James, my best bud."

Robert's eyes widened. "Really! Nice o' ya to be there fo' Brucie." With that, the elder extended his hand and James shook it. That done, Robert almost said something else, but an old woman in a black dress ran toward him, interrupting him.

"Robert, there you are. The priest's lookin' fo' ya. He—" Then she stopped and her mouth gaped as if she'd noticed the two other men for the first time.

Robert pointed at the bodyguard. "Alice, look, it's Brucie!"

For a fraction of a second, her brow wrinkled as if she failed to recognize the name. Then she brightened up and touched his chest with her palm. "Oh my God, Brucie! All grown up! And you're huge! I'm Alice, your aunt! So glad ya came, we weren't sure ya would. Ain't this place beauti-ful? Onel's a historical church, it's like a miracle Hank's getting his funeral here. Oh, and, Brucie—"

The family reunion lasted about five minutes afterward. Since the reverend needed both Robert and Alice, they soon had to leave. Once they walked far enough that they wouldn't hear, I grinned.

—Thoughts of James Hunter, Hocmar 28, 2134, on the Nirnivian calendar

"So, I'm your best bud?"

"Yeah, Janice dropped a few notches."

"Uh, that's fair, I guess, but I'm sure she would've been here if it wasn't for your past."

"Yeah, I know."

Chapter 5

Talking with Robert and Alice seemed to calm Brucie's nerves a bit, and after they left, we took our places in a pew.

—Thoughts of James Hunter, Hocmar 28, 2134, on the Nirnivian calendar

No doubt given the bodyguard's status as the deceased's son, they could've chosen the front row, but Brucie settled for the third one. After they sat, silence fell over them. From up close, James noted the stained glass mounted high behind the altar and statues. Though crude, he recognized the white-and-cyan Papillon emitting light. Not just reflecting it from the sun, but producing it. The thought of Rose transforming into that creature brought him a shiver.

James attempted a couple conversation prompts to break the tension, but these went nowhere. Lucky for him, Brucie's procrastination meant the ceremony started soon after. The organ switched from a low-key background music to a louder composition, and everyone stood up. Both James and Brucie followed their lead. Then several people marched between the rows of pews, carrying the black coffin with a solemn expression. A few sobs echoed through the church as they advanced. When they arrived, they settled the coffin before the altar and opened the top part. The gap revealed an old man smiling with his eyes closed. Makeup covered his skin's imperfections, resulting in a flawless complexion. He appeared at peace, as if death provided a sweet relief.

In truth, I doubted he'd ever looked so serene when living. Funeral parlors performed miracles in Nirnivia too.

—Thoughts of James Hunter, Hocmar 28, 2134, on the Nirnivian calendar

Upon the sight, Brucie let out a whimper and averted his gaze. Concerned, James patted his back. "Are you okay?"

"Yeah, I'm fine, just the shock, ya know. Ain't seen the guy in decades."

The moment he finished that sentence, the priest exited his chamber and took his place behind the altar. Once he greeted his guests, the proceedings began. While the ceremony lacked sense for James, the structure proved somewhat familiar. The reading of scripture, prayers and song brought memories of his own Christian childhood, though he hadn't entered a church in years. Soon, they reached the equivalent of a eulogy.

"Now, let us hear from Robert, who will tell of the departed, his brother Hank."

Again the back room's door opened and the large senior James had met earlier stepped out. Instead of the smile he'd adopted then, he sported a worried grimace and beads of sweat dripped from his brow. An appropriate reaction given a thug held him from behind and pointed a pistol at his temple. Gasps resounded through the house of worship and they multiplied when a woman dashed for the priest at incredible speed and grabbed him, resting a sword against his throat before taking him away. Simultaneously, several goons encircled the attendants, aiming their weapons at them. Brucie went for his gun, but he hadn't brought it with him. James swallowed hard. The one who had taken the reverend hostage... that leather jacket and red scarf, not to mention the quickness... Wrathchild. Did that mean...?

As if to confirm his suspicion, a monstrous crimson being emerged from the priest's chamber. That massive frame and the single horn protruding from his forehead couldn't be mistaken. No question, it was Diabo. At least sunglasses concealed his hideous yellow eyes.

The beast walked to the altar, rested his hands upon it and leaned forward. "All right, men, tie up every damn one of 'em. No exceptions." Those under his command obeyed the order with disconcerting speed. When the thugs reached James and Brucie, they complied without resistance.

All along, Brucie glared at Diabo. Anger and sadness filled his stare. I remembered that the crimson beast was his brother. They hadn't met for a long time. Not since Pierre had founded BBR.

—Thoughts of James Hunter, Hocmar 28, 2134, on the Nirnivian calendar

Diabo grinned. "Now, I ain't much of a public speaker, so I'll keep this short. NISDA captured some o' my colleagues, misunderstood heroes who fight the Ostarkirans 'cause you're all too damn scared to do it yourselves. For our sacrifices, you bastards call us terrorists. The law's against us and won't never give 'em a chance. I want my friends back. That's why we're here." He groaned in a resigned manner. "Don't like it? Blame your government. It's their fault. They got their head jammed so high up their arses I'd don't got a choice. Ya all better listen, I'll only say this one freaking time: don't piss me off and you'll be okay. I'll let ya go once I got my men. Mess with me: you're dead. Issat clear?" Nobody answered. Diabo produced a sickening chuckle. "I'll take that as a yes. Any objections?" The giant paused for a moment, but the crowd hushed. "Good, didn't think so."

As the red tyrant finished his sentence, a timid voice broke the silence. It trembled in terror, but the mere fact that it could be heard proved its owner's courage. "I have an objection! You're not a hero, you're a sick brute!" The tension in the room heightened. Everyone dreaded Diabo's reaction, including James, but the ruffian didn't exhibit any rage. Quite the contrary, he chortled as if he considered the response hilarious. He scanned the area and soon spotted the one who had spoken: a feeble old man sitting across the aisle from James and Brucie. With a smirk, Diabo briskly advanced toward him. James gritted his teeth and his muscles grew tense. The senior, however, didn't even flinch.

"What are you going to do? Kill me? Go ahead!" Diabo now towered above the elder. From experience, James knew of the mutant's putrid breath, and at that distance, it must've been at full strength. How he pitied the poor old man.

Diabo waggled a finger negatively and replied with a calm tone. "Nah, I ain't gonna hurt ya. Violence ain't a solution. My mamma always said: Pierre, use your words, not your fists. So I won't break your jaw: I'll teach ya. Let's debate." He crossed his arms. "You first, explain yourself."

"You and your organization, you're just out for revenge. At best, you're reckless vigilantes, at worst terrorists. In the name of fighting evil, you've become as despicable as the ones you hate!"

"I see... interesting." The crimson beast rubbed his chin. "That's a tough one. I ain't too smart, I'll have to think 'bout it. Hmm... all right, I got it. Here's my rebuttal." With that, Diabo grabbed a nearby young woman and twisted her neck, snapping it. The move came with such strength that James heard every detail of the resulting crack. Blood splattered on her neighbors. His stomach churned, and he covered his lips with his palm, afraid he might throw up. As he fought the urge to vomit, the elder broke into tears.

"Why? I didn't even know her."

"'Cause you're a self-centered asshole!" a furious Diabo yelled while pointing an accusing index finger. "You're old. You're close to death anyway. You figure, I ain't got anything to lose; why not end with a bang? You ain't even thinking 'bout how your actions will affect others. Well, ya ran your mouth and got that woman killed. That's on you. If ya'd shut your trap, she'd be fine. You'll have to live with that fo' the rest o' your pathetic life. So, yeah, in case my rebuttal is too intellectual for ya, here's the simple version."

Diabo snatched the elder by the collar and lifted him about a foot above the ground. Any trace of courage vanished from the senior as he whitened and his feet danced in the air. "I'm the boss and there's nothing you can freaking do 'bout it, so shut up and do what I say or I'll make you pay. Any more objections? No? Okay, then."

Satisfied, Diabo let him go and began to return to the altar. Along the way, he stopped and stared right at Brucie. He changed course, heading for the bodyguard. James gulped as his heart rate sped up. With a sob, he cowered, pushing himself as far away as possible on the bench and covering his face.

"Brother!" Diabo shouted, his voice filled with enthusiasm. He spread his arms wide in a mock-welcoming gesture. "How nice to see ya! Hey, do ya like my new sunglasses?"

Unflinching, Brucie looked Diabo straight in the eyes. Though he attempted a strong demeanor, the tremors in his voice betrayed his anguish. "Ya told me yourself long ago: you ain't my brother no more."

"True that. Whatever, I'm glad you're here. In fact, I kinda counted on it."

"Ya can't win! Pierre, get outta here! They'll never give ya Plague and the others. Ya'll get yourself killed."

"Oh, I'll win. All thanks to you..." After a laugh, Diabo reached out and rubbed Brucie's cheek. The bodyguard remained still, showing no signs of being touched. The display of self-control impressed James. If it had been him... "Ah, brother, I chose this place 'cause I figured you'd be here."

"Ain't gonna work, dude. I ain't important 'nough. Just 'nother grunt, ya know."

Diabo frowned. "Uh, ya think? Ain't so sure 'bout that. Daniel Ricdeau won't let his precious princess cry over her dead bodyguard." He shrugged. "Either way, I ain't leaving without my men. In BBR, we care 'bout each other, not like Nirnivia." He almost turned away to leave, but then stopped. "Wait, issat...?" The monster looked at James, who whimpered and attempted shrinking even more. As if to confirm what he saw, Diabo seized his sunglasses and crushed them. Those yellow eyes. It was as if they burned into James's very soul. In comparison, Doctor Death's ravaged body failed to bring such disgust.

"The human! Ah, little boy, I'm so glad to see you too!" James gulped. Meanwhile, Diabo extended his arm and ruffled his hair as if he was a child. "Relax; I ain't gonna harm ya. Not yet." Diabo glanced at Brucie and bobbed his head at James. "Ya brought him here, huh?" The bodyguard gritted his teeth and bent his neck. "Oh, brother! Thanks! What a gift. No way I'm losing now!"

With a self-satisfied smirk, Diabo then returned to the altar. Brucie leaned toward James and whispered, "Sorry, dude. I shouldn't have brought ya here."

I wanted to reply that it wasn't his fault. That he couldn't have known. How I wished to tell Brucie I didn't blame him for this. The shock ended up so intense the words refused to come. Instead, all I could manage was to sit there and mumble nonsense.

—Thoughts of James Hunter, Hocmar 28, 2134, on the Nirnivian calendar

***

As Diabo talked to his brother, a twitching Wrathchild stood near the altar. Resisting the temptation to pace along the room demanded an effort, but she feared such a display of nervousness might anger her boss. "Gotta intimidate hostages, Melissa, don't show signs weakness."

This mission left her with a churning stomach. What potential for disaster. With Plague captured, if things turned south, that implied the death of all three founders. In addition, she'd also perish. Not to brag, but she was one of their best combatants. And they'd lose Allison too, their living weapon. BBR would crumble. Since the image of the telepath entered Wrathchild's mind, she spun her head and glanced at her. The poor girl sat in a corner beside a bookcase. Still restrained by a straitjacket, she bobbed her head and mumbled something, oblivious to her environment. Allison's fear proved beyond obvious to Melissa. She must have realized that eventually, Diabo would bully her into using her powers.

The sight of Allison brought tears to Wrathchild's eyes, and so she averted her gaze and began fidgeting her fingers. Soon, Diabo finished his discussion and returned. He glared at her cross-armed and said, "Worried, huh? So ya don't trust my plan?"

In truth, she didn't as she deemed it too risky. Yes, Melissa liked Plague and wanted him out, but she doubted this would work. Still, she judged it best not to show her doubts. Recently, Diabo had punished her for disobeying his orders. Between the choice of killing Doctor Death and saving Diabo's life, she had chosen the latter. The resulting beating had left her in shambles, and she feared being honest now would rekindle his fury.

"No, no. All good."

"You're fidgeting."

Denying it at this point would only infuriate him, so she might as well come clean. "Okay. A bit worried. No biggie."

"Relax. This can't fail. Rose ain't gonna let Brucie die. She's grown fond o' him." Diabo gestured toward the bodyguard, or more precisely the man next to him. Wrathchild believed she had met him before, but she couldn't recall where. "'Sides, my stupid brother brought the human kid with him! Lucky us. I wanted to experiment on him back then. It pissed me off when we lost him, but that turned out fo' the best. If my sources are right, Rose's even fonder o' him." He joined his palms together and rested the back of his hand against his cheek as he faked a tender smile. "Her best friend! Ain't that sweet? She'll do anything to save 'im. They'll give us Plague and the others in no time."

"But Rose not in charge! Won't lead negotiations."

"Yeah, but ya think her daddy will make his baby girl cry by sacrificing her best friend? Daniel Ricdeau eats out of her hand like a freaking slimy dog."

That statement might have been correct, but it failed to calm Wrathchild's anxiety. Still, she nodded and sealed her lips. Then Diabo wrapped his arm around her shoulders and dragged her toward the altar.

"Hey, Wrathchild, come over here." Once they arrived, he pointed at a map of the church resting on it. The crimson beast jabbed his index finger at an area in the basement. "Would ya mind joining the guards patrolling there? If NISDA infiltrates the place, that'd be our weakest spot."

"Sure thing, boss."

Guards didn't need help. Diabo sent there to calm worries. Fine with me. Everything stable, hostages wouldn't cause trouble. As useless here as downstairs. Before leaving, peeked at human. Didn't talk much him, but seemed nice guy. Glad escaped BBR, too bad captured again.

—Thoughts of Wrathchild, Hocmar 28, 2134, on the Nirnivian calendar

Chapter 6

Stuck inside a small cell, Plague lay on a bed as hard as stone. Compared to where he'd slept in some of his past hideouts, this proved almost comfortable. Plus, he'd never suffered from claustrophobia, so the tight space didn't bother him. Boredom served as the biggest annoyance of his imprisonment. He had no source of distraction and no one to converse with except two disgruntled guards. Still, given how agitated his daily life could be, the relative calm of prison offered a chance to relax. Well, it would have, but he worried about BBR's fate. Officially, Diabo had always been in charge, and with Plague captured, nobody controlled him from the shadows. Plague admitted he'd often failed at that task, but he'd mitigated the crimson beast's rage. Without him, Diabo found himself unrestrained and that would spell doom for BBR. Perhaps Stalker or Wrathchild would rise and usurp him once it became clear the group's survival depended on it. However, while they'd be a better alternative than Diabo, they lacked the required qualities for a great leader.

The various interrogations NISDA had subjected Plague to provided his only distraction from these dark thoughts. As a BBR founder, he had access to a wealth of information about the organization, and the Nirnivians sought it. So far he'd refused to talk, and NISDA had little means of forcing him. The Council had declared torture illegal years ago thanks to Rose. Though, somehow, waterboarding remained legal, his physical deterioration saved him from that torment as it might kill him. His death would deny the

Nirnivians the intelligence they desired. No doubt his captured colleagues didn't share his luck, and he prayed for them.

Even without his fragility and the fear of breaking the law, Plague suspected his jailers would hesitate to torture him. That kind of treatment implied bleeding, and they feared infection. Yes, they'd developed an antidote against his poisonous nature, and with proper precautions they wouldn't need it, but they still dreaded the sickness he carried within. Not that he blamed them. Plague himself had learned years ago of the dangers his new body posed.

In appearance, today was like every other day since his arrival. Yet Plague sensed a restlessness in the air. The blurs representing the guards kept fidgeting and mumbled to each other. Though it was subtle, Plague noticed. What if he tried extracting some information? Guards weren't always the sharpest tools in the box, so to speak. Employers often selected them for their physical strength rather than their mental abilities.

"Hey, boys. When's dinner?" he asked to test the waters. "I'm getting hungry. You don't want me to starve yet, do you?"

"Shut up in there, will ya?" the guard on the left shouted. Plague took his impatience as a confirmation that his suspicions were correct and something troubled them.

"Geez, you're in a rotten mood. Something wrong?"

"I said shut up! I'll break your freaking jaw if you don't pipe down!"

"Really?" Plague chuckled. "Fine, come get my blood on your hands." The guard considered the veiled menace and muttered a harmless curse. Plague knew he wouldn't dare do anything. With the goon's armored uniform and gloves, his venom posed a limited threat. Plus, the soldiers had a cure. The illness progressed slowly; there'd be plenty of time to administer it. As such, the men might brave the disease, except their superiors had ordered them to ensure the captive remained unscathed. If they disobeyed, they'd be disciplined later. Plague understood that much; it was common sense. He deduced he could yap for hours and they'd tolerate him with no physical retribution. For the moment, though, he chose silence and stared at the sentries. Sometimes, silence ended up being more effective than words.

"It won't work!" the watchman roared after a short delay. "Your friends at the church of Onel—they're all gonna die!" Under his bandages, Plague smiled. That foolish guard had revealed too much, and he now guessed what was happening. Soon, though, his smile turned into a frown. While Plague appreciated that Diabo struggled to rescue him, it was a reckless move. The Nirnivians wouldn't surrender him for a few hostages.

"You're the one who should shut up!" the other guard yelled as he slapped his colleague in the back of the skull. "You're an idiot." The guilty party hung his head in shame.

Plague chuckled. "Hey, it ain't like I can help them from here. And you're right, they screwed up."

"Your friends made a big mistake," the man on the left agreed. "They can't win. BBR's finished! You're finished!"

"Maybe." Plague shrugged to hide his trepidation. Based on what he'd discovered, it seemed likely Diabo and other key members participated in the attack. What a disaster. Their boss had rushed along without a plan as usual.

"About time. You're freaking terrorists."

Plague nodded. "It's true, we're terrorists." That surprised the two men, and their mouths gaped. "Yeah, unlike the others, I don't delude myself. I'm a criminal—a villain.

We all are. We've done some messed-up shit. What you guys don't get is, Nirnivia needs us. If you destroy BBR today, you'll regret it."

"Ah, the crap we gotta hear," the guard on the left mumbled. The one on the right, for his part, held his tongue.

"Don't believe me, huh, boys? How 'bout a story? It might show you what I mean."

"Shut up already! We don't give a shit about anything you have to say!"

"You're more annoying than him! All this 'shut up'; you're giving me a headache. Let the bastard talk and ignore him."

Plague smiled again.

Chapter 7

As he read the report Nicky had written, Daniel's muscles grew tense. It seemed another crucial mission awaited them. Hopefully it ended up better than the previous one. For a moment, he had believed the assassination attempt's failure doomed Nirnivia. Not that they intended anything as dangerous. Oh no, he wouldn't let himself be so cavalier ever again. Still, NISDA had had its share of bad luck these past months. Between Stalker's invasion of Valardir, the failed security upgrades, the strike, the murderous beast, and the botched assassination, Daniel almost wondered if somebody had put a curse on them. A success here would help raise morale, no question there, and he expected the officers working under him needed a boost. This operation might be their chance to achieve that goal.

"Well, that confirms it," Daniel said as he waved the papers. "The Doctor had it moved to Nerboros, Ed saw it with his own eyes."

"Guess our intel's right, huh?" Then Ron frowned. "But, damn, I don't understand why they'd do that. It sounds fishy."

A shrug came from Daniel. "According to Ed, the Doctor's sending an expert to do experiments for him. The guy can't get proper security clearance, some crime he committed in his younger years. So, instead of having him come over, they brought it to him."

"Yeah, I guess that checks out, but I dunno." He groaned. "Ed seems loopy to me. You sure we can trust him?"

Daniel nodded. "He's a peculiar fellow, I'll give you that, but he got this far."

"Heh, fair enough."

The Ed in question was the only spy they'd infiltrated into Ostark after the massacre the technicians' strike had caused. Since that event, the sole survivor, Erik Vandelay, had passed away. Regardless of Ron's misgivings, Ed had avoided detection, though fooling Nerboros's security wasn't a major accomplishment by any stretch of the imagination.

"Dan, should we do this? The Doctor's pissed. Maybe we should count our blessings and leave it alone. Thanks to his cover-up, we're dealing with BBR and we've captured Plague." Tigh chuckled as he shook his head. "Still feels like a dream. Holy crap, that will screw them hard. Anyway, it might not be the best idea to mess with the Doc so soon."

"That's a good point, but it'll be fine. If he didn't restart the war when we tried to kill him, he won't mind if we visit a third-rate research center working on public projects. It's not like we're stealing anything secret." A smile spread on Daniel's face. "I'm surprised you're so worried about this and didn't even flinch about the assassination attempt. That was far riskier."

Ron scoffed. "Yeah, but that was freaking important. This one, it ain't worth it."

"Rose begs to differ. Even she's on board, and you know how she is." He smirked. "I mean, you're always complaining about her, so you have to."

"Oh, that's because she's biased as shit. Listen, I understand why she—"

A loud ringing interrupted Tigh, and both men jumped in their seats. Once he recuperated from the surprise, Daniel stared at the source, his phone. "That's strange, I wasn't expecting any calls." With that, he picked up the receiver and brought it to his ear. "Hello."

A female voice responded. "Sir, we have an emergency."

"Nicky, what happened?"

"It's Diabo. BBR took the church of Onel hostage. He's asking to talk to you."

"Understood, I'll be right there."

Oh no. A shiver ran down Daniel's spine as he hung up. This must be because of Plague's capture. He grimaced. The press would have a field day. If a single person died under their watch, they'd drag NISDA through the mud. Not that image was his priority when innocent civilians needed rescue. If they wished to avoid casualties, they'd have to be smart and act fast. The church of Onel. He'd heard that name recently, but he couldn't remember where.

"Ron, we have to go to the war room ASAP."

"What's going on?"

"The shit's hit the fan again. I'll explain along the way."

As they rushed out of the office, it popped into Daniel's mind. The reason Onel had seemed so familiar. Oh crap. Things had gone from bad to worse in an instant.

***

Both Daniel and the Koporal ran along the corridor. After Daniel explained the situation, Ron fired a series of expletives just as expected. "Son of a gun!" Tigh exclaimed while clenching his fists. "The bastard's gone off the deep end. If he thinks we'll release Plague, he's got another thing coming!"

"Yes, but don't tell Diabo that. We have to make him believe he's winning or he'll start executing hostages."

"Yeah, that's how Diabo's mind works. He ain't a sharp tool that one, only knows brute strength." Ron scowled. "Hey, why is the dumbass asking to talk to you, anyway? You're the freaking NISDA Commander, not a negotiator."

Daniel forced a humorless chuckle. "Don't ask me, I don't have any idea. Well, it's not part of my job description, but if it saves innocents, why not?"

"Yeah, you're right. Better not piss off the freak or he'll kill someone. Shit, maybe he did already."

A shudder assailed Daniel. "Yes, that sounds probable."

"What are the odds? We just dealt with another dumb animal not that long ago."

Another tremor coursed through Daniel's body. "Here's hoping it goes better than with that one."

As Daniel finished that sentence, they reached the war room. A pale redheaded figure dressed in white paced in front of the gate. Had the clothing failed to identify her, the wings would have served as a dead giveaway: Rose. By his side, Ron shook his head and mumbled, "Son of a gun." Daniel ignored those words. The instant she spotted them, Rose gasped, rested a hand on her heart and rushed toward Daniel.

"Dad, they said on TV BBR is holding the church of Onel hostage." Daniel cursed in silence. Those goddamn reporters had already caught wind of the story. "Is it true?" Rose's crying rendered her throat hoarse, causing her voice to crack.

After a moment of hesitation, Daniel nodded. "I'm afraid so, princess." The poor soul trembled and almost collapsed. Before she did, Daniel seized her in a hug. Moral and physical support rolled into one.

"No! That's... where Hunter and Brucie went!" A whimper escaped her lips. "It's bad enough that Brucie's there, but at least he can handle the pressure. Hunter must be scared to death! I shouldn't have let them go!"

"Princess, you have nothing to do with this, it's not your fault."

Rose sighed. "I know." She gulped again. "And it's BBR, not Ostark. Oh dear Ulgorack, why does it have to be Diabo? If it had been him, they might have had a chance, but with that monster..."

No question concerning who the "him" referred to. Rose had a strange habit of glorifying their enemy and conferred on the Doctor an undeserved sense of morality. True enough, the mechanical man had stopped Nirnivia's extermination and ushered in the uneasy peace, but that was a choice born of cold calculation, not mercy.

"Don't you dare defend him, Rose! Don't you dare! He's a psychopath!" Daniel clutched his fist. Astounded, Ron recoiled. Through their whole career, the Koporal had rarely witnessed Daniel losing his temper. For that to happen with Rose was unheard of. Daniel acted gentle with her. Even now, he hated to raise his voice, but the cyborg stood as a delicate subject.

"I'm not defending him, Dad; he's a monster! But sometimes he can show mercy and be reasoned with. Try that with Diabo." Rose's palm covered her mouth. She almost bit her nails, an old habit she had overcome. Often in the past, she had done so when nervous. Daniel remembered how Rose used to ravage them. She'd worked hard to stop. Now, she stood on the edge of relapsing but caught herself at the last moment. "Diabo won't back down. Not unless he gets what he wants."

"That's not happening." Ron waggled a warning finger. "We can't bow down to terrorists."

"I know." Rose sobbed. "Since we can't let him win, the only solution will be force. Dear Ulgorack, it will end in a bloodbath."

Daniel patted her shoulder. "Not if we can help it. Princess, we'll do everything in our power to get James, Brucie and all the others back home safe."

"I know."

Then the Koporal tapped his watch. "Hey, Dan, we have to hurry."

"Yes." Daniel stepped away from Rose and faced the door, but she pulled on his wrist.

"Wait! Please, I want to go too." Both Daniel and Tigh froze, stunned by the request. This was beyond irregular.

After a groan, Ron shook his head. "Sorry, but no freaking way. You have no business meddling with—"

"I won't meddle, I promise! I... need to be there."

Tigh crossed his arms. "So, you're asking us to break the law? There are regulations—"

"Please, I'm begging you," Rose pleaded. "I'll be good and won't say a word; I won't bother you. Please, I'm so worried... Hunter's my best friend! Those two are my only friends!"

"Ah, goddamn it." The Koporal rubbed his brow. "Look, I'm not trying to be an asshole here, but we can't. Come on, Dan, let's go already."

Ignoring the request, Daniel remained still with his eyes aimed at Rose. Those tears running down her cheeks broke his heart. She had grown so attached to the human, and if she lost him... Daniel grimaced and stared at Tigh.

"Listen, Ron, it'd be fine. Yes, we'd be bending the rules, but the Council won't charge us. If they do, we'll pretend we used the Melkar as a consultant. We believed she could provide insights, and there's no arguing with that."

"Dan, be reasonable! Yeah, the Council won't do shit—in practice the Melkar's pretty much above the law. But this isn't just about that. It's for Rose's sake too. BBR has cameras, they'll show us the hostages! Diabo might torture them. What if they torture Hunter, huh? Rose's barely holding up now; you want her to see that? She'd never get through it. Worse, what if they kill James right there? No way, missy, go back to your quarters and pray. We'll take care of Diabo."

"Please!" Rose adopted a begging tone. "I must see him, please. It might be my last chance. If things get ugly, I'll leave. If I become a nuisance, throw me out; I won't resist. I'll stay out of your business! Koporal Tigh... I... need to know he's alive. That they're alive."

Daniel gazed at Rose with pity and caressed her shoulder. He then focused on his colleague. "Ron, I... won't let her in the war room without your consent, but will you consider it?"

"Dan... that's insane. If we let her in there, she'll regret it! We'll do things she won't like."

"Please! I won't interfere. If you can't do your job with me around, I'll leave, but I must see them."

Daniel could tell Ron was still against it. Yet Tigh had a soft spot for his pal, much like Daniel had a soft spot for his daughter. Even in the beginning, when they'd bickered constantly, Ron had taken a shine to him. Through the years, Daniel had saved his life on several occasions, not to mention the favors he'd granted. In truth, the Koporal had repaid each one; Daniel recognized this. Yet Ron felt grateful, and he hoped that'd play in his favor. And, yes, soon enough, Ron's scowl softened and he sighed.

"Ah, freak it. It's a mistake, but whatever." Tigh pointed his index finger at Rose. "You better be on your best behavior, missy."

"I will."

"You better or I'll literally kick your holy ass out the door."

Daniel exhaled in relief. "Thank you, old friend."

"Oh, don't thank me yet." Ron crossed his arms and frowned. "If she influences you somehow, if you can't do your job because of her, I'll do mine."

The menace in Ron's tone was clear and Daniel understood his meaning. As Koporal, Ron had the responsibility to take the Commander's place temporarily should his judgment become impaired. That had never happened so far, but Ron made it obvious he feared that might change.

Daniel responded with a slow nod. "Hey, it's part of your duties, so that's fair."

Rose forced a sad excuse for a smile. "Thank you, Koporal Tigh. I owe you one."

"When you see firsthand why I didn't want you there, you'll wish you'd listened. Besides, no offense, but I'm not doing this for you. Nah, keep your favor, I'll put this on your dad's tab." He winked at Daniel. "Feels great to have you in my debt."

Chapter 8

Tied up and stuck in a pew, Brucie gritted his teeth. How humiliating—a trained bodyguard restrained with no resistance. Despite his training and physical abilities, the BBR goons had handled him as if he had been a mere kid. Sure, fighting back would have endangered everyone present, and that explained his refusal to do so. Still, to go from a weakling to a force to be reckoned with, only to realize that he could do little when it mattered most, proved infuriating. In truth, he focused on that fact not because it annoyed him but because doing so helped him ignore the real horror of the situation: that his own brother had planned to use him as bait. No matter how hard he tried, that thought crawled into his mind, festering, growing.

Difficult to imagine that during Brucie's childhood, Pierre had been the reasonable sibling, the role model who had watched over him and kept him out of serious trouble. Brucie admitted that task had demanded constant effort. What an obnoxious brat he used to be—some would say still was, except they changed the word beginning with a *b* for one starting with the letter *a*. Regardless of their opinion, thanks to Pierre, he'd improved. The fact that he'd found a respectable career served as proof. For a time, Brucie had intended to depend on social welfare programs and commit the occasional petty crime for extra cash. Without Pierre's guidance, that outcome seemed plausible.

Pierre was much older than Brucie, a twelve-year age difference to be exact. While his mother had never confirmed his hunch, Brucie assumed an unplanned pregnancy explained the gap. His parents probably hadn't intended on having a second child. Perhaps that was why their father had left when Brucie was six. The bastard had run off and never returned, a sad but common story. As a result, Pierre had grown up fast and become the new man of the house. At his age and with a job, he could have lived on his own, but he had stayed and supported his family. The extra money he had provided helped, but despite this, they'd remained below poverty level. Beyond that, he'd handled Brucie better than their mom. No question, Brucie loved her, but they didn't always see eye to eye. Often he felt she didn't understand him. With Pierre, however, it was like he could read his thoughts.

Every major event Brucie had experienced, his brother had influenced. Pierre had insisted he finish school, prevented him from falling in with a bad crowd. When Rose had given Brucie the opportunity of becoming her bodyguard, Pierre had encouraged him to accept. Without him, Brucie would have declined. He had judged he lacked the skills, but Pierre had countered that that was why Rose offered him the proper training.

Even Brucie's several romantic conquests he owed to Pierre in a way. Far from the smooth talker he had grown up into, at twelve, he had been overcome by an intense shyness whenever a girl stood in proximity. His brother had helped change that.

***

Earlier that day, Brucie had misbehaved in school, a common occurrence. Tired of his bad conduct, the principal had sent him home and threatened to suspend him for a week if he didn't stop. When he had arrived at his house, his mom had locked him in his room as punishment. The instant Pierre had finished work, he'd visited Brucie, wearing his trademark sunglasses. After he'd stepped through the door, Pierre had approached him and kneeled so they would be nearly the same height. He'd then removed his shades and smiled. "Hey, bro, got yourself grounded, huh?"

Crossing his arms and sitting on his bed with his feet dangling in the air, Brucie bent his neck. "Yeah..."

"Roberta Harris again. Mom said ya pulled her hair. Issat true?"

Brucie nodded. He'd learned before that he couldn't lie well to Pierre, so he decided he'd be honest. "Brucie, you're harassing the poor girl." Pierre groaned. "Last week, ya pushed her in the mud. Yesterday ya stole her doll. What's going on, bro?"

"Um..." A frown formed on Brucie's brow and he shrugged. "She's annoying."

"Hmm, annoying, huh?" Pierre rubbed his chin. "Is she teasing ya or sumthing?"

"Nah, she doesn't talk to me."

"Ah, I ain't no fool, I gotcha." Pierre then rested his hand on Brucie's shoulder and winked. "You like her, don't cha?" Brucie denied it, but no doubt the way he blushed confirmed Pierre's suspicions. "You want her to notice ya, huh?" After a whimper, Brucie agreed. "Well, she noticed ya all right, but that kind o' noticing ya ain't wanna get, ya know." He paused for a second. "Hey, that friend o' yours, Dickson, ain't it?"

"Uh-huh."

"Lemme ask you, bro: if Dickson pushed you in the mud and punched ya, would you wanna be his friend?"

"No."

"Same fo' Roberta. How 'bout ya be nice to her instead? Ever tried talking to her? Get to know her?"

"I... I can't do that. She's a girl... I'm too nervous..."

"Ah yeah..." Nostalgia filled Pierre's eyes as he evoked a few of his past awkward moments. "Girls did that to me too at your age, ya know? But they ain't that scary, bro. They're people, like us. Sure, girls and boys are different, but not that different. We're all Gorumars here. So, give it a shot, try to talk to 'em. Gets easier with practice." Brucie let out an unconvinced grunt and Pierre chuckled. "Ah, ya don't believe me, do ya? Well, 'member when you started training?" Brucie nodded. "At first, you sucked, but you got better. It's like that for everything. Even talking to girls."

"Maybe, but... but..."

"Don't worry, I'll help ya."

***

And so he had. Pierre had excelled at the seduction game and taught his brother one step at a time. Brucie discovered it did become easier with practice. He took Pierre's advice and eventually improved on it. Soon enough, he'd surpassed his mentor and evolved into a veteran player. Pierre warned he should find a good woman and settle down, but he wouldn't listen. Why restrict himself to a single mate when he could have them all?

Chapter 9

When Rose, Daniel and Ron entered the war room, everyone present saluted. A young Perz woman turned toward her dad and said, "Sir, we have a direct connection with the church ready. We can start the negotiation whenever you want." Based on her appearance, Rose assumed she was Nicky. According to her father, she displayed great competence, and he considered her a protégé of sorts.

"Excellent, Nicky." The Commander rubbed his chin. "Before we deal with that, please send a message to Altiar prison. Tell them I recommend increasing security measures around Plague, just in case this is a distraction and Stalker shows up. They probably already did, but better safe than sorry."

Ron scowled and scratched his head. "Wait, why the freak would they distract us? We're not in charge of Altiar. It won't do shit."

A smirk formed on Daniel's face. "It's Diabo."

"Oh yeah, I forgot, he's a dumbass."

With that, Daniel returned his focus on Rose and touched her shoulder as he gestured at a nearby desk. "Princess, how about you sit there while we deal with the situation?"

"Yes, all right." A shaking Rose obeyed and walked toward the empty chair. With every step her tremors increased. Once she reached her destination, she sat and grabbed her head with both hands. Various emotions overwhelmed her: fear, sadness, anxiety. Maybe Tigh had been correct and she shouldn't have come. Part of her regretted her choice; she dreaded what she would witness. Yet Rose refused to leave. She had to be there. It might be her last chance to see them.

In the distance, Daniel looked at Nicky again. "Well, we better get started before Diabo kills someone."

"Understood, sir."

She pressed a few buttons on her keyboard, and a large monitor turned on. At first, it displayed gray static, but after a few seconds it cleared up and revealed a monstrous red figure leaning against an altar. Behind him appeared two golden statues, one of Rose and one of Misha, her predecessor. Though Rose had seen such effigies on countless occasions, witnessing herself depicted as a sculpture always gave her a shiver. The camera failed to provide the glimpse of Hunter and Brucie she desired. Instead, it granted her a full view of a grinning Diabo.

***

Under Rose's watchful gaze, both Daniel and his Koporal remained standing to face the crimson beast. Ron glared at the screen with crossed arms. As for the Commander, he joined his fingers in a pyramid and observed the scene with barely opened eyes. That classic posture showed he scanned the image for any potential detail that might signify weakness. Rose wondered if Diabo realized this. Either way, Rose understood the negotiation process was a bluff to buy time and distract the terrorists while they prepared a rescue operation. NISDA wouldn't grant BBR's demands, not even if it cost every hostage their life. Thank Ulgorack she wasn't in charge as she'd cave in. She could never abandon all those people to their fate. That her father could make that choice filled her with both respect and uneasiness.

"Commander Ricdeau, Koporal Tigh, glad ya made it." A scowl formed on Diabo's brow. "Issat... Your Holiness! What an honor." He offered a mocking bow while sarcasm dripped from his lips. "Ain't that a surprise? You're so busy, didn't expect ya to be here; I'm happy ya found the time."

A grunt came from Ron. "Cut the crap, won't you, Diabo?"

"Straight to business, huh?" The red beast snickered. "I like your type, Tigh. A man o' action, like me. Anyway, I think you guys know why I'm here. NISDA attacked one o' our camps. That kinda stuff happened 'fore, ain't a big deal 'cept you took a few o' my pals and I want 'em back. BBR's a family; I protect my family."

Rose suppressed a groan. While he'd save his thugs if possible, he only cared about Plague. The decrepit mutant served as a brilliant strategist and proved to be a valuable resource BBR couldn't afford to lose.

"I'm sure ya got a bunch o' bullcrap reasons, but I ain't interested. We fight the same enemy: that freak Doctor Death. You don't like our methods? Fine, we'll answer for our crimes after we're done. Ostark's busting our balls: we don't need trouble from Nirnivia. And ya don't need trouble from us. Let's be friends for now, it's good for both of us, huh? What do ya say?"

Daniel scoffed. "It almost sounds as if you forgot you're the one who breached our temporary truce, Mr. Garland."

"The name's Diabo." The red monster growled while he glared at the Commander. Perhaps realizing he should be on his best behavior, he forced himself to calm down with a visible effort. "Yeah, we killed Nirnivians in the past. It's a shame, but shit happens. Hey, war is messy."

Rose determined that last sentence was aimed at the Koporal, and based on the way he recoiled, so did he. After the military had freed the three founders and discovered that the Ostarkirans' experiments had disfigured them, they had organized a ceremony for the miserable souls. The former prisoners were to receive medals. As he'd conversed with another officer, Ron had mentioned those men didn't deserve any distinction. "War is messy," he had explained. To him, they were nothing but three casualties among thousands. Tragic, but it didn't make them heroes. Unbeknownst to Tigh, the man who'd later become Stalker stood behind him. That evening, Rose had chastised Ron. Yes, he had a right to his opinion, but why bring it up during the service? Now his venom tongue returned to haunt him.

Ron winced. "Listen, I meant no disrespect. I'm a blunt guy who talks too much."

"Heh, we got that in common. Ain't no need to be sorry 'bout it, you were right. We weren't heroes. We didn't deserve medals. Was bullshit to make us feel better. Didn't work. I'm using your words 'cause it's the same thing: civilians die in our raids, but that's just how it goes."

"We're men of war, Diabo. We're well aware of the concept of collateral damage." Daniel clenched his fists. "But, that's not what we're talking about anymore. BBR mounted direct attacks against Nirnivia."

Diabo bent his neck. "Yeah... okay, blowing up that apartment building for a goddamn spy was a mistake, my bad. 'Cause o' that, we lost support and needed resources. We didn't have much choice but to take 'em from Nirnivia." He exhaled. "Thing is, that's no problem no more, so it ain't gonna happen again. No point getting your panties in a bunch. Sure, I screwed up, but I don't wanna harm Nirnivians."

"That's hard to believe you when you have a room filled with Nirnivian hostages."

"I don't want this. Ain't no other way you'll listen to me."

"How about this? You release your prisoners and then we'll discuss calmly like gentlemen."

As Rose had anticipated, Diabo laughed at the suggestion. "Come on, ya think I'm a dumbass? They're my only leverage. The minute I let 'em go, it's over: you'll slaughter us like dogs. No way."

Daniel shrugged. "Ah well, I expected as much, but you can't blame an old man for trying."

"Oh, I could, but I ain't gonna. Don't push your luck, my patience got limits. Want us to free the hostages? No problem: gimme back my men. Simple, huh? Hey, here's some extra motivation for ya." With that, Diabo waved for the cameraman to follow him and he headed toward the pews. Soon after, he stopped beside James and Brucie. Rose's heart rate increased as she gasped. Hunter...

The instant he glimpsed Diabo, his muscles tensed up. Despite the low quality of the footage, she discerned the sheer terror in his eyes. How she wished to get him out of there. She prayed they would find a solution. Poor Brucie didn't display the same level of fear. Rather, he went for defiance and gritted his teeth. Still, Rose knew he suffered. Captured by his dear brother, what a cruel fate. Diabo smiled. "Ain't that sweet? Two good buddies. Think 'bout how your daughter would cry if something happened to 'em. You won't do that to her, would ya?" He rubbed James's hair as if he was a child. Hunter squirmed. "It's no secret: I wanted that human. Gimme my men and I'll even let him go. Test me, and he ain't getting outta here. Got it? Guys, I messed up, okay? Let's bury the hatchet. BBR won't attack Nirnivia again. We'll limit the collateral damage. Win-win, really. Deal?"

A sense of pure desperation filled James's features, as if he considered himself dead already and didn't dare hope he might be rescued. That sight tore Rose up inside. Never mind her promise to stay silent, she hopped to her feet and yelled, "Hunter! It will be okay! You hear me? It will be okay!" Ron warned her with a furious glance and she hushed. Better not test him or he'd throw her out. That satisfied the Koporal, who glowered at Diabo.

"You think we'll release Plague for the human? You're an idiot. Yeah, I guess he's a nice guy, but not that nice." Unfortunately, Rose understood he meant it. Tigh wouldn't back down for the sake of a hundred lives, let alone a single one. As for her dad, he seemed concerned, but he'd agree with his Koporal. While he liked James, that wouldn't interfere with his judgment.

"Nah, I don't expect that. I expect you'll free him 'cause it's the right thing to do. Hey, I'm a reasonable guy." Then Diabo hesitated and presented a flat horizontal hand, which he tilted from one side to the other. "Kinda, anyway... talk 'bout it together, I'll give ya an hour. If I don't hear from ya after that, I'll waste a hostage." He snapped his fingers. "Oh, and if you assholes send men after us, they'll die and I'll be freaking pissed."

The camera moved and showed Allison sitting against a bookshelf in a corner. The telepath breathed at a rapid pace and mumbled to herself. A wave of sadness crashed into Rose as she witnessed the shadow of the girl Allison used to be. The blond woman had grown up since then, but when Rose had met her, she had been a kid. If memory served right, Allison had been fifteen, but her species aged at a slower rate, so that was roughly equivalent to an eleven-year-old Gorumar. Back then, Rose had visited her often; they'd played together. Now she was BBR's slave: an unwilling living weapon.

Rose couldn't imagine what torture those brutes subjected Allison to, but the glimmer of insanity in her eyes suggested it had been quite an ordeal. For her, Allison's presence took its toll, but that was the least of their worries. The telepath complicated their task. They'd all hoped she wouldn't be there but expected her to be. Diabo would have been foolish not to bring her. The question was: what were they going to do about it?

Chapter 10

Feeling Diabo's hand on my head made my skin crawl, and I grimaced. Had I not been tied up, I might have attempted to run away. That would have landed me in trouble, so maybe I should be thankful for the restraints.

—Thoughts of James Hunter, Hocmar 28, 2134, on the Nirnivian calendar

James closed his eyes and took several deep breaths, imagining himself home. The technique offered meager results. If only he had been able to reach for Nadia's picture, maybe it would've been more successful. Then Rose spoke, promising everything would be okay. At first, James's mouth gaped in shock since he hadn't expected her to be there, but soon he remembered Diabo had mentioned her presence. Thanks to his anxiety, he'd paid little attention to the negotiations and had forgotten that fact.

Such concern filled Rose's voice. Plus, she'd uttered James's name rather than Brucie's. If he required further proof she cared about his well-being, she just delivered it in spades. The sincerity in her trembling tone couldn't be denied. Deep down, James realized Rose lied to cheer him up. He understood she worried he'd die, or that BBR would take him away. Both cases meant they'd never see each other again. James knew those things because he shared the same fears. Yet the false hope she provided offered some level of comfort.

In a rare display of mercy, Diabo removed his palm from James's body and returned to his altar. James exhaled as relief filled his mind. Not that the effect lasted long.

When the red beast ended the communication, despair overcame James once more. His eyes watered and though he attempted to fight them, warm tears soon rolled down his cheeks. He was just an all-time loser who'd accomplished nothing. He had no business in a hostage crisis.

When he perceived the sobs, Brucie whispered, "Dude, it ain't over yet. We might get outta here alive. Don't give up."

"Brucie..."

"Ya think I'm happy 'bout this, man?" The bodyguard winced. "That guy's my bro. I'm so messed up inside, ya know. But I ain't crying. No time fo' that: can't cry till it's over. Ya gotta be strong, dude."

"For what?" Because of the tension he endured, James almost yelled those words aloud, but somehow he kept his volume reasonable. "What the hell does it change? There's nothing I can do."

"Wrong, man. Watch, observe. Ya may notice a detail that can help us escape." Brucie groaned. "'Sides, dude, those douches prey on weakness. Don't ya show 'em any."

While uncertain he could follow that advice, James nodded. Weakness overwhelmed him, so concealing it seemed like an impossible task. Still, Brucie's speech inspired him somewhat. He stopped weeping and observed as suggested.

Chapter 11

Just their luck. The second the communication with Diabo ended, Nicky informed Daniel and Ron that Moderator Doug Thomson wished to talk to them. For a moment, Daniel considered ignoring the message. Yes, Doug served as a major politician, and his link to the Council implied he contacted them for an important matter, but in their situation, delays could be fatal. Diabo had given them a mere hour. That was too little time to prepare already; cutting it short would make matters worse. Except Daniel understood he had no choice. Should he ignore the moderator and miss out on crucial information, it would be a crippling blow to his career. Thank Ulgorack Nicky had ordered the video conference room be prepared in advance while they'd debated with the crimson beast.

When they arrived on the premises, Doug Thomson appeared on the monitor. The large Perz twiddled his fingers as he waited. Even with his normal senses, Daniel deduced whatever the moderator wished to discuss brought him anxiety. With his mutation, it became beyond obvious.

"Commander Ricdeau, Koporal Tigh, thank you for meeting with me on such short notice."

Daniel smiled. "It's a pleasure as always, Moderator Thomson, but with all due respect, we're facing an emergency, so I'm afraid we must be quick."

Doug nodded. "Yes, I understand. Let me cut right to the chase." Thomson leaned forward. "I'm aware of the crisis at the church of Onel, and I'm here to warn you there's a VIP hostage present—Councillor Jade Carlson."

"Really?" A scowl formed on Daniel's brow. "I had no idea she knew Brucie's father."

"Well, they went to college together." The moderator licked his lips. "Back then, Jade identified as a boy, at least publicly. When she debated whether she should go through surgery and hormone therapy, Hank Garland supported her. They haven't seen each other in decades, but Jade never forgot what he did and wished to pay her respects."

Tigh rubbed his chin. "Hmm, that's freaking weird. Diabo got a councillor. Why ain't he rubbing it in our faces?"

"Because he doesn't know." Doug waved his own comment away. "No, let me rephrase that: he probably doesn't know. When you're a councillor, you can cause quite a stir by just showing up somewhere. Jade preferred not to turn Mr. Garland's funeral into a media circus filled with journalists and bodyguards, so she kept her visit secret." He grimaced. "Well, mostly, anyway. She disguised herself, brought two guards dressed in normal clothes, and planned on sitting in the back so she wouldn't draw attention."

"I see." Daniel crossed his arms. "That complicates matters."

"Yes, I suppose so. Jade is a respected councillor and a beloved political figure. Her rescue is considered a top priority."

"Wait a goddamn minute!" Tigh clenched his fists and gritted his teeth. "Are you saying we have to give Plague back to Diabo to save Jade's ass?"

After he closed his eyes and sighed, Doug shook his head. "No. The Council believes Commander Ricdeau and you are the best people to make that call, and we won't interfere. However, if you do so, we will support you and shelter you from any repercussions. No matter what you choose, please take Jade into consideration and try to bring her back alive along with everyone else. On a personal level, if you save her, I'll owe you one. Jade is a friend."

Daniel nodded. "I understand, Moderator Thomson. Thank you for warning us, we'll do everything we can."

Chapter 12

Why Plague bothered telling his story to the blurs guarding the cell, he had no idea. On countless occasions he'd recounted the events that had led him to BBR, mostly to therapists. Regardless of their good intentions, their efforts had never helped. In fact, they'd made matters worse. Remembering the details of that sordid day left his soul as broken as his physical body, so he preferred to forget them. The experts claimed that tactic pushed the pain deep into his subconscious, where it would poison his mind. That might have been true, but the denial felt better than the alternative. At least the damage he caused remained concealed beneath the surface. Despite his reticence, he babbled about the past even though these two men displayed no interest. His intuition told him he should.

"I used to be a normal guy. Norman Orwell, that's what they called me." Whenever Plague spoke, his throat hurt, one of many side effects brought on by his condition. On this day, the emotional torment exacerbated the pain. "I had a family."

"Yeah, yeah." The blob on the left performed some kind of motion. "Like we give a damn."

Plague ignored the disruption and continued. "I was a forensic scientist with the cops. Life wasn't perfect, but it sure was nice. I was married and had a daughter: little Mary, my pride and joy, my reason to live."

A groan came from one guard. "Ah, cut the crap. I'm so tired of parents who say corny lines like that."

"If you had kids, maybe you'd understand why we do it," the other sentry mumbled. Again, Plague blocked out the distractions.

"Back then, Ostark kidnapped Nirnivians. Those bastards caught me. I guess it was just bad luck; there ain't no real reason they chose me. My family didn't know what happened. That freaking laboratory was a nightmare. They experimented on us and the torture never stopped. We didn't get anesthesia either. The drugs could've screwed the results. Every day, more and more died." He shuddered. "There was this woman, her head started getting bigger and bigger until it exploded. That got blood and brain pieces everywhere. It was disgusting. And this guy, it's like roots grew inside him and tore him apart. The crazy thing is, they were the lucky ones."

"Look, no offense, but we heard it all before. At least NISDA did its part. We rescued you, didn't we?"

Plague doubted prison guards had aided in that operation. The "we" referred to the organization in general. "Yeah, you did." He coughed. "Months later."

"Hey, it's not like it was easy. You're lucky we freed your ass. We could've let you rot there."

A sad chuckle escaped Plague's lips. "Heh, I wish you had."

Chapter 13

The unexpected meeting with Doug Thomson cut the hour Diabo had granted in half. That left them in a hurry to prepare a plan, and Daniel wished the councillor hadn't contacted him. Sure, learning of Jade Carlson's presence served as important information, but short term, it didn't change the situation.

The instant Daniel and Ron returned to the war room, they assembled a small crew of talented officers comprising themselves, Nicky, a man named David Phillips, and Timothy, a scientist who studied Allison and assisted as a consultant. As they gathered around the conference table, Daniel shot Rose a glance. His daughter still sat at the desk he'd assigned her and remained silent as she'd vowed. Her face had faded to a sickly white because of stress, and she chewed her nails, ravaging them. Years of resisting the urge undone in a flash.

She had grown so attached to the human boy. Most disapproved, and Daniel admitted the relationship didn't thrill him, but given the happiness James provided her, he'd learned to accept it. Unfortunately, her friendship exacerbated the current ordeal. Ron had been right—Rose shouldn't be in the war room. As he pondered convincing her to leave, David said, "Sir, what about Diabo's promise not to attack Nirnivia if we return his men? I know we don't give in to terrorists, but it's tempting."

The question interrupted Daniel's reverie, and he returned his focus to the meeting. A sigh escaped his lips as he considered David's query. "Don't be foolish." A smile appeared on his face, the same he'd often adopted as a father lecturing his children. "Diabo's a liar. I've watched him carefully with my special eyes, and while I'll admit the picture quality was lacking, there's no doubt he hates our guts. He told us what we want to hear. If we give in, he might honor his words for a while, but he might just as well stab us in the back. It's possible he'll kill all the hostages even if we cooperate. He's a loose cannon."

"All right, that puts an end to that." Ron crossed his arms. "What about snipers?"

David shook his head. "No good. There are windows, but they're stained glass and the shooters can't see through them well. There's an experimental thermal scope we could try, but BBR has tied-up hostages against the windows. Besides, we can't kill everyone fast enough to ensure the hostages' safety."

"That doesn't give us many options except brute force." Tigh shrugged. "Fine by me!"

"That's not so simple anymore. Not with Allison." Nicky rubbed her chin. "Her only weakness is the thirty-seven-minute-a-day limit on her telepathy, but that's too long. We can't power through and wait it out. The hostages wouldn't survive and we'd lose so many soldiers. If only we had telesthesia blockers like Doctor Death."

Tigh scoffed. "They're the size of a building. How the freak would you bring it to her?"

"No idea, but we'd have a potential weapon. Right now we're stuck."

"Yeah, we're screwed. But it's not surprising. BBR brought their biggest 'gun'? Damn, who would have imagined? At least there's no sign of Wrathchild or Stalker, but it's likely one of those rats is there, if not both. Those bastards are trouble too."

"Not as much as Allison."

"Yeah, yeah, thanks for pointing out the obvious." A groan escaped Ron's lips. "Listen, kid, don't underestimate their threat." He waggled a lecturing finger. "Happens all the time—you focus on the stronger foe and you forget the small fries and they end up killing you. Stalker will slit your throat before you realize he's there. That Wrathchild bitch is worse. She doesn't need stealth, she'll kill you fifty times before you hit the floor, then she'll crap on your corpse." Skeptical glares answered his claim. "Hey, she might: she did it to the Lobotomizer."

Daniel nodded. "True, but in fairness, he pushed her to the limit. She never made a habit of it. Anyway, we're out-gunned, we can't change that. No point crying over it. Let's concentrate on the positive. Location-wise, we have an advantage. Onel is filled with secret passages."

The church of Onel hadn't been founded by the Timanites, who couldn't afford such a monument, but rather the Progressive branch. However, the group in charge of Onel consisted of several closeted Timanites who had a plan. Through their influence, they managed to replace those they knew wouldn't collaborate with people sharing their views, even if it meant breaking the law and betraying their own branch.

Long story short, Onel had been a clandestine sanctuary for Timanites. There they could hide and even organize an escape to Ostark if they desired, though that implied considerable risks.

Eventually, the Timanites had earned their freedom. While they still experienced discrimination, their conditions had improved. Immigration remained illegal though, and the leaders of Onel decided to stop their clandestine operation, judging the risks weren't worth it anymore. Eventually, the secrets of Onel were revealed to everyone.

"We have maps showing every passage. It's unlikely BBR knows them all, but it's not impossible since it's public knowledge now. Still, it's our best bet. We can send troops through them—that's the easy part. Problem is: with Allison there, we can't surprise them too well. She's a telepath, so she'll detect the soldiers' minds and warn Diabo. Then he'll make her use her power and they'll cower in fear like babies."

David scowled. "Are you sure she'll warn him? Allison's a prisoner more than anything. What if she sees our attack as a chance to escape?"

Daniel shook his head. "No, we can't count on that. Diabo destroyed her will. Allison's his puppet now. She fears him so much she'll never betray him, even if she wants to."

"Sounds like there's nothing we can do," a desperate David said.

"No, there's always a way. Timothy, you studied her when she lived in Nirnivia. You know more about her power than anyone else here. If you have any ideas, we're listening."

The scientist slipped his hand through his hair. "Well, she's not omniscient. If we send a large group she'll notice, but since there are so many people in the church, a single man might slip by. I can't guarantee it, though."

"Could we send more?"

Timothy grimaced. "Um, I'd guess three at the most."

"That's ain't enough." The Koporal clenched his fist. "We'll need more than that to finish the job."

Nicky tapped her index finger against her chin. "If we try to subdue the terrorists, I agree, but a small squad can assassinate Allison. Then we storm Onel."

At the mention of assassinating Allison, Rose gazed toward their group and opened her mouth. Despite this, she remained silent and stilled her tongue. It seemed she remembered her promise not to interfere. Daniel smiled at her. "Anything to say?"

"No... I just feel bad for her. If only we could rescue her instead."

"I understand, princess. Allison's story is tragic. I'd like to help her too, but under these circumstances..."

A scowl formed on Rose's brow. "Yes, I know." The prophet sighed. "But it's okay. Allison is like a daughter to me and I don't want her to die, but she's better off dead than with BBR. If death is the only respite we can provide, so be it." As Rose spoke, Daniel squinted and studied her body language using his mutation. Every movement, every twitch implied she downplayed her disdain. No doubt the notion of killing Allison troubled her, but she'd decided not to meddle. Yet he sensed it would hit her hard, and a touch of apprehension seized Daniel's heart. Was this a mistake? "Never mind me, Dad! You have to hurry." Filled with reluctance, Daniel nodded.

"The little missy's right for once—let's focus, people." Ron frowned. "You make it sound easy, but killing Allison ain't so simple. Got a plan, Nicky?"

"Sort of... she's sitting close to a bookcase behind the altar. When Diabo is speaking to us, he faces away from her." With a pencil, she tapped on the map lying before her. "There's a secret passage behind the bookcase. It might be possible to sneak a soldier through there and shoot her."

"Great idea!" Sarcasm tainted Tigh's tone. "Except that's like phoning Diabo and telling him we're in the church.

He'll see Allison die and we'll lose any chance of a surprise attack. The bastard will kill the hostages."

Everyone lowered their neck and hushed. The Koporal raised a valid objection. Yet another issue to deal with. A few seconds passed before Nicky licked her lips and said, "How about a tranquilizer gun? It's less obvious, and she'd survive."

Daniel grinned. What a stroke of genius. Nicky had done it again. He glanced at Rose once more, wondering if she'd heard. The hopeful glimmer in her eyes suggested yes. What a weight off Daniel's shoulders. Now she wouldn't be crushed by Allison's demise.

Then Timothy's voice echoed in a yell, "No tranquilizers!" The instant he uttered those words, Daniel's spirits sank and Rose crumpled in her seat. "We can't judge the effects. They weren't tested on her species. They might not work. Or what if they give her strange lucid dreams?"

"What's so wrong with that?"

"Maybe nothing, but considering she's a telepath who terrorizes people with visions, you'd better not risk it, trust me."

As much Daniel wanted to fire a counterpoint, he had to admit that made sense. "Fine, no tranquilizers. We'll use poison instead. I have a suitable weapon in mind, but it's risky, and I'd rather have an alternative." A moan escaped his lips. "But, I suppose we don't have a choice: we have to contact Diabo soon."

"If only we could trick him in believing he's winning and yet have him lose..." Everyone around the table turned toward the source of that sentence, Rose. The prophet rubbed her chin in a pensive manner. Once she noticed the attention aimed at her, she blinked twice. "Oh, I'm sorry, I was thinking out loud; please ignore me, I don't want to interfere."

Daniel smiled. "If you have any ideas, we might as well listen. Is that okay with you, Ron?"

"Uh?" The Koporal rolled his eyes. "Yeah, whatever."

"Um... it's not so much an idea—more of a thought." Rose blushed. "It's just, what if we could return Plague to Diabo so he releases the hostages and still not give him what he wants?"

Ron produced an annoyed click with his tongue. "And how do you propose we do that?"

"Well, I'm afraid I don't know. Like I said, I was thinking out loud. I'm very sorry."

"With all due respect, missy, you're not helping. Please, stop dis—"

A relieved laugh from Nicky interrupted him. "Actually, she's a genius and doesn't realize it. Plague is a sick man. We can rig it so he dies in a day or two. This way, BBR rescues their men but loses the one that matters most, and assuming Diabo keeps his word, we save everyone."

Again, Daniel exhaled in relief. That scheme appeared safer than the assassination attempt and would keep Allison alive for Rose's sake.

"That might work, but only if Plague doesn't notice whatever we do to him." Ron's mouth contorted in a grimace. "Besides, I hate losing the prisoners. We could get valuable information from them."

Daniel shrugged. "No, they're ignorant grunts. Plague's the exception, but he's not talking. With his condition, we can't loosen his tongue. Even injecting him with truth serum might kill him. Those prisoners are worthless."

"You know"—David leaned forward—"maybe we should push them and propose they exchange Allison for Plague.

We save her and BBR ends up losing two key members. Without them, they'll be far less dangerous."

"Yeah, like Diabo will fall for that. Allison's more valuable than Plague." Ron scoffed with disdain. "He's a dumbass, but give him some credit."

"Yes, I doubt he'll agree, but why not propose it anyway? It's a negotiation. If he refuses, we'll present another offer. Besides, if we release Plague too soon, he'll be suspicious. It's better to make him work for it."

Daniel brought his hand to his lips. "An interesting argument. Our time is up. All right, David, Nicky, you two plan the assassination. Choose whoever is best for the job. With any luck, we won't have to go through with it. Ron and I will contact Diabo again. We'll see how it goes."

Chapter 14

When Daniel and Ron resumed the communication with the church, a grinning Diabo greeted them, sitting on the altar. On his lap lay a trembling little girl. The poor child's mouth gaped and her eyes darted in every direction as if seeking an explanation for how she'd stumbled into this situation. Despite her obvious terror, she resisted the temptation to sob and didn't dare produce any sound. She must have been seven, eight at most. Against her temple, a red hand held a pistol, ready to pull the trigger.

Daniel gritted his teeth. "Is there no low you won't reach, Diabo?"

"Didn't think ya'd make it, so I prepared."

"You goddamn son of a bitch!" Ron yelled while brandishing his fist. "Let her go right now or I swear we'll freaking kill Plague this second!"

A chuckle escaped Diabo's lips. "Relax, Koporal, ya got here in time, so I ain't gonna hurt her." With that, the BBR founder released his grip on the kid, who hopped off his knees and dashed toward the pews. The tears she'd held at bay finally flowed while she shouted for her mommy. "There ya go!"

Daniel mumbled a curse. No doubt this event would scar the girl for life. And Diabo stared at them with that insincere smile filled with arrogance, as if proud of his actions. How Daniel wished to wipe that disgusting smirk off his face, but the hostages' safety stood as the priority. Revenge would come later, and it would be sweet.

"Now that you're done threatening an innocent child, Diabo, let's begin. We've considered your deal, and we'll release your men, but we need more than the hostages in return."

With a scowl, Diabo left the altar and returned to his feet. "I'm all ears." The words proved agreeable, but the tone warned they should not push their luck.

"Allison isn't part of BBR but your prisoner. She's legally a Nirnivian you abducted. We'll give Plague back, but in exchange we want her."

"Ya think I'm freaking insane?" Diabo roared as he pounded on the altar with his fist. A loud crack echoed as the wood splintered and Daniel winced. The furniture in Onel cost a bundle. That punch alone might've brought a hefty cost. "That ain't happening. You wanna pull shit like this? Fine, I'm gonna waste a hostage! It'll teach ya a lesson."

"Whoa, whoa, calm down." Ron presented both his palms as a shield. "It's a negotiation. We made an offer. If you don't like it, we'll compromise. No need to get violent. This is still the talking stage."

Diabo grunted and then exhaled while shaking his head. "What do ya have in mind?"

"Well, let's see"—Daniel shrugged as he answered in his Koporal's stead—"you could surrender Wrathchild or Stalker instead of Allison. Whoever suits you better."

"That's even worse! They're family! I ain't gonna betray 'em like that."

Daniel nodded. "Believe it or not, I understand how you feel. Our main concern is the hostages' safety. Forgive the distrust, but what's stopping you from killing them after you receive Plague? We're willing to accept your terms, but we want insurance."

"Speaking 'bout that"—the crimson beast snapped his fingers—"there's something on my mind too. I ain't no genius, but I've been thinking... Plague's a dying man. When we get him back, maybe he ain't gonna be in mint condition, if you catch my drift."

Daniel stifled a curse and struggled not to frown. The bastard had predicted Nicky's plan. The monster acted like an unsophisticated brute and showed a lack of intelligence on multiple occasions. Still, while not smart, he wasn't a complete idiot either. He possessed a certain level of street smarts, and they shouldn't underestimate his mental capabilities lest he surprise them again.

"Don't insult us. We're soldiers, not murderers."

That reply brought a laugh out of Diabo. "Please, I ain't a free man 'cause I'm trusting. I need insurance too. Tell you what: I'll bring a few people along. No worries, I'll send 'em back in one piece once we're sure Plague's okay. How 'bout the human and Brucie?"

As Rose heard those names, she gasped and stepped closer to the display, about to voice an objection. A cold sweat covered Daniel's brow. He almost pleaded for her to return to her seat, but before he did, Ron blocked her with his arm. The Koporal adopted a harsh stare and without having to utter a word, Rose hushed and retreated. Daniel produced a relieved sigh. Thank God Rose honored her promise and didn't stir up trouble.

Diabo chuckled once more. "Relax, Your Holiness, I ain't gonna dissect the guy or anything. Gonna take self-control, but I'll manage. I guess. What do ya say, Commander?"

"No, that's unacceptable. We have no way of knowing you'll release them."

"I won't cross ya. If I don't return 'em, you guys'll be pissed, get revenge, and we'll be back at square one. One thing, though—James and Brucie ain't enough. You might sacrifice 'em to get rid o' Plague. I need someone irreplaceable." He rubbed his chin. "How 'bout Her Holiness? I'll be nice with her."

Outraged whispers spread across the war room. As for Daniel, he remained still except for a slight shaking that increased with every passing moment. Stay calm; focus. But, regardless of his effort, an intense rage coursed through his whole body, gripping his chest. Blood rushed to his face. All his life, Daniel had battled against sadistic urges. In his youth, he'd succumbed to them often. Sophia and to a lesser extent Madeleine had shown him how to resist them. Now that he was an adult, controlling his savage impulses had become second nature and posed no challenge. Yet at this moment, restraining his anger proved impossible, and he exploded while pointing at Diabo.

"You won't get your filthy hands on her, you hear me? We'll storm the church and slaughter you all like animals even if it means the death of every damn hostage! Even better, I'll go down there personally, skin any BBR thugs and any hostage still alive, then I'll kick the crap out of you!"

The whole room fell silent as everyone looked at Daniel with their mouths gaping. The outburst stunned the entire staff. Even Ron, who'd experienced such tirades on rare occasions, stared at him wide-eyed. Rose covered her lips with her hand and whimpered. Shame seized Daniel. He'd always shielded her from his darker side.

A horrid chortle echoed as Diabo slapped his knee. "Relax, I'm messing with ya. Payback fo' the Allison thing. Keep your freaking Melkar; she'd be a pain in my ass. But I do want an important hostage. How 'bout a high-ranking military officer? I'll let you choose someone. Now, I get you need insurance too... hey, propose something reasonable and I'll listen."

After several deep breaths, Daniel regained enough composure to answer without shrieking like a lunatic. "All right, we'll find you someone. But, please realize I can't decide just like that. We must talk among ourselves."

"Sure." Diabo grinned with contempt. "Don't make me wait too long: I ain't patient." The monitor went black. Daniel groaned and faced Rose.

"I'm sorry you had to see that."

Though still pale, she appeared calmer. "It's okay, I understand. Diabo pushed you to the limit, and you said things you didn't mean. I know you wouldn't harm an innocent." Rose quivered. "It's just I never saw you lose your temper like that before."

"Don't worry, princess, I won't let them have you."

"I didn't think you would." Rose closed her eyes and Daniel sensed a sadness growing within her. Perhaps she wished he would abandon her for the safety of others. Noble intentions, but Rose undervalued her importance as usual. At any rate, Daniel had more pressing concerns, so he focused on his Koporal.

"The assassination is on. We'll keep a mock negotiation going to distract Diabo, but BBR aren't getting their men no matter what."

"You spoke my mind, old friend."

Chapter 15

As Janice advanced in the darkness, a high-pitched squeak reached her ears. Out of curiosity, she aimed her flashlight toward the source. A flurry of animals scurried away while squealing, terrified by the three soldiers invading their domain. The size of a pissack and a half, the rittles proved less than intimidating, yet they possessed sharp teeth and didn't mind using them. Since the sewer was their natural habitat, such a bite implied a risk of infection and disease. Good thing they avoided Gorumars by instinct.

That they hadn't met a bunch of those creatures already surprised Janice. They littered the Nirnivian sewer systems despite the efforts to curb their reproduction. It seemed the buggers had heard them from a distance and made a premature escape. Smart and convenient for both parties.

On Janice's left stood a solid brick wall, on her right a river of brown gunk some might dare call water. The narrow passage offered little space, and so losing footing and stumbling in the goo became a too-real possibility. Anyone falling in there would receive a heavy dose of bacteria that would no doubt bring consequences should the poor fellow manage not to drown. Because of this tight path, they walked in a line. Behind Janice followed Bertrand Gormier, and Charlie closed the march. Both competent soldiers she could depend on. Bertrand she didn't see often, but she knew him well enough. As for Charlie, he tended to loiter in the fifth level's rec room and watch TV, to the point where he had been present the first time she'd dragged James in there. Janice chatted with him almost every day.

The deeper she progressed, the more Janice thanked God for the respirator she'd received for this mission. The mask blocked the smell, though her imagination still produced a convincing memory of the odor. Back during the war, Ostarkirans had caught her in an ambush and she had jumped in the sewer to survive. The act had saved her life, but at a price. The sordid air had taken the breath out of her lungs and she'd soon thrown up. It had felt like having your nose assaulted by thousands of public toilets, which she supposed was accurate. She only hoped they wouldn't drag the scent along with them or the stench would make infiltrating Onel an imposing challenge.

At least the underground trip should be short. A secret exit connected Onel's basement to this tunnel, which they'd use as an entrance. What a dangerous mission, for them and the hostages. If anyone spotted them and raised the alarm, Diabo might lose his temper and slaughter half of his captives. Even if they succeeded and assassinated Allison, should a BBR goon notice she'd stopped moving, it'd be over.

As the telepath's image entered Janice's mind, she shivered and glanced at the two trailing her. They were lucky, for they'd never met Allison. Janice had, however, and murdering that innocent young girl made her sick to her stomach. Give her a gun and she'd slay terrorists without reticence, but Allison was a Nirnivian prisoner like those they tried to save. Many would disagree with her assessment. Most didn't consider visitors to be true Nirnivians, not that she cared about their opinions.

Distracted by her musings, Janice slipped in a puddle. One of her legs flew in the air and the other bent backward, sending her toward the toxic goop. With a sharp in-hale, she extended her arms and through her mutation stabilized herself. For a second, she silenced that voice in her head asking if acting ethically can get you killed. Janice exhaled, straightened and wiped the sweat off her brow.

Behind her, Bertrand and Charlie stared at her acrobatics with wide eyes while reaching out to grab her. Once the shock passed, Charlie burst into laughter. "Ha ha ha! Too bad: I like dirty girls."

With a groan, Janice shook her head and rubbed her forehead. "Ooh la la, that's like Brucie's level of humor. You should be ashamed of yourself."

Charlie lowered his gaze in mock shame. "Yes, you're right, I'm sorry. Please don't dick punch me."

"Ah, don't worry, buddy." Janice winked. "Everybody gets one free." Then she formed a fist. "Next one, though, you gotta pay." The three of them laughed as they knew the threat to be toothless. That treatment she reserved for the bodyguard. Then she remembered Brucie also served as BBR's hostage. The chuckles stopped, replaced with concern.

***

Traversing the sewer brought Janice, Bertrand and Charlie to a hidden ladder leading to a trapdoor. After a deep breath, Janice climbed, trailed by the others. Soon, she reached the hatch and undid the latch. Then she prepared herself to push it open but stopped. What if guards patrolled the area? They'd be caught, and it was impossible to check. With a groan, Janice shook the notion out of her head. The passage led to a secret room, implying a low risk of ambush. Gritting her teeth, she shoved through and emerged inside Onel.

As promised, they arrived in an empty chamber lacking doors. Though in appearance they were trapped, Janice knew better. A lever decorated one of the walls. A quick pull would retract the facade, revealing a path. Beside it, she spotted a sliding peephole. She'd be able to ensure the way was clear thanks to that. Once Charlie emerged from the hole, he used military sign language to say, "Now's the dangerous part." Janice nodded and then she slid open the peephole, which revealed a pair of legs walking by. With a discreet sigh, Janice presented her index finger in a manner suggesting her companion should stay put. Bertrand signed, "Somebody there?" She answered yes and added that they were just passing by.

After the guard vanished in the distance, Janice and her cohort exited the concealed chamber and entered Onel proper. Careful, they advanced at a slow pace and avoided producing any sound. A single loud footstep might cause failure. Before long, they reached an intersection. Charlie carried a minicomp displaying a map and Janice signaled for him to give the correct direction. Left, he motioned back. Again, she gestured for her fellow soldiers to wait. She hugged against the wall and crawled forward. Once close enough, she extended her neck and peeped around the corner. Two BBR thugs chatted in the middle of the hall, enjoying a smoke. Cigarettes in a church; those bastards respected nothing. Several minutes passed, and the goons showed no signs of leaving.

Sweat covered Janice's brow. No choice but to delay, but that risked being discovered. Charlie and Bertrand observed the other paths to avoid that outcome, but if a guard drew near, they'd have limited options. Perhaps sensing her apprehension, Bertrand slipped his index finger against his throat. While Janice wished to agree and kill the assholes, they'd have to hide the bodies and deal with the blood. No, too complicated, so she shook her head. Instead, she stared at Charlie. "Is there another way?"

With a frown, Charlie poked on his minicomp. "Yes, but it'd be twice as long."

Janice winced. Under normal circumstances, they'd reach their destination in ten minutes. Because of the obstacle they faced, that time frame might double or triple. The longer they took, the bigger the danger, yet increasing speed could also spell doom. Worse, what if Allison detected them with her telepathy? Yes, that expert hoped the large number of people would confuse her, but there were no guarantees. Should that happen, no doubt she would warn Diabo. Ah well, no point complaining about it. Covered in perspiration, they retraced their steps.

Chapter 16

By that point in his tale, Plague's throat grew parched. Even under the best circumstances, speaking set his esophagus on fire. A long speech with no hydration equaled torture. Though Plague attempted to request water, his jailer denied him. Not that it would stop him from continuing. "Yeah, so NISDA saved us months later. By then, only six of us lived. One of them died a few days after. Two were brain-damaged and paralyzed. The last three were Diabo, Stalker and me."

Along with a groan, the guardian blur on the left twitched in an undecipherable motion. "The bastards who became terrorists!"

"Yup! Heh, I figured I was lucky. Diabo was a monster, Stalker looked like some animal, but me, I was pretty much the same, except for a couple gross scars. NISDA sent us to a military facility to run tests. Nice guys that they were, they prepared a surprise for me."

***

Two soldiers flanking him, Norman strolled down the corridor. The walk lasted five minutes and already his legs hurt. Not that surprising. Ever since the experiments he'd endured, any light physical effort resulted in aching muscles. While it was painful, he understood he had gotten off easy compared to the others and counted his blessings. What annoyed him in this case was that his escort refused to explain where they headed or why. Based on what they'd told him, someone wanted to see him. As for their identity, the guard declined to reveal it.

Soon, the trip concluded in a small room with the same gray walls forming the facility. Whoever had requested Norman's presence hadn't arrived yet, as the chamber stood empty. Well, not quite, he supposed. A sofa rested against a wall, and a flowerpot sat on an end table beside it. Out of breath, Norman sat on the couch and leaned back, eyes closed. He just waited, inhaling and exhaling. The tests the NISDA scientists had performed exhausted him. Still better than what he'd suffered in Ostark, though. Regardless, he yearned to return home, but that assumed he had one. Norman had vanished for months. What if Alphonse believed him dead and had started a new life? With a shake of the head, Norman pushed the idea away. He'd worried about that if it became reality.

For a moment, sitting there doing nothing proved beneficial. The forced rest helped Norman recuperate and regain his bearings until he found himself refreshed. He opened his eyes, twiddled his fingers. How long did they intend on making him wait? As those words popped into his brain, the door opened. A Jonilan man with short black hair and a mustache entered. Sticking close to him, a Perz little girl with pigtails also approached while sucking her thumb. Norman recognized them in an instant. His husband, Alphonse, and adopted daughter, Mary.

Norman gasped and his eyes widened. Then he twisted his neck to conceal his facial scars. In addition, he raised his palm to cover his face. This was too early. His family needed time to adapt to his new appearance first. While he was not nearly as disfigured as his friends, the torture had left traces.

None of them moved. They stared at each other in awe and without a word. Their frozen state lasted a few seconds, but it felt like hours. Little Mary must have been terrified. She'd have nightmares for months—perhaps years.

As Norman mulled over these dark thoughts, the child dashed toward him, arms outstretched. "Daddy! Daddy!" A large smile formed on her lips. Instinctively, Norman stood up. A fortunate premonition, for Mary jumped on him and he seized her. The poor kid clenched so hard it almost hurt. Norman couldn't believe it—she recognized him and accepted his appearance in an instant. Tears of joys ran down his cheeks. What a wonderful daughter. In less than a minute, Alphonse joined the hug and kissed him. "Oh, Norman, we were so scared! You disappeared; we feared the worst! Thank Ulgorack you're back!"

"I swear I'll never leave you again."

***

Outside the cell, the two blurs hushed. Whether they listened or ignored him in silence, Plague couldn't tell, but it didn't matter. By this point, the words needed to come out. "We were so happy. I didn't believe it: Alphonse waited for me. He didn't know what happened, or if I survived, but he waited anyway." Plague's voice faltered. "We were a perfect family reunion. We hugged, cried tears of joy. But it wasn't meant to last."

***

What a difference a day can make. Yesterday, Norman and his family had enjoyed a happy reunion. Today, he watched them lying immobile in hospital beds. Both had fallen unconscious by then. While unbearable, the silence might have been better than the alternative. Earlier, they had spoken to him and tried to show a brave face, but it had been obvious they'd endured agonizing torments. By now, their physical appearance had deteriorated further. Pus-filled abscesses covered their flesh, and they breathed with difficulty, explaining the respiratory masks attached to them.

Part of Norman wished to run away from this nightmare, but he refused to abandon them. Sometimes he sat in a chair next to their mattresses. Sometimes he paced around instead, though his aching muscles kept those bouts of activity short. Twin beeping from the heart monitors served as the only sounds. Under normal circumstances, that would've become annoying, but in this context, it meant his loved ones were alive, and so an irritating noise morphed into a beacon of hope.

While he waited, Norman couldn't help but ask, why had this happened? Hadn't they suffered enough? Didn't the gods have any mercy? Apparently not. Frustration and rage grew inside him. Unfair—it was unfair. Overwhelmed by emotions, he jumped on his feet and grabbed his head with both hands. Then he let out a furious roar. Even that didn't satisfy his anger, so in search of a target, he kicked a small garbage can. A metallic clunk echoed as the cylindrical shape collapsed. Soiled papers, carton plates and cups spilled on the floor.

Observing the mess he'd caused, Norman sobbed. That was when a weak voice reached his ears. "Daddy?"

Breathless, Norman spun and gazed at his child. Her eyes... they'd opened. And her lips moved, though no other words came out. Without delay, Norman rushed to her bed and crouched beside it.

"Yes, dear? What is it?" Then her features froze. After a gag, yellow liquid dripped from her mouth while her eyes rolled back. "Mary?!" He stared at the door reflexively. "Doctor, we need help! Hurry!" Before anyone answered his plea, the rhythmic beeping turned into a constant piercing shriek. With horror, Plague realized both monitors flat-lined. Soon, his screams joined the electronic cries. Nurses dashed into the chamber. Most headed for the patients, a few grabbed Norman and pulled him away. He attempted fighting to stay, but his weakened body proved to be no match.

***

"The soldiers who rescued me caught the same disease. They died not long after. Turns out Doctor Death's experiments made me poisonous. Direct contact with my skin causes a lethal infection." Plagued paused while he sobbed. "The two people I cared for the most in the world were gone. I killed them with my own hands—with a freaking hug. Even now, their ghosts haunt my dreams."

One of the blobs twitched and Plague detected a touch of sympathy in the vague shape. That must have been his imagination. How could a blur communicate empathy? "Um, I'm sorry."

"Thanks. You see why I wish I'd have rotted in that laboratory? My family would be alive."

The other guard grunted. "Hey, that's hardly our fault! Is that why you kill innocent Nirnivians?"

"No." Several coughs escaped Plague's lips. "I only blame the Ostarkirans. Sometimes we kill Nirnivians, but those are accidents."

"Oh yeah? And when you raided grocery stores? That was an accident too?"

With a sigh, Plague lowered his head and closed his eyes. "No, that's 'cause we screwed up when we blew up that apartment building. I told Diabo it was a mistake, that it wasn't worth it just to off a spy. The boss, he ain't the listening type." He grunted. "Anyway, my family isn't the only thing I've lost. The poison's killing me too. It's a painful, degrading death. My body's slowly eaten away. These days, any small movement feels like I'm tearing my muscles apart. I get more disfigured as time passes. Under these bandages, I look like a freaking zombie. Diabo and Stalker don't find me lucky anymore. The poison gets more potent too. Back then, it took a day before Alphonse and Mary became sick. Now a poor bastard who touches my skin will have symptoms in an hour and he'll be a goner in three. If he touched my blood instead, he'd throw up right there. I don't have much time myself. A year, maybe, but I'd guess six months."

"Listen, what happened to you is horrible. It's the saddest thing I've heard and I'm disgusted by what Doctor Death did, but you're not helping Nirnivia, You're murdering people out of revenge."

"Revenge, huh?" Plague chuckled. "Yeah, that's true, I ain't denying it. Making Ostarkirans suffer is my only pleasure. Part of me knows most of them are low-ranking grunts with families of their own, but I can't stop hating them. Still, there's more to it."

Chapter 17

Peeping from a corner, Janice gritted her teeth. That BBR goon ended up being a major pain. The guy refused to budge, blocking their path. All the while, the long-haired fool smoked cigarettes and picked his nose as he hummed lame tunes. Over ten minutes had passed now, and they needed to progress before a different guard walked in on them.

Out of desperation, she had lurked out of her hiding place when the thug gazed in another direction and planted a special distraction. The tricky part had been staging it so it appeared like it had been dropped by mistake. The trap had to be visible, yet hard enough to spot that the terrorist would assume he'd missed it without growing suspicious. Now she waited for results, but so far the move proved futile. But wait, he turned his head... and, yes, that puzzled frown he adopted...

A touch of perspiration forming on her brow, Janice clenched her fists and smiled, filled with anticipation. She'd leaned forward too much already but risked edging an extra half inch.

As Janice hoped, the terrorist stepped toward the lure and kneeled. "Huh? What the freak?" he mumbled as he picked up the object. Then, magazine in hand, he straightened and paged through his new reading material, giggling like a child who'd pulled a prank. Janice had trouble not laughing herself. And to think her companions had insisted her plan wouldn't succeed.

Now that the guard failed to pay attention, they slipped by behind him. Once far enough, Charlie tapped Janice's shoulder and signed, "I can't believe that worked."

"I knew it would, I tested it on Brucie."

"Uh, yeah, but he's a special case."

Janice shrugged. "That's debatable."

Chapter 18

For Brucie, meeting Pierre, or rather Diabo, unleashed all his memories. As the brothers shared a substantial history, he found plenty of material to recall. Currently, he reminisced about a party that had ended up turning his life around.

***

While Brucie never saw Pierre enter the house, from what he heard later, his sibling had searched in there for a while, questioning the guests. That had proven futile, since Brucie chose not to waste his time inside. Instead, he lingered near the pool, not because he fancied a dip, but rather several babes in bikinis hung there. Why not enjoy the view, he figured. Before long, a decent-size group of girls surrounded him. They giggled and made pretty eyes as Brucie regaled them with past exploits. Between stories, he indulged in sips of beer.

Brucie had no illusion and realized he served as their eye candy as much as they did for him. That seemed fair, so he stood there shirtless and his "fans" admired his pecs. The workouts he shared with Pierre had sculpted him into a fine figure. One girl, a short-haired brunette with blue eyes wearing a pink bathing suit, displayed more enthusiasm than the others. She remained as close to Brucie as possible and touched his shoulder while laughing at his jokes. Sensing an invitation, he risked wrapping an arm around her hips. If that gesture offended her, she didn't show it. In fact, she kissed his cheek, and that soon turned into his lips. Before long, she whispered an offer into his ear and Brucie smiled.

"Yeah, I'm up fo' that. Let's—" Then he spotted a large guy, larger than him even, advancing through the crowd. "Ah, just gimme a sec, babe. That's my bro, I gotta see what he wants. Don't worry, I'll get rid o' him quick." With that, Brucie waved. "Hey, bro!" Cued in by his greeting, Pierre started walking toward Brucie. "New sunglasses, huh? I like 'em!"

With a frown, Pierre pointed a questioning index finger at Brucie's torso. "What're ya doing here? Ya got an important exam tomorrow, and ya swore to Mom you'd study."

"Ah, come on, man. Ya know I ain't the studying type. Besides, lookit all the freaking sweetness around ya!" As Brucie winked, he patted the brunette's bottom. With a laugh, she kissed his neck.

"Brucie, fun is nice and all, but you gotta think 'bout the future."

"Don't sweat it, dude, ya can get me a job!" Since their father had abandoned them, Pierre hadn't pursued his education to completion. As a result, he specialized in manual labor, hard but honest work.

"Yeah, but maybe it ain't a bad thing to keep your options open? Won't ya at least try? You're smarter than you think, Brucie. You ain't no genius, but you're not stupid."

Brucie shrugged. "Test scores disagree with ya!"

"Heh, well, that's 'cause all you do is hang out with losers." The girls surrounding Brucie grumbled at the comment and extended their tongues in protest. "Nah, didn't mean ya gals. I'm talkin' about jerks like that asshole Craig who put this party together. All ya do is drink yourself stupid with guys like 'im and sleep with any whore you can find." Pierre scowled. "Say, got a burning sensation when you pee, bro? I'd get that checked out."

Cheeks reddening, the brunette stared at Pierre, pulled away from Brucie, slapped the large man and stormed off.

With a wince, Pierre rubbed his assaulted face. "Uh, yeah, sorry 'bout that, didn't mean ya either, just in general." He sighed. "Whatever, she ain't here no more."

Brucie crossed his arms. "Well, ya screwed me over, bro, thanks."

"Hey, I gotta do what I gotta do."

"Ah, come on, dude, ya sound like a freaking PSA! Stay in school! Don't screw any chick or it'll fall off! I love you, man, but you're embarrassing me. Please go."

"Oh, sure, I'm leaving, but you're coming too."

"No way, ya can't make me."

"I just wanna show you something. I'll drive ya back after. You lost your shot with that babe, so you ain't in a hurry, are ya?"

After he rolled his eyes, Brucie nodded, if only to get Pierre off his case. He owed his brother a lot, but sometimes he could be overbearing. Wherever they headed, the car ride ended up silent and awkward. When they reached their destination, a gasping Brucie realized Pierre had brought him home.

"Hey, bro, what gives?"

"You'll see." Pierre gestured for Brucie to follow and led him toward a window. The elder sibling jabbed his thumb at the glass and spoke a single word: "Look."

"Huh, dude, that's Mom's room. Yeah, I'm a dirty perv, ya know, but come on! I ain't gonna peep on Mom! You're sick, man, freaking sick."

Pierre groaned and slapped his brow. "Nah, she's dressed, look." Brucie sighed and obeyed. His mother sat on the bed, hugging her pillow and dampening it with tears.

"What's wrong? Why's she cryin'?"

Pierre tapped his shoulder. "Cause o' you, bro."

"Huh? Why?"

"All ya do is get drunk and woo gals. Mom worries you might be on drugs too. She's watching you piss your life away and there ain't nothing she can do 'bout it 'cause ya don't listen." Brucie hushed as a grimace formed on his face. "You and Mom never saw eye to eye, but ya can't tell me you want this."

"You suck, man!" Brucie threw his hands in the air. "Now I can't enjoy the evening! Son of a bitch! Hey! Lookit what ya made me say—she's my mom too!" Pierre burst in a vigorous chortle, which frustrated Brucie even more. "Don't laugh, bro!"

***

As Pierre had hoped, Brucie didn't return to the party that night. He stayed home and studied out of guilt. As a result, he passed the test with his best grade so far. That made him feel good, and he began trying harder. Of course, he didn't stop celebrating or drinking, and he certainly continued fooling around with the ladies, but he struck a better balance thanks to Pierre.

Chapter 19

Janice was dead—simple as that. Worse, her mistake had doomed Bertrand and Charlie. Allison would survive. The hostages wouldn't be rescued. In fairness, the BBR goon had surprised all of them. The trio scattered in various directions, searching for hiding spots. Despite her best effort, he spotted Janice. Now he aimed his automatic weapon at her. By pure reflex, she raised her hands, still holding her own gun. The guard glared at her. "Drop that thing, handle first. No funny business or I'll shoot!"

After a hard swallow, Janice nodded. "Okay, you got it, buddy. Stay calm, I'm surrendering."

"Shut up and put it down!"

Slowly, Janice bent to obey the order. Around midway she paused and glanced at her firearm. Should she rush him? That would no doubt result in death, but what if she could take him with her? Sure, the commotion would get them discovered, but capture implied the same. Plus, her mutation granted her an edge. As she deliberated, the thug reached for his radio and brought it to his mouth. That settled the matter, then. Gritting her teeth, Janice hopped forward. Before she even came close, Charlie snatched the terrorist from behind and squeezed his neck. Desperate gurgles echoed as he choked, a noise Janice had grown too familiar with. It used to sicken her, but she'd hardened through the years. Charlie covered the sentry's lips to stifle the sound. Soon, his body turned limp and Charlie let go. The cadaver collapsed on the ground like a rag doll.

Eyes open wide, Janice rested her palm on her heart and took several deep breaths. Once she recuperated, she sighed. "Thanks, you saved my ass."

"No problem."

Then Janice pointed at the corpse. "And no blood, good job."

"Heh, of course." A smile formed on Charlie's face. "That's why I did it that way. Come, we better hide the body."

"What if someone tries contacting him through the radio?"

He shrugged. "Maybe they'll think he's napping or goofing around. No point worrying about it."

Janice realized he was right. They had no alternative but to keep going and pray for the best.

Chapter 20

Once again, Daniel Ricdeau and his Koporal faced Diabo in a battle of wills. During the latest recess, they'd prepared a fake list of hostages for BBR, the idea being they'd serve as the requested insurance. While NISDA intended to deny the terrorists' demands, the ensuing negotiations should delay the proceedings, allowing the squad to assassinate Allison. With her gone, a rescue operation became possible. How Daniel craved to see Diabo's dumb smirk vanish once he understood his precious telepath had died. Though that implied Janice and the others succeeded. Should they fail... well, announcing the news to Madeleine would be beyond difficult. Ah, who was he kidding? Accepting the fact himself would be much harder. A large part of him had wished to object when they had selected her. Nicky and David had sure taken him literally when he'd said they should pick the best available regardless of who they were. And yet, his professionalism meant he couldn't display favoritism. Janice was a soldier; this was her duty. All he could do was distract Diabo and pray it would help. That thought in mind, he stared at the red monster.

"All right, Diabo"—Daniel forced himself to adopt a calm tone—"I have good news. Jade Carlson, a councillor, volunteered." A chuckle attempted to escape his lips as he contemplated the notion that Jade already lay at BBR's mercy without them realizing. Somehow, he kept it inside. "You don't get much more high-profile."

"Generous of 'em, but councillors can be replaced."

Daniel nodded. "I know. That's why I'll join her. While I can be replaced too, it should be enough to convince you of our good faith. The only irreplaceable one is the Melkar, and that won't happen."

"Didn't expect that." The crimson beast paused and rubbed his chin. "A councillor, you, Brucie and James. Yeah, I guess it's fine."

"Perfect, we're finally getting somewhere. Now that you have your insurance, we need ours." Daniel's smile widened. "We'll use hostages too, it's only fair. So, we've been thinking, and we want Wrathchild, Allison and Stalker." He snapped his fingers. "Oh, and since I'm putting my life on the line, we expect you to do the same."

A furious roar escaped Diabo's lips. "Gimme a break!" Again, he struck the altar. The first blow cracked the wooden surface. The second shattered it in two with a deafening bang. "Issat a joke? 'Cause it ain't funny. Leave the bad humor to my bro, won't ya? That's like the heart o' BBR. I give ya that, BBR's dead, ya got no reason to do what ya say you're gonna do!"

"Yeah, I guess so, huh?" The Koporal stepped forward and frowned. "Tell you what, we'll let Allison go."

"Ya freaking bastards!"

And so the talks continued. Every time Ron or Daniel proposed a compromise, Diabo refused. Not surprising given they'd prepared each one so it would be unacceptable. It went back and forth with little progress. The brute accepted rare minor concessions, but they were insignificant in the grand scheme of things. Under normal circumstances, this would have been frustrating, but considering they intended to divert Diabo's attention, it delighted both of them. BBR's boss proved as stubborn as ever, and that served their purpose. By far, the biggest challenge was not bursting into laughter whenever they revealed another ridiculous proposal. Diabo's furious expressions made that even more difficult.

Chapter 21

After another narrow escape, Janice stood in a big empty wardrobe along with Bertrand. As for Charlie, he ran in a different direction. She hoped he'd found a decent spot to hide. Outside, two BBR goons talked about various things. Sometimes footsteps echoed, showing they walked around. Based on the loudness of their shoes scraping against the floor, Janice could tell whether they approached the cabinet or went farther. Whenever the volume increased, she clutched her weapon, ready to pounce. Why wouldn't they leave? Her heart pounded hard. Plus, she imagined the walls closing on her and fought the temptation to scream. While not claustrophobic, she hated tight spaces, and Bertrand's sweating and heavy breathing suggested he didn't fare much better.

While it must have been her imagination, Janice felt like oxygen was running out and she'd suffocate. Unable to tolerate it anymore, she cracked the door open. Bertrand's mouth gaped in horror. Obviously, he dreaded the sentries might detect her. Though well aware of the danger, Janice needed some fresh air. Watching the guards pacing back and forth made it worse, yet she couldn't stop studying their movement. In silence, she prayed to Ulgorack so he'd send the men away, but her pleas remained unanswered.

After a moment, one of the thugs' eyes stared right at Janice. She froze, breathless. He must have noticed... yet he turned his head. Relieved, Janice inhaled at last. Then someone else entered the chamber. This woman seemed familiar. Wait, that sword... Janice gasped and her face whitened. Wrathchild. Despite Janice's considerable skill, Melissa outclassed her. Increased balance might offer an edge under normal circumstances, but compared to super speed, it proved lacking.

"What's wrong?" Bertrand whispered. He must've discerned Janice's terrified expression, but he couldn't see Wrathchild from his position. The two grunts saluted the warrior as she came in. Janice believed she wasn't their superior, but her reputation preceded her and her peers showed her great respect.

"Sir!"

"Hi, boys!"

Bertrand recognized the voice, and in an instant his skin tone matched Janice's. "Just passing through." So she was in a hurry. Janice wiped the sweat off her brow. How lucky. As Melissa headed for the exit, she glanced at the wardrobe and pointed her thumb toward it.

"Checked in there?"

"Nah... why?"

Wrathchild shrugged. "Precaution." With that, she approached the cabinet. Gasping, Janice readied her gun. Her hands trembled. Melissa would chop them in half without breaking a sweat. Still, she refused to go down without a fight. Wrathchild reached for the knob when her radio buzzed. Once she answered, she mumbled that she understood, declared she'd received new orders and left. That must've been an important call, for she forgot all about the wardrobe. While Janice thanked God, she feared the others might inspect the wardrobe themselves now. A bad situation, but manageable.

"Should we open it?" one sentry asked.

"Nah, why bother? Hey, that reminds me, lookit the magazine I found earlier."

"Sweet!"

"You gotta see this shit. Let's find a good place to check it out." A grin formed on Janice's lips. Though not part of that publication's target audience, she loved it anyway.

Chapter 22

With the guards appearing as blurs to Plague, gauging their level of attention proved difficult, yet he sensed their interest grew with every word. Not that it mattered; he'd keep going either way. "When what happened to us went public, we figured Nirnivia wouldn't stand for it. What Ostark did was unforgivable. We thought NISDA would step up and fight hard until Doctor Death was dealt with, but we were wrong. All we got were pointless speeches promising justice that never came and worthless medals. The kidnappings stopped, so nobody cared: they were safe. Nothing changed, except our lives were ruined. That was a dark time. No one understood our pain. We only had each other, so we got together and complained 'bout how Nirnivia's heart wasn't in the battle. After a while, I realized it was because of Her Holiness."

"What?" the two men exclaimed in unison. "What blasphemy is this?"

Plague shrugged. "The Melkar can't stand violence. Yeah, Rose realizes Nirnivia has to fight, but she wants a 'clean' war. There ain't no such thing! War's a dirty business: if you ain't gonna compromise your ethics, you're worm food."

"That's ridiculous. The Voice of God has no authority over the military. It's not like she's leading the war effort. Even as a councillor, she's not in charge of NISDA. Sure, she has input, but not much."

"True." Plague nodded. "But who's in charge? The honorable Mr. Daniel Ricdeau. I've met the guy. The

Commander's a good man and a great leader." He waggled a lecturing index finger. "But he's also the Melkar's adoptive father, and that's the problem. Rose influences his decisions and makes Nirnivia weak."

"Oh, you're insane!"

"Am I? Listen, the Melkar is Daniel's daughter; they meet regularly. It's easy for her to sway his opinion without even trying. If you had access to the Voice of God's clairvoyance, wouldn't you use it? I'm sure sometimes Mr. Ricdeau casually discusses the war with her, and I'm also sure he puts a lot of stock in whatever she says. Who wouldn't?" Several coughs escaped Plague's lips, interrupting his speech. Soon, he recovered enough to continue. "Plus, like you said, Rose's a councillor. The links between the Council and NISDA are confusing, but they influence each other. Take the decision to cut military funding not long before the war started, for example. I believe it was Her Holiness's idea, or at least she supported it."

One blur twitched. "I've had about enough. I don't like hearing you slander her, you damn heretic. Maybe you should shut up like my partner suggested earlier before I forget my orders and cut out your tongue."

"Won't be necessary. Yeah, there was a time when I was angry at Rose, may she forgive me. But I was stupid and have since regained my faith. You see, I can't blame her: she's only doing her job. The Melkar's a prophet who guides us toward the afterlife and steers us away from nothingness. Rose can't condone war crimes. She must restrain our soldiers so they don't damn themselves. Doctor Death is an atheist; many of his men are too, so he's not afraid of nothingness. To him, once you're dead, you rot in the ground and that's it. He can decide his own moral code without fear of Timagoron. Not Rose—she follows Ulgorack's rules. Her goal is to save our souls, not our lives. She might not realize it, but to her, it's better if Ostark kills every Nirnivian and most get to the afterlife than if we win the war but fade into nothingness because of our actions. That's fine, but me, I'm a greedy guy—I'd like to win and save a maximum of souls."

Plague paused for a second. He expected the men would complain, but they stayed silent. "This is where BBR comes in. We fight dirty like Nirnivia should. We're terrorists, we're monsters, we're all you accuse us of and more. I ain't got any delusions: there's no afterlife in my future and I accept that. We're sacrificing ourselves so others don't have to pay that price." Plague produced a sad chuckle. "In a twisted way, we're heroes, but you guys hate us for it. Today, you might destroy BBR. If you do, you'll lose the war or you'll have to sully your own souls. So, yeah, Nirnivia needs us quite a lot."

"That's the biggest load of bullshit I've ever heard," the sentry on the right said.

"Uh, yeah, heroes? Don't make me laugh," the one on the left added.

Plague shrugged and lay down on his small lump-filled mattress. "Whatever, I don't care what you think. Just trying to pass the time."

Chapter 23

"I've almost got it." Though Janice's words conveyed confidence, her assurance proved faked. The particular brick wall she faced served as the mechanism for the secret passage leading to Allison. In theory, they had reached the end of their journey. In practice, however, things weren't so straightforward. It remained to open the concealed door. Janice had received instructions during her briefing, and they should be simple to follow. Push three special bricks in the proper order. A scratch mark denoted the first, and from there on she needed to count five to the right, and then four down. Too bad the passing years had caused their usual damage, and several slabs ended up cracked.

Since determining the correct brick turned out to be impossible, Janice instead attempted to press each damaged one in succession. Despite her effort, this had yielded few results so far. Still, she kept trying while Charlie and Bertrand surveyed the area in case a BBR terrorist showed up. Janice gritted her teeth. If that happened, they'd be out of luck. As that pessimistic thought entered her mind, a grinding sound echoed—rocks rubbing against rocks. She found the desired stone, and it moved backward. Filled with relief, Janice exhaled and smiled. Now, it should be easy. Five to the right, yes, that worked. And four down...

While she pushed the final brick, Charlie said at full volume, "Bertrand, wait!"

What was he thinking? They were supposed to use sign language. Thanks to Janice entering the correct sequence, the door opened with a swoosh. Instead of celebrating her victory, Janice ignored the new tunnel and glanced at Bertrand. Charlie wouldn't have yelled without a reason. Immediately, she saw it—a thin transparent wire glimmering in the light. Her position allowed her to spot the trap, but from Bertrand's perspective it remained invisible. Worst, his leg stood a fraction of an inch away from the thread. Like Charlie before, Janice fired a warning, but too late. The string snapped.

A loud blast resounded, so strong Janice winced in pain and covered her ears. Confused, she closed her eyes. When she reopened them, Bertrand's upper body exploded into streams of blood and ripped organs. His legs alone remained whole, falling backward. That trap must have triggered a hidden shotgun or something similar. After a moment of shock, Janice clenched her fists. Sadness and rage for her lost comrade overwhelmed her. Then she gasped. Oh shit. With a gulp, she stared at Charlie. Both looked at each other, mouths gaping. He understood the implications as well as her. No doubt the BBR goons had heard the detonation. Enemies would surround them in a minute, maybe less.

Janice's lips moved as she attempted to say something. Before she uttered a single word, Charlie shoved her inside the secret passage and closed the door. Without delay, Janice sprang against the wall and pushed, but it refused to move. With a roar, she punched the barrier again and again. Hollow clunks served as her reward. That and bruised knuckles. Still, she continued. "Charlie, you dumbass!"

"Cap Allison's ass, I'll distract them."

"Charlie! What are you doing, you bastard? Why should you sacrifice yourself? Because I'm a woman? Don't be an idiot, you sexist jerk, I don't need saving!"

"No! Because you're a better shot than me. Now, go kill Allison. For us."

Janice bent her head downward and rubbed her brow as she mumbled. "Ah, screw you, Charlie." Why did stupid men always feel they had to sacrifice themselves? On that note, she shook her head. "Whatever." She took a few deeps breaths, then dashed forward. Through training, she'd achieved admirable physical strength, but even Janice couldn't brute force her way out of there. She couldn't help Charlie no matter how much she wanted to. All she could do was honor his dying wish and complete the mission. Grieving would wait.

Chapter 24

Of all the moments Brucie had shared with Pierre, the fondest ones were the times they worked out together. Given their lack of money, they couldn't afford an expensive gym membership. Instead, Pierre had set up a makeshift gym in their basement, though they couldn't pay for equipment either. When possible, he built his own out of random materials. For the more complex components, he salvaged them from the scrapyard. Once in a while, Pierre got lucky and found old broken machines, which he bought for a fraction of the price and restored them.

The home fitness center improved over the years. Despite its shabby appearance, it was complete. Nowadays, Brucie exercised in Valardir, using facilities filled with cutting-edge gear. Somehow it felt inferior to Pierre's crude alternatives. Perhaps the nostalgia clouded his judgment.

Since Brucie had served as a target for bullies, Pierre had shown him how to defend himself when he was still a child. More precisely, Pierre taught him how to box. Though Brucie always wished to test his skills against his brother in a friendly competition, Pierre refused: the boy was far too young. As such, Brucie clashed with a punching bag. Pierre also arranged mock fights. Those were fun, but not the real contest Brucie craved.

In the end, Brucie proved so insistent that once he was eighteen, Pierre agreed. However, the elder sibling wanted to avoid serious injuries, so he demanded Brucie wear a protective helmet. That plus a few alterations to the rules satisfied Pierre's need for caution. A single problem remained: they required a ring. One day, Pierre dragged an old, battered, stained mattress inside the improvised gym. That thing, Brucie guessed, came from the garbage dump. For sanity's sake, Pierre covered the disgusting bed with his cleanest sheet. Then in the evening, he fashioned makeshift pillars that held a lone rope instead of the standard three. The result did not impress, but it served its purpose.

The brawl turned out to be an amazing experience. Somehow, trading blows with each other strengthened their bond. It was magical, albeit painful magic. Pierre won, but Brucie had expected that conclusion. Still, based on the layer of perspiration covering Pierre's body and his shortness of breath, Brucie had performed better than he'd dared hope.

The two men enjoyed the battle so much that they made it a tradition. Brucie remembered it well. Dodging punches; dealing some; receiving them; feeling blood running down his cheeks. It was something else. Somehow, he discovered that you never quite knew someone until you faced them in combat. What strategies and tactics did they use? Did they rush in and attempt to knock you out as fast as possible? Or maybe they preferred to stay on defense until you grew exhausted. Those choices revealed a lot about an opponent's personality, whether or not they intended them to. Pierre, for instance, was a brutal fighter who didn't hesitate to strike whenever an opportunity appeared. Yet he remained cautious and kept his guard up, careful not to leave himself vulnerable. That latest aspect had vanished since he'd become Diabo.

Despite numerous attempts, Brucie had failed to achieve victory against Pierre. He hoped he'd win once, but no. That hadn't stopped him from trying. The more he trained, the more his skills increased, and he almost succeeded twice, but Pierre prevailed. At least Pierre didn't feign defeat out of mercy as some brothers would. Brucie preferred loss to pity and Pierre understood that.

Those memories filling his mind, Brucie stared at the red beast. His chance to beat Pierre in a boxing match had vanished long ago. That was fine: at that point, he considered surviving the hostage crisis enough of a triumph.

Chapter 25

Charlie had no hope; it was a fact. The mission depended on Janice. The only help he could provide was distracting the enemy so they wouldn't discover her. As far as BBR knew, he and the deceased Bertrand served as the complete attack force and he intended to keep it that way. The instant he shoved Janice through the secret door, he began yelling and running, shooting every goon who dared to cross his path. The carnage should distract the thugs and lead them away from their true goal.

At least ten minutes had passed since Charlie's assault started. That he still breathed was nothing short of a miracle, and he had slain far more terrorists than he'd expected. Plenty of cadavers littered the ground. But he never kidded himself: he wouldn't survive. Some might prefer delusion in such circumstances, but that wasn't his style. Besides, he'd reached the end of the line already as the BBR bastards cornered him.

Charlie pushed a table on its side for cover, but that wouldn't protect him for long. Bullets struck the wooden surface without respite, cracking it. Splinters littered the air, irritating Charlie's lungs, and he coughed a lot. Once the chaos lessened, he popped out of cover and fired his own salvo. A few screams resounded; it seemed his shots had hit some of his targets. But then the spray stopped as a click echoed. With a frown, Charlie stared at his gun and cursed aloud. Out of ammo. That moment of inattention ended up being a fatal mistake. A stray bullet pierced his shoulder. Charlie yelled as he collapsed backward, behind the table. After a wince, he touched the injury, causing a flash of pain. Then he looked at his red-stained fingers and forced a laugh as his eyes watered.

With his remaining good arm, he grasped his last grenade and shouted, "Okay, you got me! I surrender."

A couple terrorists approached, careful not to expose themselves too much.

"Drop your weapon."

Charlie obeyed, and that done, he pulled the pin out of his grenade. Perhaps he'd take a few of those assholes with him, his final gift for NISDA and the hostages. He closed his eyes. Three seconds... two seconds... one second...

Chapter 26

"You're being unreasonable, Diabo." Daniel's voice's resounded with ever-growing frustration. "We gave you insurance; you must do the same. It's simple."

"Yeah? Fine with me, but I need to protect my men."

Ron sighed and rolled his eyes as he muttered, "Goddamn stubborn bastard." At the same time, Daniel shook his head, hoping their acting skills gave the impression they'd reached their limit and he and his Koporal had run out of patience, when really, the current impasse pleased them. They had to delay the negotiation, and so far they'd succeeded. By now, Janice and the others must be near the final secret passage that would give access to Allison. Daniel reckoned that unless something bad happened, the telepath would soon be dead. Then a rescue operation became possible.

Despite Daniel's optimism, a niggling concern gnawed at his mind. Diabo proved beyond cautious. So far, he'd denied every single request. At first that had made sense, since they indulged in ridiculous demands. As time passed, the list they'd prepared dwindled, and they'd had to improvise. By now, they asked for reasonable things that BBR should consider, yet Diabo rejected them without a second thought. This stood in contrast to the red beast's usual bravado. A little more, and Daniel would wonder if perhaps Diabo procrastinated too. The only reason Daniel could imagine for this was that Stalker attempted to free Plague as they spoke, but the prison had gone to high alert and they'd discovered no signs of the elusive spy.

As Daniel reflected upon those things, he and Ron continued arguing with Diabo. During a lull in the conversation, he glanced toward Rose again. Pale as a sheet, she still chewed her nails in silence. So far, she'd honored her promise and declined to interfere. No question she was a wreck, yet she'd held up better than Daniel had dared hope earlier. When he returned his focus to Diabo, a loud blast echoed from what Daniel assumed to be the basement. He resisted a hard swallow as his muscles tensed instinctively.

For a second, a scowl appeared on Diabo's brow. Soon after, he gritted his teeth and glared at the camera. It seemed the brute had reached the same conclusion as Daniel. Several more bangs then resounded. Mouth foaming, Diabo advanced toward the camera, thus appearing bigger on the monitor. While already red, his cheeks seemed to turn a shade darker. However, Daniel admitted that might have been his imagination.

"You bastards!" An accusing index finger Diabo brandished.

Without meaning to, Daniel recoiled and shielded himself by raising his palms. "That wasn't us!"

"How dare ya? How dare ya screw with me and lie 'bout it?"

"Diabo, I swear it's not us! Allison's there, we're not crazy enough to risk—"

A groan escaped Diabo's lips. "Think I'm a damn fool? Ain't nobody else who'd attack us here." On the monitor, Diabo trembled with rage. "Ya know what you did?" With a growl, he seized his pistol and three bangs echoed. Simultaneously, a trio of hostages tied up in the front row fell limp as blood stained their clothes. Daniel's mouth gaped as Diabo shouted, "You killed 'em! You sons o' bitches killed 'em hostages!"

"You freaking lunatic!" Ron yelled while clenching his fists.

Daniel stepped forward, interrupting his tirade. "Wait, Diabo, let's talk about this." But the mutant ignored him and kept firing at random targets. Old or young, man or woman, it didn't matter.

"That boy was four at most. Why did ya kill him, huh? Why?" As Diabo said that, Rose hopped to her feet and rested her hands on her hips. Tigh warned her with a glare, and she returned to her seat.

Then Diabo's radio beeped. With a grunt, he stopped his carnage, reached for it and brought it to his ear. The content remained unknown to Daniel and Ron, but based on the smirk on Diabo's brow, it appeared to be bad news for them. Before long, the red beast pushed the close communication button and glared at them. "Hope you're happy, your two men are wasted. We're sweeping the place. If ya got more in here, we'll have 'em soon 'nough."

These words filled Daniel with hope, but he resisted the coming sigh of relief. Two men... one was still alive. How he prayed Diabo meant "men" literally, since in that case Janice would be okay for now. Except he doubted she'd survive for long.

"You're lucky I still want my men back," Diabo howled. "Don't ya pull any shit like that again, ya hear me? Or are ya still pretending NISDA got nothing to do with it?"

Daniel exhaled and bowed his head. "Fine, it was us, but it wasn't an attack! They were scouts, only reconnaissance."

Not taking the bait, Diabo laughed. "Yeah, right. Ain't like I care anyway. You're gonna pay for this."

"We already did." Ron groaned and shook his head. "Our men are dead and so are those hostages."

"Ain't 'nough!" Diabo snapped his fingers at one of his thugs. "Bring me the human kid."

***

The guard dragged me toward Diabo and he wasn't gentle. Sweat covered me. I wanted to cry but the tears wouldn't come. Diabo would kill me to teach them a lesson. I prayed it'd be quick, but somehow I wasn't hopeful. When he got close, the red monster grabbed me and rubbed my head again. I almost threw up.

—Thoughts of James Hunter, Hocmar 28, 2134, on the Nirnivian calendar

A mad grin formed on Diabo's lips as he caressed James's hair. "Your precious Melkar's friend—"

"Please, don't!" a voice echoed. James gasped. That sure didn't sound like Daniel or Ron. Holding his breath, he glanced at the monitor Diabo used to communicate with NISDA. Poor Rose stood shaking in front of the camera, hands linked as if in prayer. That confirmed James's suspicion.

Behind her, Ron Tigh fumed and yelled, "What the freak are you doing?" The Koporal pointed toward the back of the room. "Go sit down, missy!"

After a chuckle, Diabo's tone softened, but mockingly. "Oh, Your Holiness, I ain't gonna kill the guy." He wiggled his finger. "Nah, I'll do worse... the boy's coming with us and we'll experiment on him." The crimson beast shrugged. "Your fault."

While he attempted to recoil, James gasped. That fate proved far more frightening than death. Despite the effort he put into maximizing the distance between himself and BBR's boss, Diabo's muscular red arm blocked him.

"Please, have mercy!" Tears ran down Rose's cheeks, and the slight bow she adopted implied begging. "He's innocent! Hunter has nothing to do with this! Don't punish him for our sins, please!"

Diabo rubbed his chin for a second before nodding twice in quick succession. "Hmm, I got a bit of a soft spot for ya, Your Holiness. Yeah, I'll keep him alive and I swear I'll send him back once we're done." A maniacal laugh resounded. "But he ain't gonna be in mint condition no more!"

"Please!" A sob escaped Rose. "If you let Hunter and the others go, I'll be your hostage."

She meant it; I was sure of it. Rose meant every word. She'd sacrifice herself for my safety without a second thought. Over time, I had come to suspect that woman. The Doctor had proven she'd lied to me, so I couldn't trust her. All those doubts disappeared in that instant. It didn't matter if she had hidden information about the first human. I didn't even care if Doctor Death himself was from earth as he claimed. Rose was a noble soul who'd risk her own life for someone from another world. That single act convinced me she couldn't be the bad guy the mechanical freak wanted me to believe. I was ashamed. Ashamed for distrusting her. Ashamed for considering she might be...

While shame is a powerful emotion, it's nothing compared to terror. To hear Diabo explain I'd be his guinea pig petrified me. Still, her proposition was worse and I couldn't accept it. I was a nobody—just a loser. An all-time loser. Rose was a religious icon: a symbol of hope for a whole nation. To me, "Melkar" was only two meaningless syllables strung together, but this was beyond me or her. Nirnivia needed her. There was no way, no way I could have lived with myself if she'd ended up dying for me. Thinking back now, it's all too clear her father would have stopped her anyway, but at the moment, her offer felt like a dreadful possibility.

—Thoughts of James Hunter, Hocmar 28, 2134, on the Nirnivian calendar

"Rose, no! Don't do this! I'll go with them; don't be stupid!"

Intrigued by the prophet's suggestion, Diabo covered James's face with his palm, preventing him from speaking. The grip ended up so strong it stopped his breathing and he began suffocating. In desperation, he struggled, but he lacked the strength. Still, his squirming relayed the message and Diabo let him go, though the warning glare he fired made it clear James should stay quiet.

Chapter 27

Though stuck in a less-than-ideal situation, Janice reached her destination. By this point, BBR had discovered two infiltrators, and that put the hostages at risk. At least Janice might kill Allison. After that, the outcome depended on her father. Janice understood she wouldn't survive; not with what had happened. She accepted that fate, not that it pleased her.

A small TV rested in the secret passage, showing the room where Diabo held his captives. The monitor helped determine if one could open the concealed bookshelf door safely. On the screen, a glowering Diabo talked and gestured. Without sound, Janice could only guess why, but she figured he'd learned about the assault. To his knowledge, NISDA had sent two men. That was her only hope. Through his sacrifice, Charlie had given her that chance, and she refused to waste it.

Janice cracked the bookcase open, just enough to see Allison. Although she sat so close, the telepath didn't hear. Instead, she focused on the crimson beast's outburst, wide-eyed and whimpering. That made sense to Janice; when he yelled, he often hurt her.

Without delay, Janice seized the silenced pistol her superiors had provided. That weapon didn't shoot bullets but microdarts so tiny it would be tough to spot one lodged in Allison's cadaver.

Under normal circumstances, the projectiles contained a tranquilizer intended to knock out enemies, leading to their capture. This time, however, a poison labeled

H43A23 filled them. The name didn't roll off the tongue, nor did it do the substance's lethality justice. Taken from a notorious sea serpent and boosted by scientists in a laboratory, it served as the deadliest toxin known to Nirnivia. No antidote existed, because it'd be useless. Allison would be dead as soon as the metal tip pierced her flesh. No screaming or reacting possible, let alone administering a cure. If all went well, nobody would remark her demise since they were so busy. While H43A23 cost a ton of money and proved limited in quantity, NISDA judged this operation vital enough to warrant its usage.

Fighting the sickness in her stomach, Janice raised the gun and aimed for Allison. At this range, missing was inconceivable, yet she hesitated. She'd met that girl and remembered when Rose and she had accompanied young Allison to a carnival. The lights, the food, the rides, the almost impossible games—the child had gazed at everything with an astonished expression, disbelieving the wonders she witnessed. Never had Allison glimpsed such a cheerful place. They'd had a ton of fun. Between the snacks and the crazy rides, it had been a miracle Allison hadn't thrown up. Janice hadn't been so lucky, but whatever.

Allison had such a short life devoid of happiness... it was unfair. Janice swallowed hard and chased those thoughts away. Life was what it was. She began to squeeze the trigger when an arm wrapped around her neck while a hand pressed a handkerchief against her nose. That powerful smell... the odor overwhelmed Janice, and her eyes watered. She struggled, but the assailant held strong. In a desperate final effort, Janice jerked her elbow, hoping to strike them. The first two attempts failed, but the third one landed. The force of impact propelled the assaulter backward. Now freed, Janice attempted to get to her feet, but she wavered. Her head spun and her vision blurred as she collapsed on the floor. The cloth had been dipped in gorthaca, and she'd inhaled a large dose already. Before Janice sank into unconsciousness, she realized someone had crept up on her. She had been careless.

***

Janice's body lay unconscious in the secret passage as Melissa gazed at her. With a sigh, she patted Janice's back and mumbled, "Sorry." Wrathchild lacked Stalker's infiltration skills, but she had a ton of experience and sneaked better than the average thug.

Felt bad for Janice. Didn't want kill her. Didn't want hurt Rose's sister. Hated me already. Didn't want more hate. Would've let her go. Couldn't let Allison die. Saw Janice open secret passage. Guy pushed her inside. Decided not raise alarm. Followed Janice, captured her. Diabo wouldn't mind: make good hostage anyway.
　　　—Thoughts of Wrathchild, Hocmar 28, 2134, on the Nirnivian calendar

Filled with regrets, Wrathchild picked up Janice and opened the hidden door. Then she took a few steps forward and entered the main room.

Chapter 28

From the start, Ron had expected Rose to meddle in the negotiation. Yes, she had promised otherwise, but he doubted she'd keep her word. Oh, she might have intended to, but she was soft. The moment she saw that James fellow, she'd waver. No question, if Rose had been in charge, she would have granted Diabo's demands in a heartbeat. Still, that she offered herself as a hostage surprised him, and he stood there mouth gaping like an idiot. The same held true for Daniel. If anything, the proposal out of his daughter shocked the Commander even more. The already pale Zarg complexion grew a shade lighter, bordering on pure white.

For a moment, Tigh wondered if perhaps he misheard, but the next sentence uttered confirmed his ears proved accurate. "Please, with me as your hostage, you'll get your men back for sure!" That was enough. Ron's confused expression morphed into a scowl and he gritted his teeth.

"Princess, don't—"

Ron ignored Daniel's objection. Instead of listening, he dashed toward the prophet, grabbed her and covered her lips with his palm. A few garbled sounds escaped his grip, but nothing coherent. All around him, gasps echoed. The officers looked at each other, shook their heads, and even face-palmed. To dare handle the holy Melkar so brutally, they must've deemed him crazy. Tigh shrugged their reactions off. Often in the past his behavior had caused outrage, and he had become immune to it.

"You're out of here," he mumbled to Rose.

Daniel winced. "Don't hurt her!"

"For crying out loud, Dan, I'm not mad! You!" Ron shouted to two nearby soldiers. "Lock the Melkar in her room." The women glanced at each other but didn't move. "Now! It's an order." The two shuddered and approached Rose. To be terrified of Rose—how ridiculous. Then something pierced Ron's flesh, and he screamed as pain flared. In horror, he jerked and glimpsed the teeth marks on his hand. She'd bitten him. "You little"—at the last second, he silenced the "bitch" he'd intended—"rascal."

Now free, Rose stepped away from Tigh and waggled her index finger at him. "I'm not leaving! I'd rather die! You can't stop me: it's my life, my choice—"

A deafening noise interrupted her, as if something large rubbed against the floor. Curious, they all stared at the screen. Ron's heart sank while Daniel held his head with both hands. As for Rose—well, she breathed so hard she might hyperventilate. Wrathchild walked toward Diabo. In her arms, she carried Janice Ricdeau.

***

The next book, The Cyborg's Identity, is available for preorder and releases on January 6, 2025.

Do you want a free short story that serves as a prequel to The Cyborg's Crusade? Then, join the cyborg's fan club on my website, https://thecyborgscrusade.com/fanclub.html

Please consider leaving a review. Those help a lot. Note that you can buy books, and follow me on social media with this link:

https://thecyborgscrusade.com/hub.html

Thank you for reading, I hope with all my heart you enjoyed The Cyborg's Fortune.

ABOUT THE AUTHOR

My name is Benoit Lanteigne and I'm a French Canadian (outside of Quebec) who's trying to write in English. That can be tricky. I'm a computer programmer and I enjoy it. I see many inspiring writers who hate their day jobs and hope to quit someday, but that's not my case. Mostly, I've worked on websites and web applications.

Back in school, I enjoyed writing and according to my teachers and classmates; I had a talent for it. Well, not so much for grammar and spelling, but they liked my stories. Once I went to university, I dropped writing as a hobby. There were other things I wanted to focus on, such as my career. Then, in the early 2000s, around 2006 I'd say, I had a flash of inspiration. At first, it was a single character: a winged woman with red hair. I didn't even know who she was, but the image stuck with me. From there, I began figuring out details about her origins and her world, but I only started writing for real in 2009. After over ten years of hard work, books of The Cyborg's Crusade are finally ready for release.

www.ingramcontent.com/pod-product-compliance
Lightning Source LLC
Chambersburg PA
CBHW060652190726
48289CB00002B/373